"Trudy, are you in there?"

Linc! Trudy spun around in surprise as he opened the door.

They were alone in a public rest room.

One of her books had mentioned several sexy possibilities if a woman ever found her guy in the ladies' room.... It had sounded *very* naughty—and a lot of fun! Trudy would never have dared anything like it back at home, but New York City was a different story. But it was too soon for her to try anything like that with Linc. Wasn't it?

She gazed into his eyes and decided the least she could do was explain her behavior. "I walked into this nightclub and realized I didn't have the New York nightlife look. So I came down here to see if I could make myself look more presentable." She watched as the corners of his mouth started to twitch. "And don't you dare laugh."

"Who's laughing?" he asked, stifling a chuckle.

His grin was a little too cocky to suit her. She wanted to wipe it right off his face. And she knew exactly how....

Dear Reader,

Just as we all have fantasy lovers (you might as well go ahead and admit it—you're among friends), we all have fantasy beds. If you're lucky, you might be sleeping in it, but if you're like the rest of us, the reality isn't exactly what you had in mind. There's the cost issue.... Do you have any idea what some people pay for sheets? And the space issue... Yes, you might be able to wedge that canopied four-poster into the room, but you'll have to vault into it from the doorway.

My heroine, Trudy Baxter, is determined to have her fantasy bed exactly as she pictured it when she was dreaming about living in the big city. So I gave Trudy her fantasy bed, maxing out her credit card in the process, and let her figure out how to fit it into her tiny apartment. I also gave her a fantasy man to go in the bed. This is a Blaze novel, after all! And I discovered that this particular man in this particular bed is a pretty good combo. I hope you'll agree.

Enjoy,

Vicki Lewis Thompson

P.S. Harlequin has a cool new Web site called www.tryblaze.com. Check it out!

Books by Vicki Lewis Thompson

HARLEQUIN BLAZE
1—NOTORIOUS

HARLEQUIN TEMPTATION
744—PURE TEMPTATION
780—THE COLORADO KID
784—TWO IN THE SADDLE
788—BOONE'S BOUNTY
826—EVERY WOMAN'S FANTASY
853—THE NIGHTS BEFORE CHRISTMAS

ACTING ON IMPULSE
Vicki Lewis Thompson

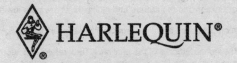

HARLEQUIN®

TORONTO • NEW YORK • LONDON
AMSTERDAM • PARIS • SYDNEY • HAMBURG
STOCKHOLM • ATHENS • TOKYO • MILAN • MADRID
PRAGUE • WARSAW • BUDAPEST • AUCKLAND

To Katherine Orr, for more years of support and friendship
than either of us is willing to admit!

ISBN 0-373-79025-2

ACTING ON IMPULSE

Copyright © 2002 by Vicki Lewis Thompson.

Visit us at www.eHarlequin.com

Printed in U.S.A.

Prologue

OKAY, SO ALL HER cherished plans were in the dumper. Trudy Baxter grabbed another plastic glass of wedding reception champagne and vowed to make the best of it. Obviously she and her best friend Meg wouldn't be single girls sharing a New York flat this coming January, after all. Trudy would have to experience that long-awaited lifestyle change solo.

For six months she'd secretly and selfishly hoped Meg's wedding would be canceled. But nearly everyone in Virtue, Kansas, had crowded into the Baptist church this morning to watch Meg marry her "city slicker" Tom Hennessy. Then they'd all hurried to the Grange Hall for the reception.

Now that it was a done deal, Trudy realized how right this move was for Meg. Brilliant and bossy, she'd always been a redhead with an attitude. She couldn't have made a better choice than a mellow, funny guy like Tom, someone who could tone her down a little.

Of course Meg had assured Trudy that she'd still be there for her when Trudy arrived in New York. But Trudy knew it wouldn't be the way they'd planned it in junior high when they'd decided to be career girls together. That wasn't Meg's fault. Meg had left this one-horse town three and a half years ago, right on schedule, ready to experience big-city living and big-city men. Trudy was the slowpoke, tied down by family obligations she hadn't had the heart to ignore.

While Trudy had struggled to finish her college correspondence courses and help out at home, Meg had met Tom during a Christmas shopping trip to Saks. And despite his well-tailored tux and Manhattan address, he was anything but slick. Two nights ago Trudy had watched him chugalug a pitcher of beer at the Pizza Palace and then line up with everybody else to dance the bunny-hop. Trudy figured Meg had fallen in love with his goofy side. The fact that he was a talented securities trader was a bonus.

Still, he *was* a securities trader, not a hayseed, and Trudy wondered what he really thought of this reception in the Grange Hall with disposable tablecloths and crepe paper streamers. According to Meg, he'd wanted the guests to be comfortable.

As a result, they'd served Jell-O salad and pink champagne instead of caviar and Dom Pérignon. They were using a tape deck instead of hiring a live band out of Kansas City, and the favors were tulle bags filled with M&M's instead of gold boxes of Godiva. By all appearances Tom didn't seem to object to any of it.

Trudy objected. She was cringing inside wondering how Tom truly must be viewing all this. His parents came from a small town in Indiana, so they were probably cool with it. But Trudy was glad Tom's best man, also a securities trader, hadn't made it. She hated to think of anybody getting chicken pox at the age of thirty-one, and Tom must miss having his best buddy at such an important moment in his life, but a guy like Linc Faulkner wouldn't fit in. From what Tom said, Linc's family was loaded.

"Hey, Trudy, Irish jig time!" Tom called across the dance floor. "You ready?"

Her brother Kenny laughed. "Who said she could dance an Irish jig?"

Because it was a wedding and she was all dressed up, Trudy gave him only a light punch on the arm. "I did." She vaguely remembered making the boast at the Pizza Palace after she'd had a fair share of beer, herself.

But she could do this. She'd watched her *Riverdance* video at least a hundred times. While doing chores in the barn she'd worked off some of her frustration, sexual and otherwise, by kicking and stomping up and down the wooden aisle. Her dance step sounded exactly like Michael Flatley's, if she did say so herself.

"Look, sis, watching a video isn't the same as—"

"Hold this." She handed her glass to Kenny. "And prepare to be amazed." She'd had just enough champagne to be confident and not enough to affect her balance. She adjusted her flowered headpiece, which insisted on slipping down over one eye.

Kenny thought he was such a hotshot because at the last minute he'd had to fill in as best man. With a safety pin here and there, he'd been able to wear the tux meant for Linc. A seventeen-year-old wearing his first tux could be a real pain in the ass.

Her little sister Sue Ellen, barely three, clapped wildly. "You go, girl!"

"I will!" Trudy had taught her to say that. It was so damned cute. She loved the little tyke, loved her to pieces, even if Sue Ellen was the anchor that had kept her in Virtue those extra years. Without Trudy around, her mom wouldn't have made it after Sue Ellen was born, not with five other kids under fourteen and a husband who had his hands full earning enough to feed them all.

"I have ten dollars says she can't do it!" hollered Clem Hogarth. "Any takers?"

"You'll lose that money, Clem." Trudy figured he was nursing a grudge because she'd broken up with him six months ago. He'd said he had a surprise for her and she'd thought he'd finally decided they'd drive the hundred-mile distance to a motel. Instead he'd had the back seat of his car reupholstered.

Trudy had refused to have sex with him that night or any other night since. In fact, she'd vowed that she would never

have sex in the back seat of a car again as long as she lived.
For single girls in Virtue, that meant becoming celibate.
New York would be a different story. A *totally* different
story. She could hardly wait.

"I'll take your bet, Clem," Tom said. "If Trudy says she
can do it, then I figure she can."

"And here's another ten from me," said Meg. She gave
Trudy a grin and a thumbs-up.

Trudy flashed them both a smile as the fiddle music
started. Ever since high school she and Meg's motto had
been Fake It Till You Make It. That philosophy hadn't failed
her yet. Lifting her skirts, she gave it all she had.

1

Six months later

"OH, TOMMY, you have a drop of gravy on your chinny-chin-chin." Meg leaned toward her husband and tenderly dabbed at his face with a napkin.

Tommy. Linc took a manly bite of his pot roast and thanked God he was a free man. Nauseating nicknames were only the tip of the iceberg in this marriage business. Tom had gone completely crazy when he'd met Meg a year ago, leaving Linc to stand by helplessly and watch his friend abandon all the fun guy stuff.

Gone were the weekly racquetball matches, nights at the Knicks games, even their Sunday afternoons watching football, drinking beer and eating Cheez Doodles. After six months of wedded bliss Tom was slowly starting to act a little more normal, but Linc doubted he'd ever be a hundred percent.

They'd started playing racquetball again and had watched a few football games on the tube, but it was nothing like the old days. Meg had become the center of Tom's world, and in Linc's opinion that made Tom so damn vulnerable. Marriage was such a risky venture. Tom might *seem* happy, but that was because he was so blissed out floating down the marital stream of steady sex and home cooking that he couldn't hear the thunder of the waterfall he was heading toward.

Tom gazed lovingly at his increasingly pregnant wife.

"Maybe I dripped gravy on purpose to see if you'd come over and lick it off."

Linc put down his fork. "Are you sure you two wouldn't rather be alone? This being your six-month anniversary and everything?" Linc hadn't realized they were celebrating when he'd accepted the dinner invite. It had never occurred to him that anyone would celebrate semiannually. There he discovered they'd been celebrating monthly.

It was all foreign territory to Linc. He never remembered his parents celebrating any anniversary. Of course they wouldn't, now, with his mother living permanently in Paris and his dad batching it at the mansion Upstate. A long time ago Linc had heard the phrase *a marriage of convenience,* and had recognized that was what his parents had. He'd noticed that most wealthy couples seemed to have that kind.

He wondered how many of them had started out like Meg and Tom, gaga about each other. Maybe most of them. Meg and Tom were far from wealthy, but Linc knew divorce was rampant in other parts of society, too. He hoped Meg and Tom wouldn't end up like his parents, but he wouldn't make book on it.

"We can be alone later." Meg winked at Tom. "Besides, we asked you over tonight because we have a special surprise."

"Oh?" He couldn't imagine what kind of surprise they could have left. He already knew about the baby. He'd have to be an idiot not to know, considering that Meg was six months along. Then it hit him. "Twins?"

Tom laughed. "Not unless the other one's hiding."

"No twins," Meg said. "Our wedding album finally arrived!"

"Really?" Linc tried his best to look overjoyed. Wedding pictures made him nervous. All that cheerful optimism in the face of terrible odds. It seemed too much like plunking down your life savings in the midst of a bear market.

"Since you didn't get to be there, we thought you'd like to see the pictures, at least," Meg said.

"They're nice pictures." Tom looked encouragingly at Linc. "Trudy's brother looks halfway decent in your tux."

"Yeah, I'm really sorry about that chicken pox thing," Linc said. "Who would have thought?" He'd contracted chicken pox at thirty-one because he'd been so overprotected as a kid that he'd never been exposed. Still, ever since that canceled trip he'd wondered if getting the chicken pox had been fate stepping in to keep him a safe distance away from marriage-ceremony vibes.

Hanging out with Meg and Tom was bad enough, but watching them actually tie the knot would have been way too close to the altar for comfort. Some guys said they never planned to get married, but they were bluffing, trying to act macho about the whole deal. Linc was not bluffing. The idea of ending up like his parents was a very real fear.

"Trudy's in a lot of the pictures," Meg said. "And with her moving to town next week, I thought you might be curious."

"Oh?" Linc went on red alert. He was not curious about Trudy, but he had a feeling Meg was about to give him a reason to be.

Meg pushed her plate aside and leaned her arms on the table as she smiled over at Linc. "I have a confession to make."

"Is that right?" Warning sirens sounded in Linc's head. He hated confessions. This was not going to be good.

"I'm hoping you might be willing to watch out for Trudy in the beginning, when she first comes to town."

As Linc stared at her and tried to come up with a gentlemanly, considerate, compassionate way to tell her to go to hell, Tom leaped into the breach.

"What are you talking about, Meg? You never said anything about this to me."

"I didn't tell you," Meg said, "because I was afraid if I

gave you any time to think about the idea, you'd read all kinds of things into it.''

''Which I'm now doing, anyway.''

Linc found his voice. ''Yeah, let's talk about that. Tom and I made this rule years ago, but he might not have told you. We promised we would never, ever fix up each other.''

''Don't worry, buddy,'' Tom chimed in. ''I definitely told her. No fix-ups. I told you, right, Megs?'' Tom looked worried.

''You told me,'' Meg said.

''See?'' But Tom still looked worried. ''I told her.''

''This is not a fix-up,'' Meg said. ''I just need someone I trust to take care of her, at least for a little while. I would be eternally grateful if you'd do it, Linc.''

''It feels like a fix-up,'' Tom said, gazing at her.

''Well, it's not, because Trudy is even more commitment-phobic than Linc after helping raise all those kids.''

Tom looked relieved. ''Oh. Well, that makes sense. How many brothers and sisters does she have again? They wouldn't hold still long enough for me to get a final count.''

''Six,'' Meg said. ''Trudy makes seven. She's been expected to help take care of them for, like, forever. She's up to here with domesticity.''

''Seven kids.'' Linc couldn't imagine such a thing, unless it was a blended family, like in *The Brady Bunch*. He'd watched that on reruns. He'd never missed *Family Ties* or *The Bill Cosby Show* either. He'd been pretty damn lonely growing up as the only child in that huge house. ''Is it because of their religion or something?''

Tom gave Linc a conspiratorial glance. ''It's 'cause there's not much else to do in Virtue.''

''Yeah,'' Linc said, ''but you can do that and not have consequences.''

''Not in Virtue.'' Tom gestured toward Meg's round belly. ''Exhibit A.''

''Oh, for pity's sake,'' Meg said. ''We do know about

birth control in Virtue. It's just that Trudy's mom and dad make beautiful children and they can't seem to resist the temptation to keep doing it. Plus they hate the idea of Trudy moving to New York. I think they hoped if she had to stay and help out, she'd eventually give up her plan, marry some nice farm boy and settle in Virtue.''

"Obviously that didn't work," Linc said.

"Obviously not, since she's arriving next week. Thank goodness we had an opening at Babcock and Trimball, or I'd have to worry about her job situation, too.''

Tom cleared his throat. "Personally, I think you've done a lot by helping her get that PR job. I don't see why you have to ask Linc to—"

"You don't understand. Trudy and I have been best friends since third grade. We've dreamed of living in New York and having big-city careers ever since we saw *Working Girl* at the Virtue View Theater. Originally I was supposed to be the one hanging out with her when she hit the social scene, but I'm sure she doesn't want a pregnant married lady trailing after her.''

"I'll go along with that," Tom said. "But what's wrong with asking somebody at work, some other woman?''

"I can't think of anyone I'd feel right asking. It's sensitive. She's never been east of the Mississippi, never dated a guy who wasn't a corn-fed plowboy. She's anticipated her move to New York for so long, and she tends to be impulsive, anyway. I'm afraid she might get reckless.''

Linc began to relax a little. "She's never been out of Kansas?''

Meg shook her head. "Our sophomore year in college we went all the way to Kansas City and stayed in a hotel one weekend. That's the extent of Trudy's experience with big-city living. So do you see what I mean?''

"I guess." So Trudy was a country bumpkin. That shouldn't pose much of a challenge, after all.

Meg picked up a platter and handed it across the flowered

centerpiece. "Here, have the last slice, Linc. And take some more of those potatoes and carrots, too."

"Thanks." Linc accepted the platter and knew that he'd probably accept this assignment to baby-sit the newcomer, too. Tom Hennessy was the best friend he had in New York, maybe the best friend he'd ever had, period. Tom didn't seem to care about Linc's wealthy background, and Linc didn't find that quality often.

As a result, he'd do just about anything for the guy. Now that Tom was married to Meg, Meg's requests were on a par with Tom's. Still, he didn't have to roll over and play dead yet. "I still have to say this feels dangerously like a fix-up," he said.

Meg shook her head. "How can it be when Trudy has zero interest in finding a steady boyfriend? Listen, it won't be so bad, squiring Trudy around. As her best friend I'm sort of prejudiced, but even Tom would say she's funny and cute, right, Tom?"

"Yeah, but—"

"Let me go get those wedding pictures."

Once she was out of the room, Linc leaned over toward Tom. "You can tell me. Is she a dog? I don't care, you understand, but it would be good to know in advance. I'm probably going to do this thing, but—"

"She's not a dog," Tom said. "I wouldn't say she's your type, though, since you go for tall and elegant and she's…well, short and perky."

"But if this isn't a fix-up, it doesn't matter if she's my type or not." Linc held Tom's gaze.

"Right."

"Do you think it's a fix-up?"

"Meg says it's not."

Linc knew Tom had to be loyal to Meg. He decided to let the matter drop. He could handle a Kansas farm girl with one hand tied behind his back. "Okay, so she's perky. I guess that's a good trait for somebody in public relations."

"Yeah." Tom seemed glad to abandon the subject of fix-ups. "She'll do well. Meg sort of steamrollers people into doing what she wants, but Trudy tends to charm you into it by making you laugh."

Like you, Linc thought, and felt even better. He ought to be able to get along with a female version of Tom for a few days of New York orientation.

"She has this curly hair thing going, and dimples, and she loves to talk. She'll talk your ear off."

Linc began having reservations again. "She's a pain in the butt, right? You can tell me."

"No, not a pain in the butt, either. Unless you get in her way when she has a plan. Underneath that charming grin of hers, she can be *extremely* focused."

"Perky yet stubborn," Linc said.

"You could put that spin on it, I guess. Or you could just say she's determined. Like Meg had decided on pink rose-buds for the wedding bouquet and the bouquets for the bridesmaids, and when the flowers arrived they were full-blown roses, not buds. Meg was kind of upset and was ready to take somebody on, but Trudy promised to get it fixed without making a big deal out of it. I don't know what the florist had to do, or how they did it, but we had pink rose-buds by the time the organist started playing the proces-sional."

"Here's the album." Meg appeared and plopped a leather-bound volume the size of an unabridged dictionary on the table.

Linc braced himself for the pictures. There were a gazil-lion of them, and looking at them all at once was like being forced to eat an entire plate of cookies without a strong cup of coffee to cut the sugary taste. If only he believed that the pomp and circumstance portrayed in these pictures would guarantee a happily-ever-after, but he didn't, so it seemed like a colossal waste of time, money and energy.

"Okay, here she is coming down the aisle."

Gazing obediently at the picture Meg pointed to, Linc saw a woman who definitely seemed too sweet for a cynical guy like him. The outfit didn't help—pale lavender with puffy sleeves, it made her look like a princess in a fairy tale. He'd outgrown the prince-and-princess fantasy years ago. She wore a wreath of flowers on her head, and sure enough, she had the curly brown hair and dimples Tom had mentioned.

She looked like a woman who dreamed of white picket fences, not a woman who could hardly wait to experience big-city sex. Maybe Meg was overestimating her impulsiveness in that regard.

"See how pretty she is?" Meg gestured toward the picture of Trudy. "It'll be no hardship to hang out with her for a little while, will it?"

"I guess not." Linc studied the picture more closely. Definitely perky, like Tom had said. She had the kind of smile that made you want to smile back. He realized he was doing exactly that—smiling at a picture—and he composed himself.

"You'll like her, Linc," Meg said. "She's easy to talk to."

"So Tom said." A chatterbox, according to Tom. But that was better than someone who was the silent, moody type, and Linc had to admit he liked the way she carried herself, with her shoulders back and her head up. She had full breasts and a small waist, but he couldn't tell about her legs, because the dress came down to her ankles. Her figure didn't matter to him, of course, but she'd have an easier time constructing a social life if she looked decent.

"So you'll do it?" Meg asked.

"How long are you thinking I'll need to keep an eye on her?"

"Oh, I don't know. A week, maybe two at the most. She's a quick study."

Linc nodded. That wasn't such a big chunk out of his life, now that he knew Trudy didn't present any kind of threat to his carefully guarded single status. If he hadn't been carried away by the charms of women who spoke three languages and wore only designer labels, he sure as hell wouldn't have a problem with someone who was still combing hay out of her hair. "And she's arriving next Thursday?"

"That's right. Thursday." Meg flipped through the album. "Over the weekend Tom and I are helping her move into her apartment." She glanced up at Linc. "If you could lend a hand on Saturday, that would be a low-key way to introduce the two of you. Then maybe you could grab a pizza or something Saturday night and get acquainted."

"Uh, okay." Linc's attention had been captured by a candid shot in the album, one that must have been taken during the dancing at the reception. "That's her?" he asked, pointing to the picture that had caught his eye.

Meg laughed. "Yep, that's Trudy. We'd all had plenty of champagne by then, and Trudy was making good on her claim that she could dance an Irish jig worthy of *Riverdance*. There was even money riding on it."

"And she was terrible," Tom said, laughing, "but the guy who bet she couldn't was so busy looking at her legs that he didn't realize she wasn't doing any of it right, so Meg and I won the bet."

From the picture, Linc couldn't tell whether Trudy was terrible at dancing a jig, but now there was no mystery about her legs. She'd hiked her skirts up to show off her footwork, and her legs were quite…tempting. No wonder she'd mesmerized some poor fool by showing them off. He felt a stirring that he definitely didn't want to feel, one that might spell trouble. Her flowered wreath had slipped so that it dangled over one eye, and she had an expression of pure glee on her face.

Looking at this version of Trudy Baxter, he felt a little less sure of himself. He also understood why Meg might be worried about Trudy on her own in New York.

NEW YORK! Trudy grinned at Meg and Tom as the three of them rode up in the somewhat shabby elevator to the fourth-floor apartment, her very first, all-to-herself apartment. Her pad. The few things she'd had shipped from Virtue were in boxes piled at their feet and on the hand truck Tom had rented for the occasion.

What a moment. She couldn't help herself; she started singing "New York, New York."

"Come on," she said to Meg, "sing it with me, girl!"

Meg obliged, while Tom rolled his eyes.

She kept singing as they reached the fourth floor. She propped open the elevator door with one box so that Tom could back the loaded hand truck out of the elevator. Meg wasn't allowed to help, but she kept up her end of the singing.

"Remember your *neighbors,*" Tom called out over the ruckus.

"Oh, they'll understand," Trudy said. "A girl only moves into her first New York apartment once, you know."

"She's right," Meg said. "We grew up singing that song together. It was like a ritual whenever we'd get discouraged about making it to the big city."

"Which is why we have to sing it now," Trudy added. "To mark the occasion of me *finally* getting here."

Tom shrugged. "Okay. But don't come crying to me if somebody reports you to the super on your very first day."

Trudy glanced around at the closed doors of the apartments on her floor. Maybe Tom had a point. She'd never lived in an apartment building before, and she supposed if everyone got off the elevator singing at the top of their lungs, it could get a tad bit noisy.

"Sorry!" she yelled out. "It's my first day living here! I'll keep it down after this!" Then she turned to Tom. "How's that?"

"Oh, that's *much* better," he said, grinning.

"Probably nobody's home, anyway," Meg said.

"They're out getting coffee and a newspaper. Where's your key?"

"Right here." Trudy whipped off her snazzy little backpack, something she'd bought yesterday after noticing that purses were *so* last century. She dug in a section of the backpack and came up with the key. "You gorgeous little devil, you," she said to the key. Then she kissed it soundly before turning to unlock the door.

"Is that another ritual?" Tom asked.

"Not exactly," Trudy said. "But you have to understand the significance. This is my first-ever key that opens the door into a place that's mine, all mine." She flung open the door. "Ta-da! Brrr. It's cold in here. Let's have some heat." She ran over to the thermostat and jacked it up several notches.

So what if it was chilly and not especially cheerful inside her new apartment on this gray January day? So what if the windows were bare and so was the room, with no furniture in it? She'd fix that once she moved up from her entry-level job in the PR firm and got a couple of raises. The most important piece of furniture would be delivered in a couple of hours. Yesterday, besides a backpack, she'd bought a bed.

And what a bed she'd found—a king-size, four-poster, canopied wonder of a bed. She'd closed her eyes and charged the whole thing to her credit card, right down to the black satin sheets and comforter.

Take that, Clem Hogarth! No more back-seat couplings for this girl. Her next love affair—with a good-looking city man—would be conducted on a real mattress sitting on a solid hardwood frame. Sex with substance was what she had in mind. She was going from country to cosmopolitan.

"This will be nice, once you fix it up," Meg said, standing in the middle of the empty living room.

"Sure it will." Trudy became aware that while she'd been daydreaming about her bed, Tom had hauled all the boxes in from the hall. "Thanks, Tom." She gave him a smile. He really was a sweetie-pie, and Meg had done the right thing, marrying him. Trudy kind of regretted how she'd hassled Meg about Tom at first, but she'd been horrified that Meg was getting serious about someone before Trudy could make it to town.

She glanced at her friend. Her pregnant friend. "You should sit down," she said. "I don't have any chairs, but you can sit on that box. It should take your weight."

"Thanks, thanks a lot." Meg walked over to a box and sat down on it. "Remind me to make cracks like that when you get knocked up."

"I didn't mean it that way! Oh, Meg, you know you look beautiful pregnant. Doesn't she look beautiful, Tom?"

"Yep. She doesn't think so, but she does."

"Okay, okay," Meg said. "I'm gorgeous. And hungry. Tom, would you run down to the deli and pick up some sandwiches? By the time you get back we'll have found some plates to put them on." She took off her coat and laid it on the floor.

"We sure will," Trudy said. "Oh, my gosh. My first meal on my first day in my first apartment."

"Should I buy champagne, Megs?" Tom asked.

"No, because it wouldn't be any fun if she can't drink it with us," Trudy said. "But you could get some beer, maybe. Would you be sad if we had a beer without you, Meg?"

"I would be sad, but not as sad as if I had to miss champagne. A hot decaf latte would taste almost as good."

"I'll get you that, and I'll get beer for Trudy and me," Tom said. "Linc could probably use some beer, too."

"Linc?" Trudy thought the name sounded vaguely familiar, but she couldn't place it. "Who's Linc?"

Tom shot a glance at his wife. "You haven't said anything about him?"

"I was going to," she said tightly, "once you took off. This is girl talk."

"But what about when you talked to Linc? That wasn't—"

"The deli, Tom."

He shrugged. "Okay. I'm only saying—"

"Pastrami on rye for me," Meg said. "Trudy?"

"That'll work." Trudy also wanted Tom to leave, so she could find out what Meg was up to. She had that gleam in her brown eyes that meant she'd formed a plan, and once Meg formed a plan, hardly anybody could stop her. Trudy was one of the few who'd managed it a few times, but they'd been hard-won victories.

"I'm gone." Tom hurried out the door.

The minute the door closed behind him, Trudy threw off her parka and settled cross-legged in front of Meg. "Okay, spill."

"The other day, I had a brilliant idea."

"Uh-huh." Trudy refused to buy into Meg's enthusiasm. "Something to do with this Linc person, right?"

"Right. He's the guy who was supposed to be Tom's best man, but he didn't make it, remember?"

Trudy nodded but kept her tone cautious. "Yeah, yeah, now I do. Linc Faulkner. We had to change his name to Kenny's in the program at the last minute. Chicken pox. The guy you said was so rich his parents know The Donald."

"Yes." Meg wrapped her arms around her knees and leaned forward. "Trudy, Linc's just adorable. He has that little-boy grin, but the rest of him is all man. He works with Tom, and he's a very loyal friend."

"Hold it." Trudy put her hand firmly on Meg's arm. "This sounds like the kind of speech you give when you're trying to fix me up with someone. I don't want to be fixed up with Tom's buddy. What if he's looking for a steady girlfriend or...or a *wife?*"

"Linc's not. He's—"

"Okay, but he's still Tom's friend. I want to go out there

and meet *strangers*.'' She shook Meg's arm, for emphasis. ''Do you realize how few strangers I've come across in my life? How little mystery? How little delicious intrigue? And it's all here waiting for me. I have a list.'' She started ticking off on her fingers. ''I want to know what it's like to date a Wall Street type.''

''That's Linc.''

Trudy kept going. ''*And* an artist, *and* a construction guy, *and* a fireman, *and*—''

''Yes, but when we first came up with this plan of moving to the city, we thought you and I would find these amazing guys together.''

''Aha! You're jealous because you ended up with Tom before you could explore all those options.''

''Not even slightly. I'm worried that you'll be out there alone at first, and that might not be a good idea.''

Trudy shrugged. ''I'll be fine. I'm also four years older and wiser.''

''Older, maybe.''

''Hey, are you saying I can't be trusted in New York on my own?''

Meg's gaze softened. ''I'm saying it's a big step, going from Virtue to New York. I'm saying that you've been building up steam and you're ready to blow. I'm saying that it wouldn't hurt to spend the first week or two with a guy like Linc, who can introduce you to some of the hot spots and teach you about the unsavory parts of town while you're orienting yourself.''

Trudy eyed her suspiciously. ''You're not going to morph into my mother, are you, now that you're married and PG?''

''No,'' Meg said, laughing. ''Linc is the guy mothers warn their daughters about. He's sinfully good-looking, sexy as hell, and he has absolutely no intention of settling down with one woman.''

''Really?'' This was starting to sound more interesting. Maybe he could be her Wall Street guy, as long as the ground rules were clear from the beginning. She had so much to learn about how people lived and thought outside the state of Kansas, and she intended to learn it while having fun. Each different kind of man would add another layer to her sophistication until she was totally worldly.

But she had to make sure this Linc person fit the criteria. "You're sure that he's not trying to find a nice wife? I mean, he is Tom's best friend, you said."

"Yes, and they think alike on most things, but not on the subject of marriage. Linc's dead set against it. He would never say so to our face, but I think he's waiting for Tom and me to discover that we've made a huge mistake."

Trudy blinked. "Well, you haven't! You're perfect for each other. Why on earth would he think that way?"

"I'm guessing it's mostly because of his parents and their high-society friends. Although his mother and father are technically married, they don't live together anymore."

"Huh." Trudy drew her knees up and rested her chin on them. "But you shouldn't generalize about all marriages because one is like that."

"Maybe you shouldn't, but it's the one Linc knows best. And face it, there are a lot of unhappy couples out there, especially in the high-profile marriages, which is the world Linc's parents move in. Plus, I get the impression Linc is expected to marry into that set, which he sees as a doomed venture. He's not the rebellious type, so the easiest way out is not to marry at all."

"That's kind of sad."

"Is it? Everybody doesn't have to get married. I know you don't want to."

"Not for years and years, but that's not to say it won't happen eventually." She grinned at Meg. "After I've had my fill of new experiences."

"Look, I know you want to explore. I just think having somebody like Linc to show you around at first would be a good way to ease into your new life. He's the perfect escort, and he's also very yummy."

"I don't know. It feels like having a baby-sitter or something. I—" She paused when a buzz echoed through the apartment. For a minute she couldn't figure out what it was. "My *doorbell*." She leaped up. "It's the first ring of my doorbell on my first day in my first apartment. I know it's only Tom with the sandwiches, but still, it's exciting." She reached for the lock on the door.

"Look through the peephole first!" Meg called to her.

"Oh. Yeah, I should do that, even if I think it's Tom, right? I mean, it could be the mad slasher." Smiling, she leaned forward to squint through the peephole. Then she jumped back.

"Trudy? What's the matter?"

"It's not Tom." She didn't recognize the guy, but even elongated by the peephole lens, he looked very cute.

"Does he have dark hair and blue eyes?"

"Yep."

"Then it's Linc."

"My baby-sitter?" She peered through the peephole again. Jeans, gray sweatshirt, navy parka, running shoes. Nice package.

"Are you going to let him in?" Meg asked.

"Yes." Trudy twisted the lock open with a sense of anticipation. First male caller on her first day in her first apartment in New York. "Yes, I do believe I will."

2

THE DOOR OPENED and Linc stood face-to-face with Trudy Baxter of Virtue, Kansas. With her eager, open expression, he'd never mistake her for a New Yorker. She looked like a kid who'd just been promised a trip to Walt Disney World. She seemed innocent and vulnerable, just as he'd expected from someone who'd grown up in the middle of nowhere.

He hadn't expected that he'd instinctively want to protect her. No doubt Meg had counted on that.

Up close Trudy was more girl-next-door than princess, with her freckled nose and wide green eyes. She didn't have on much makeup and her lipstick had nearly worn off, leaving a faint pink tinge behind. Although she wasn't wearing gingham and pigtails, she still looked unnervingly wholesome standing there in jeans and a Mets jersey.

He figured they must be moving-day clothes. The women he usually dated wouldn't be caught dead lugging boxes around, but they also had the money to pay someone else to do it. Trudy probably didn't have the extra cash.

Her jeans looked old, the jersey new. Two days in the city and she was already picking up souvenirs. In a way, he envied her. He couldn't remember a time when he'd anticipated the future with this kind of gusto.

She'd meet up with her share of disappointment, of course. Some of that brightness would fade from her eyes. Although he didn't know her at all, shouldn't really care, he had the ridiculous urge to tell her to go back to Kansas, before disillusionment set in.

"You're Linc," she said. "Meg said you're willing to baby-sit me for a little while, until I get acclimated to the big city."

He had to smile at the way she'd phrased it, pretty much the way he had thought of it, too. "So, are you insulted?"

"Kind of." She smiled back at him.

Tom had said she was a charmer, and sure enough, he was being charmed. Maybe it was because she was so totally different from the women he was used to. Even Meg, who shared a similar kind of Midwest accent with Trudy, had become a city woman by the time he'd met her. Trudy was definitely still country. He doubted they had anything in common, and that was just as well.

"Oh, she is not insulted," Meg said. "In her heart she knows—"

"Food's here!" Tom said, coming up behind Linc. "Let's move this party inside. Trudy, you're going to have to learn not to stand with your door open, or you'll be heating the whole damned hallway. Hi, there, Linc. I got a pastrami on rye for you, just in case you showed up. And I bought three kinds of imported beer to stock Trudy's refrigerator."

"Three kinds of imported beer? Did you take a look at that tiny refrigerator, Tom?" Meg stood and came over to get the fragrant bag of sandwiches. She set them on the counter that separated the small kitchen from the living room. "She won't have space for food it you put all that beer in."

"I can store the beer in a closet," Trudy said. "It's good to have imported beer. Let's see, we still need plates." She turned and started rummaging through boxes.

"Have a beer, buddy." Tom twisted off the lid of a bottle and handed it to Linc. "We have to reduce the inventory so Trudy has room for meat and veggies."

"Thanks." Linc welcomed the distraction of the beer. Until that moment he'd been far too interested in the fit of

Trudy's jeans when she leaned over to sort through the packing boxes. Okay, maybe he felt a slight attraction to her, but he could deal with it.

"I doubt I'll be cooking much." Trudy continued to search the boxes. "Take-out. That's what I'm talking about."

"That gets old after a while," Meg said.

"It should take me months to get tired of it." She glanced over her shoulder at Linc. "In Virtue, even McDonald's is a twenty-mile drive." She returned to digging in the box. "Well, I can't find the plates. I thought they were in this box, but they must—"

"Let's forget about plates," Tom said. "We can use the napkins I brought and be careful not to drip."

"Works for me," Linc said. This whole starting-from-scratch experience was something he knew little about. Until now Tom had been the most poverty-stricken person he'd known who'd moved to New York, and even Tom had begun with more stuff than this. After a lifetime of wealth and excess goods, Linc was intrigued with the idea of such minimalist living.

Sandwiches were handed out, and soon Linc was sitting on the scarred wooden floor next to Trudy with a box in front of them to serve as a table. Tom sat on the floor, too, but Meg claimed she'd never make it back on her feet if she did that, so she was perched above them on another box.

"I guess I need to think about getting a table and chairs," Trudy said.

"I have a card table and folding chairs you can borrow," Linc heard himself say. Now where had that offer come from? Loaning her something was not the way to keep this relationship free of entanglements. But in the face of her lack of resources, he couldn't seem to help himself. He'd had so much. Too much, probably. In comparison to the lightness of Trudy's lifestyle, he felt suddenly weighed down.

"That would be terrific," she said. "I went sort of overboard on the bed, so I'd rather not have to buy any more furniture for a while."

So that's where her priorities were, Linc thought, feeling the tickle of arousal grow stronger. But hell, most guys would get excited by the prospect of a woman who put all her resources into buying a great bed. His reaction was perfectly normal.

"Speaking of the bed, when's that puppy due to arrive?" Tom asked.

Trudy glanced at her watch. "Soon."

Tom looked over at Linc. "The bed's what I could use some help with. The store charges extra for setup, so I told Trudy you and I could put the thing together for her. She has a toolbox, so we have what we need for the job."

"Be glad to help." Linc didn't have a clue how to do things like that, but he'd never told Tom. In their ten-year friendship they'd drunk a lot of beer, played a lot of racquetball and seen a lot of Knicks games. They'd spent zero time working with tools, so the subject hadn't come up.

He could admit as much right here and now, but he had a feeling a down-home gal like Trudy, a woman who came prepared with her own toolbox, would think less of him for not possessing such a manly skill. So he kept quiet. Tom could talk him through it.

Besides, it was a bed, for Pete's sake—some sort of frame, either metal or wood, a mattress and box springs. Setting up a bed probably required muscle, not expertise, and he had the muscle thanks to regular workouts at the gym with Tom.

"I figured while you guys set up the bed, Trudy and I would unpack these boxes," Meg said. "Before you know it, she'll be all set."

"All set," Trudy repeated, looking very pleased with herself. "I don't know if you noticed, Linc, but from that window, if you lean a little to the right, you can see the trees in Central Park. They're far away, but you can see them. Of course there aren't any leaves right now, but in the spring, it'll be awesome."

"Yes, it will." Linc thought of his apartment, which was a mere block from Central Park. He decided not to mention that. He'd never had to struggle financially, thanks to a trust fund that had kicked in when he turned twenty-one. After ten years of working on Wall Street he made enough to afford the apartment without using the trust fund, and he was proud of that.

Still, he knew it wasn't the same pride that Tom or Meg took in their success. With no cushion like he'd had, they could have bombed out, but they hadn't. In a city like New York, that was no mean feat.

Trudy cocked her head to one side. "Listen, do you hear that?"

"Hear what?" Meg took a sip of the latte Tom had brought her.

"Traffic. Just listen to that traffic going by. Buses, taxis, limos, trucks, delivery vans. It's Saturday, and still there's all that traffic. There's even traffic at *night*."

Tom sighed. "I know, but there's not much you can do about it. The alternative is living outside the city, which means a long commute."

"I can help you put up some drapes," Meg said. "That will cut the noise a little. And you could try one of those white-noise machines."

"You'll also get used to it." Linc figured she was used to crickets and birds and stuff like that. She was probably in for a bout of homesickness when she turned off the lights tonight and heard only traffic. "Just now, when we were sitting here, I wasn't even aware of it until you said something."

"That's true," Tom said. "Give it time, and you won't even notice."

Smiling, Trudy gazed at them. "I don't want to get used to it. I *love* it. You know how some people dream of living by the ocean, so they can hear the waves? I've dreamed of living in New York, so I could hear the traffic."

Linc stared at her in disbelief. "You're kidding, right?"

"Nope."

"This is a first for me," he said. "I've heard people say they don't mind the traffic noise, or that they're used to it, but I've never known anybody who actually *liked* it."

"I didn't say I liked it. I said I *loved* it." She glanced over at Linc. "Have you spent much time in a small town?"

"Sure." Little villages in the French countryside and along the coast of Spain, small towns in Northern California, in the heart of the wine country, hamlets in Switzerland. Technically he'd grown up in a small town in Upstate New York, but it was a small town with amenities. Lots of amenities.

"So be honest—if you had to pick a place to live, would it be in that tiny town where nothing happens and you know every person you see, or in a big city like this, where something is always happening and you have the possibility of meeting all kinds of new and interesting people every day?"

"The city." But Linc doubted his reasons were the same as hers. In the small town near his parents' estate he didn't know everyone in town, and the population changed a lot, anyway. But everyone knew who he was. The Faulkner name caused all kinds of reactions in people, few of them good. They were curious, deferential, envious or rude. Only a small minority seemed to be able to take him at face value.

"There you go," Trudy said.

"I'd take both," Tom said. "That's my dream, to have enough money to own a summer place in a small town where a commuter train runs."

"But if a town has a commuter train, it doesn't qualify

as the kind of small town Trudy and I lived in," Meg said. "Then people work in the city but they live in the town, and that's totally different."

"Totally." Trudy took a swallow of her beer. "In Virtue, everybody works, lives, loves and plays bingo right there. Nobody commutes anyplace. And I am so outta there."

The place sounded very backward to Linc. And yet towns like those contained families like the ones he'd envied on TV sitcoms.

"Aw, Virtue's not so bad," Tom said. "I had a pretty good time there."

"As evidenced by my current condition." Meg patted her stomach.

"Besides that," Tom said. "The slower pace was nice for a change."

"Exactly," Trudy said. "For a *change.* Try living that way for twenty-six years. I've seen enough wheat fields to last me the rest of my life."

"Yeah, but those lonely farm roads are great for watching submarine races," Tom said. "Right, Megs?"

Meg rolled her eyes. "I still can't believe you actually wanted to park."

"Nostalgia."

"You can have your nostalgia," Trudy said.

"Oh, come on, Trudy." Tom grinned at her. "The back seat boogie is as American as mom and apple pie. It's got everything—forbidden pleasure, maneuvering in close quarters, the danger of getting caught—it's great, right, Linc?"

"Um, yeah." Linc had never had sex with a girl in the back seat of a car, and now he wished he had, both for the experience and so he could feel like a regular guy instead of the rich kid who'd lost his virginity in an expensive hotel room. Also, he wouldn't be so damned curious about the custom if he'd tried it out a few times.

Unfortunately, he was very curious. He figured Trudy must have participated in her share of back seat sex with some of the local boys. She'd probably left a few broken hearts in Virtue. Maybe at this very moment somebody was sitting on an old tractor, plowing a wheat field, and yearning for Trudy's curvy little body.

Well, maybe they wouldn't be plowing in January. He was kind of hazy about farming schedules, but even he knew you didn't plow when the ground was frozen. Okay, so this heartbroken farm boy could be feeding the chickens and longing for Trudy. Linc was reasonably sure chickens were a year-round deal on the farm.

Regardless, all this talk about having sex in the back seat of a car was making him picture Trudy doing that. Damn it, the concept was turning him on. He didn't want to be turned on.

The doorbell buzzed, and Trudy leaped to her feet. "My bed!" She hurried toward the door.

"Check the peephole," Meg called out.

"Right. Oh, it's the guys with my bed! I can hardly wait."

Linc glanced over at Meg and lowered his voice. "Is she always like this?"

Meg grinned. "Like what?"

He leaned closer. "You know. So…high octane."

"Oh, she's more revved up than usual because of this move, but yeah, she has a high energy level." She gazed at him. "Think you can keep up with her?"

TRUDY COULDN'T BELIEVE that a guy who looked like Linc was already in her bedroom on this first day in her first New York apartment. True, he was in there to help Tom set up her bed, and that might be the extent of his connection to her bedroom, but still, she was thrilled to know that her fantasies about New York men hadn't been so far off. Since he'd popped up right away, that meant there had to be a bunch more where he came from. The town was probably full of fantasy men.

"I can tell you like him." Meg stood at the sink giving Trudy's dishes a quick wash before they put them in the cupboard. They'd decided not to use the dishwasher, which was too small to hold everything, anyway.

"And you knew I would." Trudy had climbed to the counter so she could wipe down shelves. She'd begun making a list, and a step stool was on it. She'd always lived in a houseful of people, several of them taller than she was. Now, if anything had to be fetched from a high shelf, she'd have to do the fetching. "He looks like that poster I had of Harrison Ford in *Working Girl.*"

"You should see him in a three-piece suit. Oh, baby."

Trudy glanced down at Meg and grinned. "I'm not sure you should be making remarks like that, married and preggers as you are."

"Hey, I can still look! No law against that."

"Come on, admit that you're a *little* bit jealous because I'm just starting to shop, while you've made your final purchase."

"Nope."

"I say you are." Trudy dried the shelf with a paper towel. "I say you can hardly wait to get some vicarious thrills from my soon-to-begin adventures."

"I know you won't believe me, but I'm having more fun in bed now that I'm married to Tom than I ever had as a single girl."

"You're right, I don't believe you." Trudy finished drying the shelves and climbed down. "But I think that's how it's supposed to work. When you marry a guy, it's like the minister has that zapper they used in *Men in Black.* Your previous sex life gets wiped from your memory bank." She picked up a dish towel.

"That is so not true! It's just that—"

A thump came from the bedroom, followed by a loud oath.

"Maybe we'd better check on the guys." Trudy put down the dish towel and started for the bedroom.

Before she got there, Tom came out looking frustrated. "Well, it won't fit."

Linc followed, a screwdriver in one hand. "That's right. It won't fit."

"You mean the parts don't match?" Trudy asked.

"The parts match," Tom said, standing with his hands braced on his hips.

"Sure do," Linc added. "They match great."

"But the bed's too big for the room," Tom said. "We tried it both ways, and it just won't go."

"Let me see." Trudy looked through the doorway into the bedroom. Sure enough, the headboard was leaning catty-corner, and she could tell from here that it was too wide for the room. "I don't believe this," she said. "This is a bedroom, so why won't a bed fit in it?"

"A bed would, but not *this* bed," Tom said. "You could sleep a family of six on that thing, Trudy. Why'd you have to get such a big one?"

"Because it looked nice in the store, that's why." Trudy wasn't about to answer truthfully with Linc right here, looking like he'd like to know the answer as much as Tom. She'd bought the huge bed because it was the exact opposite of the back seat of a car. She would never, ever feel cramped making love in that bed. Tom and Linc might still be hung up on the quaint custom of parking, but she wasn't.

Meg came up behind her and peered over her shoulder. "Maybe you could call the store and see if they have a queen in the same style. A queen would fit. It would still be tight, but it would fit."

"Nope, I don't want a queen." Trudy made her decision. "I'll put it in the living room."

Everyone looked a little surprised, but fortunately the guys set right to work moving the pieces of the bed into the living room without trying to talk her out of it.

The more Trudy thought about the new arrangement, the more she liked it. "Could you put it up against the right-hand wall, so I can lie in bed and look at the trees in Central Park?"

"Sure thing," Tom said. "Linc, would you hand me the Allen wrench?"

Trudy loved watching men work with tools. She probably could have put the bed together herself, but it would have been a struggle because the sections were heavy. Besides, as she drifted off to sleep tonight she could think about the fact that Linc, a gorgeous Wall Street studmuffin, had tightened the screws holding the bed together. She'd also remember how he'd leaned over to search Tom's toolbox for the Allen wrench, providing her with a nice view of his buns. He really was a terrific specimen.

Meg sidled closer and spoke in an undertone. "Caught you looking."

"I'd like to lick him all over," Trudy said. She was delighted that he was having trouble finding the Allen wrench, which gave her more time to admire the fit of his jeans.

"Nobody's stopping you," Meg murmured.

"I doubt he'd want a girl fresh off the farm. He's probably used to more sophisticated—" She paused to stare in astonishment as Linc pulled a pipe wrench out of the toolbox and handed it to him. It not only wasn't an Allen wrench, it wasn't even vaguely similar to an Allen wrench.

Tom looked at the large tool and gave a slight shake of his head. Then he drew a subtle little diagram in the air. Immediately Linc put the heavy wrench back, dug around some more, and came up with the Allen wrench. Tom gave a little nod and took it.

Trudy exchanged a glance with Meg. The little tableau she'd just witnessed definitely needed dissecting.

Meg jerked her head toward the bedroom to signal that they could duck in there for a conference. "Come on,

Trudy," she said, raising her voice. "I'll help you hang your clothes in the closet."

"Great." She followed Meg into the bedroom and over to the closet. "Did you see that? Linc doesn't know a pipe wrench from an Allen wrench."

Meg nodded. "And even more significant, he didn't want you to know he didn't know. I think we have to conclude that your opinion of him matters."

"So what do I do about that?" Trudy's pulse raced with excitement.

"I have to tell you?"

She clutched her stomach, which was fluttering madly. "I'm not ready for this."

"Why not? I thought you could hardly wait to start sampling the exciting men of New York."

"That's true, but I don't want to screw it up, especially with a guy like Linc. He may not know a pipe wrench from an Allen wrench, but he's used to New York women, women who have that big-city polish. Eventually I might have that, but I don't yet."

"What happened to your motto? Fake It Till You Make It. I could help you. We used to be pretty good at coming up with seduction plans."

"Nope, nope, nope." Trudy waved both hands as absolute panic set in. She might be able to fake an Irish jig, but she wasn't prepared to fake being a New York City girl. Not yet.

"Come on, Trudy. What do you have to lose?"

"My pride, that's what! Besides, it's too late. He's already seen me like this." She held out both arms. "Here I am, your average Kansas farm girl."

"There's nothing average about you and you know it."

"Not on the inside, maybe, but on the outside I'm looking pretty damned homespun. You know how important first impressions are. I could never transform myself enough to erase his image of me as a cute little country mouse."

Meg frowned. "I think it's worth a shot."

"And I don't think it's doable. He can be my buddy for the first couple of weeks, if that would make you feel better, but that's as far as I can see it going. He's already met the *before* version of Trudy Baxter. I could never sell him on the *after*."

"Hey, he's a guy! Fulfill some of his dearest fantasies and he'll forget all about that homespun image."

"The first time I try that maneuver, I want it to be with somebody who doesn't know I'm from Virtue, Kansas, where it's a twenty-mile drive to the nearest McDonald's."

Meg shrugged. "Okay. We'll forget it. He can just be your buddy."

"Good." For a brief moment she was irritated at Meg for bringing Linc on the scene too early. But then her irritation passed. Meg had only been trying to help.

THE PLAN HAD HIT a slight snag, but Meg wasn't about to give up now. From the moment she'd met Linc, she'd known that he was crying out for the right woman, someone who could shake him up and break through that protective shell. With her dynamic personality, sensuous nature and traditional roots, Trudy was everything he needed.

Getting Linc and Trudy together served so many purposes. Linc needed a wife and family no matter how vehemently he denied it, and Trudy could date every eligible man in New York and not find anybody better than Linc. Meg couldn't see the point in wasting all that time. Her best friend married to Tom's best friend made so much sense she got goose bumps thinking about it.

Besides, Meg had lived the single life that Trudy seemed to think would be paradise, and it wasn't what Trudy imagined. The search was painful and traumatic, and Meg wished she'd met Tom a long time ago. Tom had told her the same thing. Meg was simply trying to save Trudy grief.

And get revenge. Trudy had teased her unmercifully

about "selling out" during the six months she'd dated Tom. Meg wanted to watch Trudy fall just as hard for someone, and Linc was the perfect guy to sweep her off her feet. Trudy was so damned sure that she wasn't going to get caught the way Meg had.

But she was. Meg smiled to herself. It was payback time.

3

"SHE SAW ME FLUB UP with the wrench," Linc said, glancing over at Tom. He'd never felt so out of his depth with a woman. And the worst part was, he wasn't supposed to care, and he did.

"It's no big deal." Tom finished connecting the side rail to the headboard.

"I'll bet it's a big deal with her. Hell, she's the first woman I've ever met who owns her own toolbox."

"Well, you're probably the first guy she's ever met who owns his own stock portfolio, so get over it. Besides, what do you care what she thinks of you?"

There was ol' Tom, hitting that bottom line with complete accuracy. He had no choice but to lie. "You're right. I don't care."

"Good. For a minute there it sounded like you did. Now hold this together while I get the rest of the hardware."

"Okay." Stepping around the litter of foam packing squares and sections of cardboard, Linc moved to the end of the bed frame. "The thing is, I'm supposed to be showing her the ropes, protecting her in the big, bad city. I don't think it's good for me to look inept, even when it comes to wrenches." He took hold of the footboard and the side rail.

"You worry too much. I think she likes you just fine."

"Yeah, you're probably right. Besides, it doesn't matter if she does or not." The conversation was getting too weird for him, so he changed the subject to the bed, which had elaborately carved posts that rose eight feet in the air. There was something definitely phallic about those posts. "This thing is massive."

"Like I said, I don't know why she had to buy such a monster."

"Orgies?" The thought popped into Linc's head. Lots of thoughts were popping into his head today, and he didn't like it.

"God, I hope not. Meg would flip out if she thought Trudy had something like that in mind."

"Let's hope she doesn't." Linc was way too conservative to have considered multiple partners, but he wasn't about to predict what this little dynamo might have going on under that mop of shiny brown curls. She threw him off his game, with her toolbox and her enthusiastic approach to life.

Unpredictability translated into volatility. In the securities business, volatility promised greater opportunity and greater risk. He was willing to take that kind of risk in the market. After all, it was only money. But when it came to anything involving relationships, he wanted no part of risk.

"I guess you have to look at things from her angle." Tom knelt down and fastened the side rail to the footboard. "She's been living in a house with six kids, probably sharing a bedroom with a couple of sisters. What kind of life is that for a woman in her twenties?"

"Frustrating," Linc admitted. He imagined Trudy as a sexual powder keg, and the concept made him nervous.

"The little town of Virtue doesn't provide much opportunity for unmarried people to have sex, either," Tom said. "There are those long country roads I mentioned and not much else. No bed-and-breakfast, no motel, not even a campground. Even if there was, nobody would get away with staying overnight there without the whole town finding out."

"Sounds brutal."

"My folks said it reminded them of going back to the fifties." Tom moved around to the other side of the bed.

By now Linc knew the routine and held the sections to-gether while Tom manned the Allen wrench. "I guess it's not like any small town I've ever seen," he said.

"Nope. It's Middle America, buddy. Meg and I spent our wedding night in her old room in a twin bed. Prior to that I was on the foldout couch in the living room and, let me tell you, there was no creeping around possible. Squeaking floorboards, cats and dogs, booby traps everywhere. That's why we ended up taking that long drive out in the country."

"Amazing." In the world of the wealthy, such roadblocks never existed. Once he'd reached driving age he'd had a Gold Card and the freedom to use it for renting little hide-aways. His parents had been too busy with their own com-plicated lives to pay much attention. He remembered hear-ing about curfews and had sort of wished he'd had one. It sounded stable.

"It's funny to think that our first kid was probably con-ceived in the back seat of her daddy's Dodge," Tom said. "Shades of my high school days, or I should say nights. Friday night after the football games was a favorite make-out time at our school. I'll bet it was the same at yours."

Linc checked to make sure the women were still in the bedroom. Then he lowered his voice. "I've never had sex in a car."

Tom looked up in surprise. "You're kidding."

"Nope."

"Not even in a limo?"

"Good Lord, no. With Cecil in the chauffeur's seat?"

"Jeez, I would have thought you'd have tried it, anyway. Cecil or no Cecil." Tom returned to his work. "Meg and I have even thought about hiring a limo. It'd be a step up from the Dodge, but still some of the same turn-ons."

"I don't think I've ever dated anybody who would go for it." Linc preferred to put the blame there, rather than admit to himself that he'd never considered the possibility.

"That's too bad. Now that you mention it, I hadn't either

until Meg came along. Maybe living in that small town with nothing exciting going on caused her to have a richer fantasy life than she would have otherwise."

"Yeah, maybe." He thought about Trudy. From all indications, Trudy would go for it, too. But he wasn't planning to get to know her that well.

"Whatever the reason, I thank God I met Meg. I know you're not a fan of the married life, but it's great, buddy. Really great."

"I'm happy for you." And he was. He hoped Tom would be making the same kind of statements next year, and the year after, but he wouldn't bet on it.

Yet maybe they'd beat the odds. He thought about his parents' sham of a marriage as he watched Tom work on the bed. Finally, mostly to escape his thoughts, he asked if he could take over with the wrench. He thought he had the hang of it now.

"Be my guest." Tom handed him the Allen wrench.

Linc mimicked what he'd seen Tom do, and sure enough, the screws went in like they were supposed to. He couldn't believe what a sense of satisfaction that gave him. He grinned. "Who knew this kind of screwing could be so much fun?"

Tom laughed. "It doesn't compare with the other kind, but if you're enjoying yourself, somebody still needs to put the canopy rail around the top and fit the slats across it. It might as well be you, tool guy."

"How are we going to get up there?"

Tom motioned to a couple of boxes in the corner. "From the weight of those, they have to be full of books. We'll stack those and stand on them."

"Sounds good." Linc positioned the boxes and stepped carefully, making sure the boxes would hold him. "This should work. Hand me one of those rails." He wished Trudy would come out of the bedroom and see that he was the guy with the wrench now and Tom was the helper.

"We should help her put the canopy on the thing, too," Tom said. "From what I know of Trudy, she'll want the whole effect."

"Now that I see how this is done it's not so mysterious." Linc climbed down and moved the boxes to the next corner. "But it's kind of embarrassing to think that a thirty-one-year-old guy has never done anything like this before."

"Why?" Tom watched him, arms folded. "People learn this stuff out of necessity, and you didn't need to know. I'm sure Trudy has her own toolbox because she's the oldest kid in her family. Her father probably taught her so she could help take care of things around the house when she was big enough. My dad taught me for the same reason."

Linc moved the boxes again. "It all sounds so normal. My dad taught me how to scope out the Dow Jones."

"Which will earn you a hell of a lot more than understanding the difference between a pipe wrench and an Allen wrench. Trust me on that one."

"Yeah, but I miss not knowing some of those guy things. I couldn't replace a spark plug if my life depended on it."

"When you drive a Benz, you're not supposed to be changing your own spark plugs. I don't even think you're supposed to open the hood by yourself. No telling what highly sophisticated bit of German engineering you'd foul up if you started tinkering."

"Maybe I'll get a Harley and work on that." Linc started on the last corner of the bed.

"Let's not get carried away with this manly man thing, shall we? I think drinking beer and learning to operate an Allen wrench should carry you for quite a while."

Linc grinned at him. "You're just afraid if I get a Harley I'll be too cool for you."

"You're already too cool for me. I'm afraid if you get a Harley you'll run yourself into a ditch trying to look like Sly Stallone. Riding one of those things is trickier than it seems."

"Maybe so." Linc hopped down off the boxes and accidentally tipped one over. The tape on the lid gave way and several books tumbled out. "Guess you were right about these being book boxes."

"I've moved enough times that I know a book box when I pick it up."

Linc crouched down to put the books back and happened to glance at one of the titles. *Erotic Fantasies of Everyday Women.* He took a quick look at a couple of the others and found *Orgasmic Pleasures* and *Sexual Adventures for the Uninhibited.*

"Linc?" Tom asked. "Are you going to read books or help me put the box springs and mattress in the frame?"

Linc shoved the books back in the box and smoothed the tape into place. "Those aren't just books," he said in a low tone.

"What do you mean? They looked like books to me."

He stood and walked over to Tom. "They're *sex books.*"

Tom laughed. "Then I guess she's got them in the right room."

"Guess so." Linc tried to sound as nonchalant as Tom was about the whole thing, but he couldn't stop thinking about those books. Other than *Playboy,* he'd never read much on the subject of sex. As far as he knew, his girlfriends hadn't, either. Buying a book like the ones Trudy had was like admitting you didn't know what you were doing. And he knew what he was doing.

"Come on," Tom said. "Let's put that pair of box springs in place."

"Did you ever read books like that?"

Tom paused, hands on his hips. "Meg has a couple. I skimmed them."

"Anything new in them?"

Tom shrugged. "A few things."

"Just wondering." Linc wasn't fooled. Tom was being a little *too* casual. Linc would bet his bond portfolio that Tom had devoured those books of Meg's but wasn't about to admit that to Linc.

"Let's get this done," Tom said.

"Right." Fortunately, sliding both of the box springs onto the frame required muscle, not brain. His brain was currently on overload. This deprived young woman had come to town in search of a more exciting sex life. She'd brought her sex books and she'd decided to set up a gigantic bed in her living room.

She probably had no idea how much trouble she could get into if the wrong guy got wind of this operation. If somebody didn't watch out for her, she was headed for…who knows what.

He considered the problem while he and Tom wrestled with the extra-thick, pillow-top, guaranteed-great-for-sex mattress. Eventually, after some huffing and puffing and a few well chosen swearwords, they got the mattress into position. The bed was ready.

Linc stood beside Tom gazing at the expanse of mattress and trying to decide what the hell to do about this situation. "I have a king, too, but this looks bigger."

"I think it's those heavy carved posts that make it look so huge," Tom said. "Plus the bedroom is tiny, but even the living room isn't that big. She's lucky these apartments are old enough to have high ceilings. This bed belongs in a suite at the Ritz."

"It's up! Yippee!"

Linc turned in time to see Trudy make a run for the bed, kick off her shoes and launch herself on top of the mattress. "Perfect!" She flopped back, spread-eagled. "I love it. I knew I would love it, and I do."

Linc had such an overwhelming surge of desire that he had to look away. If he had that reaction to Trudy, and he was a reasonably cool and collected guy, what would happen with somebody less controlled than he was?

"It looks okay there," Meg said. "A little unconventional but, after all, this is New York."

"It'll be a conversation piece, that's for sure," Tom said.

Linc didn't think conversation was Trudy's purpose in buying the bed. But she was definitely sending a message. With this bed sitting here, she couldn't ask a guy up for coffee and actually expect they'd drink coffee.

Chancing another look in the direction of the bed, Linc discovered that Trudy was now sitting cross-legged in the middle of it. She still looked very appealing, but at least she wasn't horizontal anymore. He took a deep breath.

"Thank you, both of you, for setting this up for me," she said. "It's awesome."

"Not a problem," Linc said. "Glad to help out."

She turned toward the two windows at the front of the apartment. "I can see the tree branches in Central Park from this spot, like I thought I would be able to. And at night there'll be a little sliver view of the lights. I'll have a reminder that I'm in New York when I open my eyes in the morning and right before I close them again at night."

"Exactly what you wanted," Meg said. Then she glanced at her watch. "Whoops, we have to go, Tom."

Linc panicked. He couldn't let them leave while he was still here. He wasn't ready to be alone with Trudy yet.

Tom blinked. "Where are we going?"

"You don't remember? Connie from work is loaning me an antique cradle, and we're supposed to pick it up before three."

"I should be taking off, too," Linc said. "I have a—"

"That was today?" Tom looked confused. "I didn't know that was today."

Meg walked over and patted his arm. "It doesn't matter. I remembered. Get our coats, will you, honey? Linc, don't feel you have to rush off."

Trudy bounced off the bed. "Hey, guys, want some help

with the cradle? After all, you helped me, so I could help you.''

"Sure," Linc said. "That makes sense. So I'll just go, and the three of you can do this cradle thing."

"We're fine with getting the cradle ourselves," Meg said. "But Trudy, I'm sorry we don't have time to help put the canopy on. I know how much you wanted to see how that looked."

Tom pulled his arm back out of his coat sleeve. "Linc and I can get that thing up there in no time. We'll—"

"Can't," Meg said. "If we don't leave now we'll miss Connie. Considering that she's trusting us with a family heirloom, I don't think we want to be a no-show."

"Guess not." Tom started putting his coat on again. "You're positive it was today? I could have sworn—"

"It's today," Meg said firmly. She glanced over at Linc. "I'll bet you and Trudy could get the canopy on."

"That's silly," Trudy said. "Linc's done plenty already. The canopy can wait. Or I might even be able to get it up by myself. I'm pretty creative."

He pictured her balancing on things she shouldn't be using for a ladder and falling. She could easily hurt herself. Then he thought about her excitement when the bed had arrived and her long jump to the mattress once he and Tom had set everything up. Someone who was that into the process deserved to have the whole thing completed.

Besides, it was ridiculous for him to go tearing out of this apartment as if he couldn't handle this situation. So what if she had a trunkload of sex books? It wasn't like he was ever going to get involved with her and have to wonder if she knew more than he did.

"You guys go on," he said to Meg and Tom. "I'll stay and help Trudy put up the canopy."

"That's really not necessary," Trudy said.

He dug in his heels. "Listen, it's not a problem."

"Okay, then, we're off," Tom said. He grabbed the hand

truck and pulled it toward the door. "Trudy, if you need anything, call. The phone's working, right?"

"Yep. I checked that when I came over here yesterday to pick up the key."

"See you Monday, Tom," Linc called out as Tom and Meg left.

"And I'll see you Monday, too, Meg," Trudy said.

"Right!" With a wave, Meg closed the door.

NICELY DONE, Meg buttoned her coat as she hustled her husband and his hand truck down the chilly hall and into the elevator.

"You're up to something," Tom said once the elevator doors closed.

"Now why would you think that?" She fluffed her hair over the collar of her coat and tried to look innocent. Apparently she'd been too obvious getting them out of the apartment.

"Because you look way too pleased with yourself, and I still think we were supposed to pick up that cradle on Sunday. Are you trying to get Linc and Trudy together? I mean, like, *together?*"

"Oh, maybe I am. A little." She decided to give him a part of the truth.

"*Meg.* You told Linc it wasn't a fix-up! And furthermore, you know that Linc and me, we have this agreement that we'll never—"

"Oh, I know about your silly agreement, and it doesn't matter, because you're not doing this, I am. I didn't take a blood oath never to hook Linc up with anybody, and I wouldn't promise that, anyway, because Linc is the perfect sort of guy for a fix-up. He's nice, he has money, and he's cute."

Tom had the most adorable scowl and he used it on her now. "I can't believe you're trying to fix him up."

"Oh, come on, it's not the end of the world. It might be a wonderful thing."

"You never told me you thought he was cute."

"Not as cute as you." She walked over and cupped his cheek in one hand as she gazed into his eyes. "You're cuter than a speckled pup." He loved it when she used some of her country expressions, and she saved them for moments when she wanted him to chill, like now.

He was obviously trying to hold on to his scowl, but the speckled pup reference had softened him up some. "Now don't go trying to talk cute and country so you can get out of this," he said, but his tone had lost its edge. "What are you trying to do to my friend?"

"Nothing he won't enjoy." She combed her fingers through his hair, knowing he liked that, too. "Look, Trudy's looking for guys exactly like him, so what's wrong with having her start with someone we know is safe?"

"You had this in mind all along, didn't you?"

"Kind of." She saw no reason to admit that she'd hoped to get them together at the wedding, but that hadn't worked out.

Tom shook his head. "I should have known. Actually I *did* know, as soon as you brought up the idea of having Linc watch out for Trudy for a couple of weeks. You could have asked Shauna or Ellen, but here you were asking Linc instead. It sounded fishy from the beginning, but I ignored my instincts and let you carry on."

"Oh, Tommy." She pinched his cheek lightly. "What's so wrong with it?"

"You're breaking Linc's and my agreement, is what's wrong with it, Megs." He sighed in resignation. "Now on Monday I'll have to go into the office and tell him what's up."

She smiled. "I'll bet he already knows, and I'll bet he doesn't care. Didn't you see the way he was looking at her?"

"How? How was he looking at her?"

"Men. You never notice the important stuff." They stepped out of the elevator and walked through the tiny lobby, the hand cart rolling along behind them.

"I don't think he was looking at her any certain way," Tom maintained stubbornly. "And I need to warn him this is a fix-up." He held the door for Meg and pulled the cart through it as they stepped into the cold wind.

"I don't think that's necessary."

"Yes, it is." As they walked to the underground parking garage where they'd left the car, Tom put his free arm around Meg and tucked her in next to him. "This is guy stuff. It's a matter of honor. I have to clue him in."

"Okay, go ahead and point out that I've violated your precious code if you want. Then Linc might think he has to back out of the arrangement in righteous indignation. But if you leave well enough alone and let nature take its course, Linc can ignore that this was a fix-up and have some fun. Be honest, don't you think he and Trudy could have a good time together?"

Tom hesitated. "I dunno. That's why we've never picked dates for each other. You can never tell if people will get along or not."

"Sure you can! Think about it. He's always dating these super-sophisticated types that his parents would approve of. I don't know about you, but I find them all kind of boring. I think even Linc finds them boring."

"I guess. He never raves about anybody, that's for sure."

"So why spoil this chance for him to be with somebody fun for a change?"

Tom frowned in concentration. "I have to think about this. I don't like the idea of not being straight with my buddy."

"But it might be for his own good."

They were in the car and easing through Saturday afternoon traffic before Tom spoke again. "You're positive Trudy's not looking for anything permanent?"

"Positive."

"Well, that's something, anyway. Because you know how Linc feels about women with commitment on their minds."

"That's why this is so perfect." Meg sensed victory. "They both have the same goal—a good time with no strings attached."

"Well, I'll see how Linc is on Monday. If he doesn't bring anything up about the situation looking fishy, then maybe I'll let it alone."

"Whatever you want to do, sweetheart." Meg felt generous. If her whole scheme worked as smoothly as this day, she had nothing to worry about.

TRUDY KNEW she should have seen this coming. Meg had given up too quickly on the idea of matching her up with Linc. Now Meg had skedaddled with Tom, hoping that sparks would fly between Trudy and Linc.

They were sort of flying, too. The combination of this gorgeous Wall Street type and her fantasy bed was activating her booster rockets. But she'd meant what she'd said to Meg. When she had her first big-city sexual encounter, she wanted it to be with someone who didn't know she was a hick from the sticks. Linc already knew way too much about her to be a good candidate.

"I think Meg engineered that on purpose," Linc said.

"I think she did, too. But don't worry. I have absolutely no designs on you." Funny how saying that out loud took away her nervousness. If he wasn't a potential lover, then she could be herself.

"Oh." He looked a little disappointed. "Well, that's good, because—"

"I know. Meg told me you're a free spirit. So am I." Now that she had her head on straight about him, she was determined not to get sucked in by the cuteness of his disappointed expression. Back home her younger brothers and sisters had played her tender heart like a fine instrument, and she'd almost always given in.

He cleared his throat. "I'm not sure *free spirit* is the way I'd describe myself."

"Then how would you describe yourself?"

"Cautious."

"Ah." She wished he hadn't said that. The folks in Virtue worshiped caution. After twenty-six years of being inundated with the stuff, she automatically wanted to seek and destroy it wherever possible. Linc announcing he was cautious was like a matador waving a red cape in front of an angry bull. "I guess that's why Meg wanted you to be my baby-sitter."

"Probably."

Trudy walked back over to the bed and leaned against the mattress. Only two hours into ownership of it and she loved the damn thing. She loved it almost as much as she loved tweaking someone who billed himself as a cautious person. "I might as well tell you that she wanted me to seduce you."

4

TRUDY WATCHED with enjoyment as Linc's jaw dropped. Then for some reason his gaze flicked to the boxes stacked behind her. She wondered if he'd peeked at the contents of those boxes.

"But you can relax," she said, "because I'm not going to seduce you."

"Why not? I mean, of course you're not. You just got here. We just met." He kept looking at the boxes.

Finally she decided to call him on it. "You peeked."

"Not on purpose!" Red crept up from the collar of his Ivy League sweatshirt. "I used the boxes for a stepladder and one of them tipped over and spilled. I had to put them back in."

"Look, if you're going to baby-sit me, we need to get something straight. Here's the deal. I want to soak up the atmosphere of the big city, which includes lots and lots of dating. With different men. I want to broaden my view of the world, expand my horizons, learn to appreciate different kinds of—"

"About that, I just want to mention that if you bring a date up here, then he's going to assume a few things."

"If I bring a date up here, it's because I want to have sex with him. Present company excepted, of course."

"That's good." He looked agitated. "Because once he gets a look at that—" he swept a hand toward the bed "—you won't be able to talk him out of having sex with you."

"But, you see, I won't want to talk him out of it. He'll

be one of the people I've chosen to broaden my experience with.''

"Great! Because you won't be able to talk him out of *anything* with that bed-o-rama sitting right here in the living room, and no other furniture."

"Linc, have you ever had sex in the back seat of a compact car?''

"No. I—''

"Of course you haven't. Meg said your family's richer than God. Whoops! That was tasteless of me, wasn't it? I didn't mean to offend you. I really didn't.''

"No offense taken. They are richer than God. I don't think I've ever ridden in a compact car, let alone had sex in one.''

"It's not much fun.'' She blew out a breath. "Well, sex is always fun, but crammed into a compact is not the best way to enjoy it, believe me. One of you usually gets a crick somewhere, and odds are good that you'll get an elbow in the ribs or a bump on the head. In the winter it's freezing, and in the summer you can't keep the windows down or you'll be chewed alive.''

"In Kansas?'' He looked startled. "I didn't think bears lived in Kansas.''

"Chewed alive by mosquitoes. Then there's the distinct possibility that at a critical moment, when nirvana is within reach, the law will show up and shine a flashlight in the window. That usually deflates things in a hurry.''

"I can imagine.''

"And *that's* why I wanted the biggest bed I could find.''

He gazed at her for a long moment. "Just so you know the message you're sending. That's all I'm saying.''

Those blue eyes of his were killer. Looking into them she wished, once again, that Meg hadn't brought him on the scene so early. She would have liked to meet Linc in a few weeks, after she had her act together. "And as my guardian angel on the mean streets, you have to warn me of the messages I'm sending. I understand that. Want to check my wardrobe?''

"Uh, I guess I could take a look, but I have to tell you I'm not good at imagining what something will look like unless it's on you. I mean, on a hanger it's sort of shapeless, and—''

"Just kidding!'' She smiled at him. Meg was right, he was a nice guy. A conscientious guy. "Don't worry, Linc, I'll be careful who I let in the front door. And as for the canopy, you don't have to help me. I'm sure you have things to do with the rest of your Saturday.''

"It's okay. I can help.'' He glanced around. "Where is it?''

"In that box. But seriously, I can do this. I'd rather save you for tonight.''

He coughed. "Excuse me?''

"Oh, my mistake.'' She felt like an idiot. "We haven't figured out how this baby-sitting is supposed to go, and I just made a big assumption that we'd start tonight. But you probably have a date, considering that it's Saturday and everything. Never mind.''

"Uh, no date. Tonight's fine.''

"It is? That's great!'' She hadn't wanted to point out to Meg and Tom that this would be her first Saturday night ever in New York, because for some reason they hadn't noticed. Then again, maybe Meg had deliberately avoided mentioning it because she'd planned all along that Linc would show Trudy around tonight.

Frankly, she didn't care if Bozo the Clown showed her around. She just wanted to be out there tonight, walking along the Great White Way or sipping a drink in a jazz club, or maybe, if Linc could stand the hokeyness of it, riding the elevator to the top of the Empire State Building to get the full impact of all those lights.

"What would you like to do?'' Linc asked.

"*Everything.*'' She could hardly wait. "Piano bars, comedy clubs—oh! I'll bet there's ice skating at Rockefeller Center!''

"Do you want to see something on Broadway?"

She thought about that. "Yes, but not tonight. That would take up too many hours and, besides, I'll bet we couldn't get tickets for anything good this late."

"Don't worry about that. I could get tickets."

"Well, yeah, and pay an arm and a leg for them. That would blow my entertainment budget in no time."

"I didn't intend for you to pay."

She realized they had another point to cover. "That's sweet of you to offer, but I'll be paying my own way. I've been saving change for years for my New York entertainment fund. I lugged ten canning jars full of coins to the bank last week and converted them to folding money. So long as I don't splurge on things like dinner at the Four Seasons, it should last me quite a while."

"Trudy, that's ridiculous. I'll take care of any expenses in the next couple of weeks and you can use that money to buy furniture or something else you really need."

She crossed her arms over her chest. Having her plans labeled *ridiculous* didn't rate as one of her preferred experiences. "What I really need is a good time in the big city. The only piece of furniture required for that is already sitting here. I realize saving money in mason jars might sound quaint and silly to a man of your infinite resources, but I loved doing it, knowing what I was saving for. Now comes my reward, and the money is going for exactly what I planned it would." She leveled a glance at him. "Exactly."

"But—"

"You're doing enough by giving up your valuable dating time for this, and by rights I should be treating you. In fact, that's what I'll—"

"Don't even go there. I'm doing a favor for my friends, not running an escort service."

"All right. I can respect that." The little bit of steel in his voice when he laid down the law was actually very thrilling. A zing of pleasure traveled through her, headed for the spot where all her pleasurable zings gathered. Not only was Meg right about Linc being a nice guy, she'd also been right that he was sexy as all get-out.

Unfortunately he probably saw her as a hick. It was way too late to change that first impression, but she couldn't help wanting to stage a slight comeback. To do that, she needed to get him out of here. Now that she thought about it, allowing him to help put this bed together was like allowing a theater audience to help construct the sets. It ruined the chance to create an illusion.

Most of the damage had been done, but she didn't have to let him work on the canopy, too. Maybe once the canopy and the linens were in place she might have a shot at impressing him, even if he had been part of the construction process.

He'd never enjoy that bed with her, of course, but it would be gratifying to know that he'd like to, once he'd seen the full effect. Yes, she needed him to go home and come back in a few hours, after she'd had a chance to complete the look she was after.

"If we're going out tonight, I'd like to take a long soak in the tub first," she said. "So let's not bother with the canopy."

"Why not put it up and be done with it?"

"It's not important." She waved a hand at the bed. "It's not like I'm going to be entertaining anyone in it tonight."

"That's for damn sure! As long as we're establishing ground rules, here's another one. If you leave this apartment with me, you're coming back with me. No leaving with some stranger."

"Well, of course! Just because I'm from a little town doesn't mean I didn't learn any manners. If I meet some hottie, we can exchange phone numbers. Then if he asks about you I'll explain that you're gay."

"*What?*"

"I don't want him to think I'm the kind of girl who makes dates with other guys while she's out with someone."

"Then for God's sake tell them I'm your brother or your cousin." He glared at her with those piercing blue eyes. "New York's a smaller town than you might think."

"We don't look like we're related," she said gently.

"I don't care. Say it anyway."

"Okay, if you insist."

He sighed and rubbed the back of his neck. "You know, to be honest, I'm not wild about taking you out there so you can troll for phone numbers. I'm beginning to feel like a damned pimp."

She studied him for a moment. "Maybe we should forget the whole thing." As much as she'd begun to look forward to a night on the town with him, he might not have the right personality for this assignment. Here she was poised on the brink of her big adventure, and he looked ready to throw up roadblocks. She'd waited too long for this to tolerate obstacles.

He gazed at her in obvious frustration.

"Really, Linc. I'm sure Meg would understand if I told her we just didn't mesh. You'd be off the hook. She knows how bullheaded I can be sometimes, so she'd blame me, not you."

He shook his head. "Nope. This isn't about doing Meg a favor anymore. Now that I've met you, I can't just let you roam the streets of New York by yourself on your first Saturday night. And don't bother telling me you'd stay home, because I wouldn't believe you. You might even think you're going to stay home, but once you hear the city coming to life, you'd have to be out there."

"I really do want to go," she admitted. "I got in late Thursday night, and Friday I spent the whole day getting oriented at the agency. Meg and Tom took me to dinner last night, but I could tell she was really tired, so we went straight back to their apartment. I was awake half the night wishing I could explore."

"So how about a compromise?" He stuck his hands in the back pockets of his jeans.

"Like what?" It was quite a manly pose, and she was as susceptible as the next woman to a muscular chest and narrow hips. She was ready to compromise.

"This first night, you won't be on the lookout for potential dates. No flirting, no exchanging phone numbers. I'll show you around, get you used to the place, and then we'll renegotiate our terms tomorrow."

"Done." She liked the idea that she'd be his date exclusively for the evening. Being Linc's date wouldn't be half bad. Not even a quarter bad.

"You're sure you don't want to get that canopy on before I go?"

"Positive."

"Okay, then. I'll pick you up at eight."

"I'll be ready." He was picking her up at *eight*. That proved that she was in the big city. In Virtue, dates usually began much earlier. Of course they ended much earlier, too, because everything, even the movie theater, was closed by ten. If you stayed out any later than that, everyone knew you were parking, and there was an understood limit of two hours on that activity. Any more time and the girl involved was labeled a nympho.

"Do you have a warm coat?"

"Sure." She thought of her only winter coat and inwardly winced. It was a parka, not a dress coat. She'd put off buying any new clothes until she'd had a chance to see what was in style, but she lusted after a black leather trench coat, something that would never go out of style. Pricey items like that, however, would have to wait until she'd recovered from the purchase of the bed. Maybe she'd figure out a way not to wear her parka tonight, though.

"Okay, then. See you soon." He picked up his coat, smiled at her and headed out the door.

FIVE HOURS LATER, Linc whistled for a cab and gave the driver Trudy's address. The itinerary folded neatly and tucked in his coat pocket had taken him most of the afternoon to prepare, and he was proud of it. He didn't often get to show off his favorite town to a person like Trudy, someone who lived in a tiny place and had virtually no experience with the big city.

Now that he was into it and now that they'd established that she was his date for the night, he was looking forward to the evening more than any in recent memory. He wasn't the kind of guy to seek out novelty, but now that it had been plopped in his lap, he was discovering how intoxicating it could be. Trudy represented novelty with a capital *N*.

In the hours they'd been apart he'd had some breathing room to analyze the effect she had on him, so he felt in better control of himself now. Standing there in her living room with that gigantic bed in the background had really screwed with his mind. He'd battled fantasies that had no business cropping up in this relationship.

Frankly, he thought Meg was being pretty dumb to try and throw Trudy and him together. Nothing good could come of it. Sure, they might have some chemistry going, but both of them cherished their freedom. That meant that any relationship would be short-term. A short-term affair between him and Trudy could only complicate their dealings with Meg and Tom, both during and after.

Of course, he'd never thought of Meg as dumb. Maybe she really had been bitten by the marriage bug and thought she could interest Linc and Trudy in a walk down the aisle so the two couples could do married things together. If so, then Meg hadn't been paying attention. He'd just met Trudy and already he could tell she wouldn't go for that any more than he would.

Too bad Trudy was tied in with Meg and Tom, though. If he'd met her on his own, she'd be the perfect playmate. He'd never have thought he'd be such a sucker for a girl straight off the farm, but her lack of sophistication really turned him on. He could hardly wait to see her reaction to the night he had planned. She'd be bouncing off the walls.

He could also picture her bouncing on that big bed of hers. He could picture that way too easily, and he needed to forget about it. Much as he'd love to find out what all that contagious enthusiasm could do for a mattress party of two, he couldn't afford to jeopardize his friendship with Meg and Tom.

Well, mostly Tom. But Linc knew that if he alienated Meg by mishandling the Trudy situation, he'd probably lose Tom as a friend in the process. That was another strike against marriage—it seemed to make friendship twenty times more complicated.

No doubt it was past time for him to find another single guy or two to hang out with, but he'd procrastinated. Buddies like Tom didn't come along every day. Some might say he wasn't facing the reality of Tom's new status. They could be right.

As the cab pulled up in front of Trudy's apartment building, excitement surged through him. He checked to make sure his itinerary was still in his pocket and told the cabbie to wait for him. Knowing the meter was running would keep him from lingering in that apartment with Trudy and a bed the size of Kansas. The less time he spent inside that apartment, the better for all concerned.

As he took the rattletrap elevator to her floor he wondered if the stairs would have been faster. But he was still on time, and he could guarantee she'd be on time, too. Anybody with as much anticipation as Trudy would be standing by the door with her coat on. She'd be tapping her foot. He glanced down when he realized that he was tapping his.

When the elevator finally rumbled to a stop and the doors creaked open, he exited quickly. A few steps down the hall, and he was there, ringing her doorbell for the second time today. The first time he'd been impatient and a little irritated with Meg for putting him in this position. Tonight he was still impatient, but for a totally different reason. His breathing was different, and his heart rate was *definitely* different; his heart was acting as if he really had climbed the stairs.

Exactly as he'd expected, she flung open the door. She did not have her coat on. In fact, she didn't have nearly enough on, period. Her skirt was short, tight and black, revealing stocking-covered legs that lived up to the promise of the wedding reception picture he'd seen.

Determined not to stare at those shapely legs, he glanced at the rest of her and discovered that her black sweater was equally tight, showing off ogle-me breasts and a waist so tiny he could probably span it with his two hands. She looked...ready for action. He gulped.

"Come on in." She grabbed his hand. "Let me show you the bed."

He didn't want to see the bed. She was supposed to be ready, and then they'd just go, just leave, and get away from the damned bed. But here she was tugging him forward, into the shadowy apartment, right where he didn't want to go.

They'd never touched before, and he found the experience jolting. Her hand was so soft, so warm, so electric. But the grip of her hand was nothing compared to the scene she'd set, apparently for his benefit.

Candles flickered on the windowsills and on top of the boxes she'd arranged as nightstands. They were the only light in the room, so that the bare corners faded into the shadows and the bed stood out in all its glory. Dazed, he tried to take it all in.

She'd managed to get the canopy on. The heavy, ivory-colored material covered the top of the bed and partially curtained off the interior, giving it the look of an Arabian tent. Inside was a sinful abundance of black satin—mounds of pillows and supple sheets folded back in open invitation.

"What do you think?"

Think? No man could think when presented with something this saturated in sexual fantasy. He could certainly react, though. That reaction was going on right now and he hoped to hell that his open leather trench coat was draped in such a way as to hide what was happening to him.

"Isn't it awesome?" she prompted again.

"It's, um, yeah, very…nice."

"It's *exactly* what I dreamed of. I wanted you to see the finished product. So tell me, honestly, how does it grab you, as a man? Is it too feminine and fussy? Because I wouldn't want a man to feel as if he can't relax and enjoy himself in this bed."

"I, uh—" He stopped to clear the hoarseness from his throat. Then he made the mistake of looking over at her to give his answer. She was leaning against the counter that divided the living room from the little kitchenette. She'd placed a few candles on the counter, too, and the light flickered over her soft curls and seemed to emphasize the tight fit of her sweater and skirt.

"You're hesitating." She looked disappointed. "So I have to believe something about the bed hits you wrong. What is it?"

"Nothing…nothing hits me wrong." It was all hitting him right, ringing all his chimes—ding, ding, ding. "It's a great bed."

Her smile blazed forth. "Really? You really think so?"

"I do."

"Want to take off your shoes and lie on it? I don't care if you muss up the sheets."

He wondered if she could possibly be naive enough to ask him something like that with no ulterior motives. Maybe. Maybe not. At any rate, there was no way in hell he would stretch out on that bed. Ever.

"Go ahead, Linc! I've already spent like about an hour on it, and I can guarantee it's the softest pillow-top mattress you'll ever sink yourself into. I couldn't test it really well yesterday because I was on my lunch hour, but I picked the right bed. I trusted my instincts and there it is—perfect."

There was another reason he couldn't take her up on her

offer to try the bed. He couldn't remember what it was, but he had a nagging feeling that there was something left undone, something left running. The cab! She'd so completely mesmerized him that he'd forgotten all about the cab downstairs, meter running.

With a mental sigh of relief he told her that their cab was waiting downstairs.

"Oh! You should have said so!" She hurried around the room blowing out candles.

"It's no big deal. I just—" He stopped talking as she blew out the last candle, plunging the room into darkness except for dim light coming through the windows from outside.

"Whoops." She chuckled, a low, throaty sound. "I got a little carried away. Give me a second to let my eyes adjust and I'll find the light switch."

He wasn't about to stand around in the dark with this bundle of sexual energy. He moved in the direction of the door. Light switches were usually on the wall next to the—

They collided with a soft thud, both of them crying out in surprise. His arm connected with her breast and his leg tangled with hers. He had to grab her to keep them both upright.

"Sorry!" Her laugh was breathy and intimate. "I was headed toward the door."

"Me, too." He released her the second he was sure they were both steady again, but not soon enough to prevent his whole body from starting to hum, not soon enough to abort the rush of yearning and the tightening of his groin.

He stood in the dark fighting his urges. He'd always been pretty good at that, thanks to early training in suppressing his emotions. His parents considered emotions messy and inconvenient, and this was living proof that they were right.

"Okay, I found a switch. I don't know what it does, but we should get some light, somewhere." Next came a faint click, and a bulb set high in the ceiling by the door came on, creating a spotlight around her. She glanced up with a grin and lifted her arms. "Presenting...Gypsy Rose Lee!"

His mouth went dry. She was beautiful. Damn. Cute he could have ignored, but beautiful was a whole different ball game.

"Okay, enough fooling around," she said. "I'll get my little backpack and we'll go."

He nodded, struck dumb by the picture she'd made standing in the spotlight. He wondered how Tom could have missed that she was beautiful. But he must have missed it, because the main thing he'd said about Trudy was that she was perky. Oh, well. He'd have to forgive Tom for not warning him that Trudy possessed a sexual power that could reduce a man to begging. Ol' Tom had been dealing with other things at the time, like getting married.

She hurried into what was originally the bedroom, her shoes making a clacking sound against the bare floor. In no time she'd returned, shrugging into a little black backpack on her way to the door. The movement drew his attention to her breasts, and he felt dizzy with desire.

Somehow he managed to usher her out the door without saying that he'd changed his mind and he wanted to test out her bed, after all. Once he got out of the apartment he'd be all right, he told himself. That was the main goal, to escape that apartment with its king-size passion pit and spotlights that turned Trudy into a fantasy stripper.

Once she'd locked the door and they were on their way to the elevator, he heaved a sigh of relief.

5

As THEY RODE DOWN in the elevator, Trudy glanced with envy at Linc's leather trench coat. It made him look dark and mysterious, like an international spy. Close up the leather even smelled expensive. That look was exactly what she wanted, once she could afford a coat like his. No more bouncy little farm girl. Cool, elegant and mysterious—that would be her.

The bed was more important, though, and she was glad she'd splurged. She only hoped she hadn't overdone it.

"Really, Linc, I want you to tell me what you thought of the bed," she said. "If you think the sheets are a bit much, I could return them for something that doesn't scream out *sex!* Maybe I've been too obvious."

He cleared his throat.

She'd noticed that he'd been doing that a lot lately. "You're not coming down with a cold, are you? Because I sure don't want to impose on you if you're not feeling okay."

"I feel fine." He looked puzzled. "Why would you think I'm getting sick?"

"Well, you've been sort of quiet, and you're clearing your throat a lot, and one time I thought your voice was a little raspy. In my family, that means you're getting sick." And he was a man, which meant he couldn't be trusted to know when he was getting sick. "Let me feel your forehead."

He ducked away from her outstretched hand. "I really don't have a fever."

"Now I'm *really* suspicious. Hold still." She kept trying to get a hand on his forehead and he kept dodging out of reach. In the back of her mind lurked the possibility that she was using this as an excuse to get her hands on him. "Meg and Tom would be very unhappy if I dragged you out into the cold when you were sick."

He finally grabbed her wrists. "I'm not sick, okay?"

Oooh, she did like it when he took command of a situation like that. Very sexy, indeed. His grip was firm, his fingers warm. Not hot, though, so maybe he was okay. "Would you tell me if you were sick?"

"I would tell you." With a little sigh he released her wrists.

Immediately she was sorry they'd lost the connection. She'd enjoyed their little run-in during her unintentional blackout, and that sample of being touched by him had made her want more. His hands weren't rough and chapped like the hands of the farm boys she'd grown up with, and she doubted he'd be clumsy like some of those boys, either. No, a man like Linc would know how to stroke a woman. She shivered just thinking about it.

"You're cold," he said. "Good Lord, you didn't bring a coat. I can't believe I didn't notice that." The elevator bumped to a stop and the doors opened. He punched the button for the fourth floor again. "We need to get your coat. It's freezing out there."

"I don't want my coat." She punched the ground floor button, but she was too late. The elevator lurched upward again.

"What do you mean, you don't want it? You can't go outside like that."

She rolled her eyes at him. "I came to New York to get away from this sort of parental conversation. I'm twenty-six years old, and I'll go outside without a coat if I want to.'' She'd tried on her parka, just to see if it looked as hideous with this outfit as she'd imagined. It had looked even worse.

As the elevator clanked and groaned to her floor, Linc stared at her. ''You have to be kidding. That outfit's skimpy to begin with! I mean, look at what I have on compared to you. Slacks, a long-sleeved shirt, a jacket *and* a leather coat. You have nothing but nylons on your legs, a very short skirt and a thin sweater.''

How nice that he'd taken such detailed notice of her outfit. She'd wondered if her clothes had made an impression. His glance seemed more than casual as he listed what she was wearing, so he'd definitely noticed. Unless she was sadly mistaken, there was a teensy bit of lust in his expression. That's what she'd been going for, so the outfit worked.

''The only way you're going to survive out there is with a coat,'' he said. ''A long, warm coat.''

''I don't have a long, warm coat.''

''But you have something. Nobody comes to New York in January without some kind of coat.''

''Yes, I have something and it's super-ugly. I refuse to spend my first night out on the town wearing a blue-and-orange goose-down parka! I'd rather run around naked.''

He cleared his throat again.

''See? You are getting sick.''

''No, no, I'm not.'' His mouth twitched at the corners.

With growing horror she realized he was trying not to laugh. Oh, God, her worst fear was coming true. The big, sophisticated city man thought it was hilarious that the country bumpkin would rather freeze her ass off than wear an orange-and-blue parka on the streets of New York.

The elevator door opened on the fourth floor, and all she could think about was escape. ''You know what? I really don't feel like going out, after all.'' She bolted through the doors. ''Thanks for the thought, but I just figured out I'm exhausted. Delayed jet lag. I'm going to bed. See you later.''

He caught up to her before she reached her door and his fingers closed around her upper arm. "Wait."

There was that thrilling connection again, but it was tainted now. She couldn't get sexually aroused by a man who was secretly laughing at her. He probably thought her beautiful bed was funny, too, and that's why he'd been clearing his throat so much. He'd been trying not to dissolve into uncontrollable laughter.

When she'd first met Linc, he'd reminded her of some dragon-slaying hero with a strict code of honor. Apparently his code dictated that a lady didn't step out into the cold without a coat. She appreciated his concern, but he'd canceled all his brownie points by smirking.

He wasn't smirking now, though. His blue eyes looked troubled. "If this is about the coat situation—"

"The coat?" She waved a hand. "Heavens, no. This is about a splitting headache." If she thought hard enough about that damned coat, she could probably bring one on, too.

"I'll bet you have some aspirin in your apartment." He continued to hold on to her arm. "Let's go get some."

Despite everything, she loved the confident way he held her arm. Her sweater *was* thin, which meant she could feel his fingertips pressing gently through the knit. That generated enough voltage to warm the rest of her. She didn't need no stinkin' coat.

As he started to tug her down the hall, guilt prompted her to come clean. "I don't have a headache," she said. "It's about the coat. I know that sounds silly to you, but it would really bother me to go out the door wearing that parka. I should have thought of that weeks ago when I was fantasizing this moment, but I didn't. And I can't afford a new coat right now after I blew my next several paychecks on that bed, which you probably also think is dumb."

"No, I don't."

"It's okay." She wondered if he knew that he'd started

stroking his thumb over her inner arm. Probably just a reflex. "You can tell me you think it's dumb and overdone. It'll take a while before I pick up on all the tricks to acting sophisticated and cool in the big city. And part of it takes money. Right now I can't afford a fabulous coat like yours, so I'd rather go without. I won't get cold if I move really fast."

He blinked and looked down at his coat. "You like this coat?"

"I *love* that coat. It shouts *New York City* to me."

"That makes things simple." He let go of her arm and started taking off his coat.

"Hey, what are you doing?"

"Loaning you my coat."

"Not on your life!" She grabbed the collar and tried to get him back into the coat as fast as he tried to take it off. "Keep that on. Do *not* take off this coat!"

He paused. "Are you worried that you'll look stupid? I realize it'll be way too big on you, but you can roll back the sleeves. The length will be about right, since it only comes to my knees."

"I'm not worried that I'll look stupid." The minute she'd grabbed the collar she'd nearly swooned with pleasure at the softness of the leather. Yes, the coat would be too big on her, but that might create its own kind of panache. People might even suspect that Linc had gallantly loaned her the coat for the evening, and she liked the idea of being matched up with him in people's minds. He was quite a hottie.

"Then take it." He shrugged out of the coat and held it toward her.

She closed her hands into fists so she wouldn't reach for it. "That doesn't solve anything. Then you wouldn't have a coat. And, trust me, you don't want to borrow my parka. Aside from the fact you'd split the shoulder seams, it would not go with the Perry Ellis combo you have on." She thought he did great things for designer clothes, too.

''It solves everything. We'll make a quick stop at my apartment before we head out and I'll pick up another one. I can show you the card table and chairs then, too. Here, see how this works for you. Take off your backpack and try it on.'' He held the coat by the shoulders and shook it, sort of like a matador's cape.

She thought about putting her fingers up like horns and charging the coat, but she curbed the impulse. No doubt he already thought she was hokey, so she needed to cool it. ''I'm still not sure about this,'' she said, just so she wouldn't seem too eager. In truth she could hardly wait to slip into that coat.

''It's the best solution. Turn around and I'll put it on.''

She surrendered to temptation. Shrugging out of her backpack, she set it on the floor and turned. With a movement so smooth and suave it made her breath catch, he slipped the coat over her arms and onto her shoulders. The effect was almost as good as an orgasm. The satin lining caressed the backs of her hands, and the mingled scents of expensive aftershave and fine leather made her knees weak.

He walked around in front of her. ''Not bad. Let me roll up the sleeves for you.''

She held out both arms, and while he leaned down and expertly rolled back each sleeve, she closed her eyes and savored the experience. He would be such a skillful lover. Anybody who rolled up sleeves with such care and precision would take the same care in pleasuring a woman's body. She knew it instinctively.

''Tie the belt, grab your purse and you're all set.''

She opened her eyes to discover he was gazing at her with an expression bordering on tenderness. The look in his eyes caused little squiggles of reaction in her as she realized that he would be more than a skillful lover. He would be a sweet one, as well.

The whole concept made her tremble and she fumbled while tying the belt. Eventually she managed it and reached down for her backpack, hooking the straps over her shoulders.

"Let's go." He cupped her arm as they walked toward the elevator.

Although she couldn't feel his grip as well through the leather as she had without it, she was thrilled that he'd apparently become accustomed to touching her. Nothing would come of it, of course, but a little friendly touching here and there would make the evening that much more exciting.

This coat trade was really working out, too. Not only would she get to spend the evening in this fabulous garment, she'd also get a glimpse of Linc's apartment. She had to admit she was dying of curiosity, although she might end up intimidated as hell by the place.

But she needed to see how a sophisticated New York bachelor lived so that she'd have a better idea how to set the scene when she invited a man to *her* apartment for the first time. For one thing, she really needed to see Linc's bed and find out if hers was lacking in good taste. He kept avoiding the subject when she asked, but getting a glimpse of his bedroom would tell her what she needed to know.

When they stepped outside, a chill wind nearly took her breath away. Linc was right. Without this coat she would have been one big icicle. She had another pang of guilt when she saw the yellow cab sitting by the curb and thought of all the time they'd spent dilly-dallying around while the meter was running.

"I'm splitting the cab fare with you!" she called above the rush of traffic and the whistling wind.

He opened the cab door and helped her inside. In the process he put his mouth close to her ear. "We'll see," he said, his breath warm against her skin and his voice low and intimate.

She nearly came unglued. Then she quickly reminded herself that he'd probably murmured in her ear to avoid having to shout in the totally small-town way she'd done. As for his tone, maybe he always sounded sexy when he lowered his voice like that. He gave the cabdriver directions and they were off.

The cab hurtled through traffic as if getting to Linc's apartment was a matter of life and death. Trudy loved it. For years she'd watched movies in which people took mad cab rides through New York, and she would have been disappointed if she hadn't been thrown around a little in the back seat.

On Friday she'd been thrown around with only Meg to bump into, but tonight she had much more exciting collision prospects. Every little jolt against Linc's lean body raised her spirits a little higher. My God, she was actually in New York, riding helter-skelter through the streets of Manhattan in the back seat of a cab next to one of Wall Street's finest.

Then, to complete the picture, Linc pulled a cell phone from an inside pocket of his jacket, flipped it open and made a call. The whole scene made her tingle with delight. From what she could tell from his end of the conversation, he was adjusting a reservation.

A dinner reservation. Good Lord, it hadn't occurred to her that they'd go out to dinner when they were starting the evening at eight. She pushed back the rolled-up sleeve of the trench coat and glanced at her watch. Actually, eight-thirty.

"I hope you're not starving to death," he said. "I moved our reservation to nine."

"Nope," she said with a quick smile. "I'm good." She was determined he would never know about the deli sandwich she'd ordered up and devoured less than an hour ago. She'd found the number on the sack as she was gathering up the garbage from their lunch and had decided she'd treat herself to delivery, considering that she was so busy getting the bed arranged.

Besides, the wonder of having a deli around the corner

that delivered to her door was too amazing to resist. The only place in Virtue that delivered was the Pizza Palace, and even they wouldn't do it if Benny's truck was in the shop, which it was more often than not.

"Where are we going?" Her heart wanted someplace famous like 21 or Elaine's, but her wallet disagreed.

He turned to her, the shadows making his features look even more chiseled. "It's a little Thai place. Good reputation. The lemon-grass soup is outstanding."

"That sounds great." How totally cosmopolitan and ethnic. A quiver of delight ran through her. Even though she thought lemon-grass soup sounded kind of yucky, she'd eat it anyway. She'd never been within spitting distance of a Thai restaurant and wasn't sure what they served besides lemon-grass soup, but with luck it wouldn't be too filling.

"I think you'll like it. The restaurant's owned by one of my clients. A couple of months ago I turned him on to some really good stock, and he's been after me to bring a date down for a couple of meals on the house."

She narrowed her eyes at him, suspecting that he was making it up so that she wouldn't have to pay. "Is that true or are you trying to pull a fast one on me?"

"It's true." His smile flashed in the dim light. "But I'll admit I picked it because I wanted to go easy on your budget. I know you're prepared to pay and that you feel it's important for you to do that, but I don't think you have any idea how entertainment in this city can drain your wallet."

"Meg warned me." Sitting next to him in the cab and absorbing the sweet mystery of that smile was more entertainment than she'd had in a month of Sundays back in Virtue. She was determined to enjoy the night, and to that end she'd been deliberately ignoring the flashing red numbers on the cab's meter. "But you shouldn't be taking *me* for this freebie. You should have used it for somebody else, somebody who was a real date."

"This is a real date."

"Oh." How thrilling to hear him say that.

"And I wanted to share it with somebody who would appreciate it. I didn't want to take someone who would consider this just another meal at a Thai restaurant."

"Believe me, I won't look at it that way." She hoped they didn't serve octopus or something squirmy like that. And if Thai restaurants were a part of that whole sushi thing, she could be in trouble. But even if they put fried grub worms in front of her she'd eat them. If Linc had decided she was worthy of this treat, then she'd make sure she was worthy.

"Well, here we are."

She glanced out the window and gasped. His building had a doorman.

"Anything wrong?"

"No, no." She grinned at him. "Everything is perfect."

LINC WAS IN SERIOUS TROUBLE. Everything about this woman charmed him, and he so wanted to take her to bed. Knowing that she was looking for that kind of experience made the temptation that much greater. And oh, my God, that bed. She was right that it shouted *sex*, but he didn't want to tell her to tone it down. He wanted to jump in there with her.

As he helped her out of the cab, he was struck again by how adorable she looked in his coat. He'd meant to solve a problem, but instead he'd created a new one. Although she looked cute and vulnerable in the oversize coat, every once in a while her stockinged knee would peep out. The first time he'd seen it happen a sudden image of her naked under the coat had grabbed hold of him. Now he couldn't seem to forget it.

Her knee slipped from between the lapels of the coat as she climbed out of the cab, and his groin tightened. Maybe he was more suggestible because he'd found those sex books in her apartment. Or maybe it was because of what his last affair had been like, which had ended two months ago because of boredom on both sides.

Not a single thing about Trudy bored him. Quite the opposite. He couldn't seem to keep his eyes off her. And once he had her out of the cab, he kept her hand in his as they walked toward the entrance because holding her hand felt so damned good.

He'd never thought about it before, but some women knew how to hold hands and some didn't. Trudy knew how. She laced her fingers through his as if fitting two pieces of a puzzle together. Her grip was firm without being too tight. Without warning, his mind made the leap from holding hands to having sex. She'd know how to fit her body to his, and not only because she'd read a few books. He sensed she was naturally talented in that direction.

Greeting Ernesto the doorman with the automatic courtesy that had been drilled into him from birth, he headed into the lobby.

"A doorman," Trudy said with reverence. "I've never in my life walked through a door held by a doorman."

"He's a nice guy. His daughter's trying to make it as a dancer on Broadway." Linc was amazed that he could make conversation when all he could think about was the way Trudy's hand fit with his, and how her body would do the same. They were going up to his apartment, and he wasn't sure he'd have the restraint to keep from trying to seduce her.

That wouldn't be good for all the reasons he'd already listed to himself earlier in the day. Add to that the fact that she'd waited years for this night on the town. He was pretty good at seducing women and he might make her forget her plan for a little while. But spending the night in a guy's apartment wasn't the memory she'd planned to create for her first Saturday evening in New York.

"Look at this elevator! I can see my face in the brass. Does someone polish it every day?"

"Maybe twice a day." He knew that factoid after living in his parents' home, where the help seemed constantly to be polishing doorknobs and hinges.

Nobody got into the elevator with them, so when the doors slid quietly closed, they were very, very alone.

Trudy took a deep breath. "It smells good in here, like furniture polish."

"They probably oil the wood every day, too." He was turning into a sex maniac. The thought of oiled wood had immediately conjured up the thought of oiled bodies. He'd never used scented oils during sex. Now he wanted to. With Trudy.

Come to think of it, he'd never done anything very innovative during sex. The novelty had come from changing partners every so often. Lately, though, even that hadn't worked because the women he asked out seemed cast from the same mold. He hadn't wanted to admit it to himself, but he'd secretly begun to worry if he wasn't a very sexually oriented guy.

No point in worrying about that anymore. One look at Trudy and he felt like a seventeen-year-old pulsing with hormones. She even smelled different from the women he usually dated, and he liked that, too. Maybe now he associated hundred-dollar-an-ounce perfume with sexual boredom. Trudy smelled like cinnamon, and he wanted to begin with her mouth and start tasting until he'd covered every spicy inch.

"Even elevators are a treat for me." She gazed up at him, her green eyes shining with excitement. "I think they're so sexual, with this cylinder sliding up and down inside a shaft."

His body heated. "I, uh, never thought of that."

"Someday I'm going to have sex in an elevator."

If she kept talking like this, someday would be just around the corner. "Is that right?"

"Have you ever?"

"No." Apparently he'd been missing out on all kinds of things.

"I guess you're so used to elevators you never thought of it. You'll have to excuse me for all my crazy ideas. In fact, feel free to say anytime *Oh, Trudy, that is so hokey.* That would help with my education, so when I really start going out with city guys I won't come off as a hayseed."

"So I guess this doesn't count as going out?" he said, feeling a little insulted by that remark.

"No, it definitely doesn't count. I've barely brushed the straw out of my hair, so you're having to put up with the unvarnished farm girl I am now. But give me a little while and I'll fit in with the other New York women a lot better. That's when I'll be ready to hang out my shingle, so to speak."

He had no response to that. He wanted to tell her not to change, that the way she was now was churning him up like no woman ever had. But he couldn't say something like that. Then he'd be implying that he wanted her to stay the same for him, as if he had some claim on her, and they both knew that wasn't true.

Fortunately the elevator doors opened, so he was saved from having to say anything at all. Maybe knowing that she didn't see him as a prospect for fun and games would dampen his enthusiasm enough that they could go to his apartment and get the coat without incident. He was counting on that.

6

TRUDY WAS HAVING the absolute best time of her life. As she walked down the thickly carpeted hallway with Linc, she congratulated herself on deciding against making him her first conquest, as Meg had suggested. If she'd actually planned on that, she'd be a real stress-case as she compared his luxurious surroundings with her extremely basic flat. She'd be intimidated, which was a bad way to begin a relationship.

Instead she could view this trip to his apartment as a fact-finding mission. Chances were she'd never date somebody richer than Linc. She could get all her gosh-oh-gee reactions out of the way now, and by the time she stepped into another city guy's apartment she'd be cool and collected, much harder to impress.

"I really appreciate you taking me under your wing this way," she said as they approached his door and he took a key from his pocket. "Meg was right to suggest it."

"Glad to be of help." He opened the door and gestured for her to go in.

She stepped over the threshold into a foyer containing an antique table topped with a small marble statue. A nude woman, to be exact. The woman's head was thrown back and her hair streamed in an unseen wind. She looked bold and confident, despite not having a stitch on. Nobody in Virtue would display a thing like that right inside the front door, that was for sure.

Trudy pointed to the statue. "I like that."

"Me, too."

"Where did it come from?"

"I picked it up on a trip to Paris. The sculptor's not well-known yet, but I think she will be." He moved past her to a door at the end of the foyer.

Trudy placed a hand to her chest and sighed. "You picked it up on a trip to Paris. That sounds *so* elegant. Someday I'm going to be able to say that."

"Would that be before or after you have sex in an elevator?" He opened the door, revealing a small coat closet.

His back was to her, so she couldn't see his face. "You're not making fun of me, are you?"

"Nope." He took a gray wool topcoat from a wooden hanger. "It's just that I've never met somebody who had so many things to look forward to."

"That's because you've never met anyone who's been cooped up in Smalltown, U.S.A., for her entire life."

"It's hard to imagine." He put on the coat and turned as he adjusted it over his broad shoulders.

She loved watching a good-looking man fit his broad shoulders into a topcoat. Men didn't have much call to wear a topcoat in Virtue. Heavy quilted jackets were the usual choice. If she wanted to flirt with him, now would be the time, with him giving her the once-over, and her getting all stirred up by how urban and suave he looked. But he wasn't going to be a conquest, so she didn't.

He walked toward her. "Ready to go?"

She hadn't realized he'd just grab the coat and leave. In spite of their tight schedule and the cab waiting downstairs, she couldn't stand to come all the way up here without seeing the rest of the apartment. But she shouldn't seem nosy. That would label her as small town.

Then inspiration struck. "Did you want to show me the card table and chairs?"

"Oh, right." He turned and started through an arched

doorway on his left, taking off the coat as he went. "Come on in. The set is in the bedroom closet."

Oh, good, the bedroom. She glanced quickly at the living room as they moved through it. More antiques, probably priceless, obviously well cared for. The color scheme was burgundy and tan, the view out the tall casement windows spectacular, with tall buildings sparkling in the cold night sky. But the room didn't look as if anybody lived in it. The fireplace was covered with a brass screen that didn't have a hint of soot on its polished surface.

She followed him into the bedroom, which didn't look a whole lot more lived in, but at least a book lay facedown on one of the rich walnut nightstands. *Market Strategies for the New Millennium.* Not very stimulating late-night reading, from her perspective. "Did you meet her? The woman who made that sculpture?" she asked.

"Yeah...I did." He tossed his coat on the bed.

From the way he said it, she just *knew* that he'd slept with her. She laid her little backpack on the bed and took off her coat, too. If he was going to be comfy she wasn't going to stand around getting hot. Hot as in warm, of course. But being in his bedroom and thinking of his affair with a Frenchwoman was making her the other kind of hot, actually, too. "Was she nice, this sculptor?"

"Uh-huh. Very nice." He opened double doors to a walk-in closet and turned on a light inside.

Oh, he had definitely slept with her. Trudy wondered if this French sculptor looked anything like the marble woman in the foyer. Probably. And a woman speaking French was so sexy. Or English with a French accent, even sexier yet. Trudy could hardly be expected to compete with that, not that she intended to. Not that she would even begin to try.

While he banged around in the closet unearthing the table and chairs, she surveyed the bedroom, trying to picture it as a seduction chamber. She couldn't quite see it. The scent of his aftershave still hung in the air, and that was pretty damned tantalizing. If she closed her eyes she could imagine him naked, coming out of the shower, which had real power to start her engines.

But when she opened her eyes and looked at the scene before her, the lusty image slipped away again. He owned a sleigh bed, which she'd always thought was kind of a sensuous design, but the tan comforter and linens were way too businesslike. Or maybe his marketing book and the leather briefcase open on a small desk in the corner set the tone. She noticed a laptop computer next to the briefcase.

A couple of ties lay over a chair, as if he might have tried on both and discarded them. It touched her to think that he might have stood in front of his mirror wondering which one to wear tonight, as if he wanted her to like his choice. That made her own agony over her outfit seem less silly.

But other than the two bright ties splashed across the back of the muted geometric print on the wing chair, the room didn't have much life to it. Of course if a certain sculptor flew over from Paris and plopped her French-speaking self in the middle of that bed with a naked Linc, Trudy imagined the room would liven up really fast.

She raised her voice so he'd hear her over the racket he was making. "You must have lots of things to look forward to, yourself."

"Like what?" he answered from the depths of the closet as he continued to clatter around.

"Oh, trips to Paris. Stuff like that."

"I probably should go back. It's been a couple of years."

A couple of years? Okay, so this was no hot and heavy love affair. Not that she was concerned whether it was or not. But no wonder his bedroom didn't have passionate vibes. Somehow she believed that if the Frenchwoman had been here recently, she would know it.

Trudy's bedroom—or rather the living room she'd converted to a bedroom—had far more potential to be dynamite than Linc's, even though his was loaded to the gills with class. Maybe it had too much class to be decadent. That's what she wanted her bedroom to be—totally decadent.

"I had to move a few things to get to it," he called out. "Give me just a second."

"Sure." She didn't mind having a little time to snoop unobserved. This room was bigger than her entire living room. Her bed would have fit perfectly in here. This was the kind of room her bed was made for, and she realized that. Eventually she'd have the apartment to go with the bed, but she had to start somewhere.

Through carved double doors to the bathroom she glimpsed an elegant pedestal sink, something right out of a decorating magazine. She might not envy him his bedroom furniture, but she envied him the bathroom. Hers left much to be desired. The bathtub was old enough to be a decent size for soaking, but she'd had to take her bath by candlelight so that she wouldn't notice the cracked plaster.

A tall walnut dresser stood in one corner of Linc's bedroom, and a framed photograph was on it, the only photograph in the room, in fact. That merited going over for a closer look. Three people stood at what was probably the railing of a cruise ship. Trudy had never seen a cruise ship, but she'd watched plenty of reruns of *The Love Boat.*

The man and woman looked as if they belonged in a Ralph Lauren ad with their tanned beauty and elegant bearing. The little boy standing between them had to be Linc. He held them both by the hand and his gap-toothed grin pegged him as being about five or six. So this was the couple who now lived apart, the super-rich people who had soured Linc on marriage.

"Here's the table and chairs set."

She gave a guilty start, certain she'd been caught staring intently at the picture. "I was only—"

"Hey, it's natural to look at pictures in a room." He leaned a large, flat box against the bed.

The only picture in the room. She wondered if he liked

it because it predated his parents' separation. "You were a cute kid."

"According to my mother I was a pain in the butt."

"One kid? One kid would be a walk in the park. Try seven."

He shrugged. "At least there's somebody to play with. I probably was a pain in the butt. I had a private tutor until I was old enough to go to prep school, so I didn't have many friends when I was little. Bored kids get into trouble."

"What kind of trouble?" She was fascinated by this peek into a world she knew nothing about.

"Well, I noticed that the downstairs maid and the butler seemed to have lots of private conversations, so I pretended they were international spies. I wanted to catch them saying something incriminating, or better yet, something in a secret code I'd have to crack. Like *The top of the chandelier needs cleaning* would really mean *I hid the missile plans up there.*"

She smiled in recognition. "I used to pretend my dad's cornfield was a secret landing field for aliens, who then transformed themselves to look like the good people of Virtue. You're not telling me you got in trouble for make-believe?"

"Not exactly. I took it a step further and planted tape recorders so I could gather intelligence."

"*Oh.*" She could feel a good story coming and she moved the coats aside so she could sit on the bed to hear it. "I guess the maid and butler didn't like that, huh?"

He leaned against the dresser, his pose making him look like a page out of *GQ*. "They never found out. But it seems they were having an affair, so I got some *really* interesting tapes. Lots of moans, groans and panting, along with rhythmic thumping and some words and phrases I'd never heard before."

A zing of sexual awareness skittered down her spine. "Wow. Did you know what the noises were?"

"Not immediately." His glance met hers. He was still smiling, but a gleam of sensuality lurked in his eyes. "I figured it out pretty quick, though. I was eleven and getting very curious about stuff like that."

"Yeah, you would by that age." She was drawn to that look in his eyes, the suggestion of heat and excitement.

"When I did figure it out, I played the tape so much that my mother finally caught me listening. I didn't want the maid and butler to get fired because of me, so I told her I'd ordered the tape from a catalog. She busted me for having porn."

Trudy was touched that he'd protected the servants at his own expense. "Your mother never found out about the affair?"

"I guess not. Nobody got fired."

"It must have been wild, to know they were messing around and then watch them going about their jobs like nothing was happening."

"Definitely wild. And the maid was gorgeous. She played a starring role in most of my teenage fantasies. She left before I was old enough to act on those fantasies, or I probably would have tried."

The lust factor in the bedroom had taken a quantum leap with this new subject matter. "I'll bet she's still there in your subconscious." She'd read enough about sexual fantasies to think that was true. His story was really turning her on, which was probably a mistake, but she was into the whole thing now and couldn't seem to back off. "What was her name?"

"Belinda."

A perfect name for a sexy maid. "What did she look like?"

His expression softened and his lips parted slightly.

God, he was hot. Trudy guessed that he was picturing Belinda and she was dying of curiosity about the woman who still had the power to put that expression on his face. "Tell me," she murmured.

His gaze lost focus as the memory took over. "She had a tiny waist, and the black-and-white uniform made it look even smaller. She wore her skirts short to show off her great legs. Her uniform was always buttoned up to her neck, but those buttons in the middle always looked ready to pop."

"And you wished they would."

"Yeah."

That one word, more a sigh than a word at all, sent a ripple of sensuality through her. "Long hair or short?"

"Kind of medium and curly, and green eyes. I still remember those eyes."

The green eyes and curly hair part took Trudy aback. "What color was her hair?"

"Brown." As he said it, his glance swung to hers. Then his eyes widened.

Her chest tightened with excitement. "Do I...do you think I look anything like her?"

"Not really," he said quickly. "Your hair may be similar, and the color of your eyes, and you have a great figure like she had, but on the whole..."

"On the whole I'm not gorgeous." How totally depressing. She dropped her gaze and wished she'd never started this line of inquiry.

"Oh, yes, you are gorgeous."

Too late. She didn't want to look at him and see sympathy in his eyes. "You're saying that because you think you have to."

"No. You are gorgeous," he said in a voice rich with conviction.

That tone brought her head up, and the look in his eyes took her breath away. He wasn't saying it to be nice. He meant every word. Talk about unreal. She could barely believe she was sitting on Linc's bed listening to him tell her that she—a girl recently transplanted from the hick town of Virtue—was gorgeous.

"And the truth is, you look a lot like Belinda," he added. "That probably explains why I—" He stopped speaking and shook his head. "Never mind."

"Why you what?" Her heart thudded rapidly.

"When I first saw you, I had this reaction."

"A sexual reaction?"

"Yes." His eyes were so blue.

"Oh." Thumpity, thump went her heart, picking up speed by the second.

"But it would be a huge mistake for us to get involved."

"Absolutely." At least she used to think so. Now she wasn't so sure. She had a trump card she'd never envisioned. She wondered what his reaction would be if she dressed up in a maid's uniform. Now that he'd given her a key to unlock his private fantasy world, she wondered if she could resist trying it.

"I mean, talk about messy," he said, "considering that Tom's my best friend, and now Tom and Meg are my best couple friends. And Meg's your best friend. I can think of all sorts of awkwardness coming out of that."

"Oh, me, too. Definitely." Then there was the tape recorder idea. If they had sex while she pretended to be the maid, she could record that and play it for him another time. If he liked that, then she could consider trying something else auditory, like phone sex. This was a concept with promise.

"So that's settled, then."

"It's so settled." She had no intention of telegraphing her moves, if she should decide to make any. "No matter how much I look like your fantasy maid, we won't do anything about that because of Tom and Meg." He didn't know that Meg would love the concept. Meg would want to run out and rent the maid's uniform for Trudy.

"Right." He didn't sound as if anything was settled. He

looked as if any hesitation on her part would make him abandon all his arguments and join her on that bed.

Tempting as that was, it lacked the kind of drama she craved. Dressing up as a maid and seducing him seemed like a much more New York way to go. She needed time to consider whether she'd do such a thing. They'd better leave this bedroom soon or she'd lose the element of surprise.

Then she remembered their dinner reservations and a cab that was running up the equivalent of the national debt downstairs.

"Linc, we have to get going!" She glanced at the clock beside his bed. "We're already late for dinner, and I don't even want to think of what the meter reads on the cab by now." Cabs were becoming more of a problem than she'd anticipated while dreaming of big-city life.

He looked startled, as if he'd forgotten all about the cab, not to mention dinner. "God, I'm sorry. I'll bet you're starved."

"Famished." Famished for great sex. One thing was for sure, she'd never met a man who'd lusted after the downstairs maid in his youth. The romance of that idea was swaying her toward getting it on with Linc.

"Then let's go."

"Yes, let's."

They'd put on their coats, left the apartment and started downstairs in the elevator before Trudy realized she hadn't even looked at the folding table he'd taken so much trouble to get out for her. She vaguely remembered a picture of the set was on the outside of the box, but she'd been too involved with his story about Belinda to pay attention.

"I'm sure the table is great, from what I saw." She assumed it was great. Linc wouldn't have a crummy folding table in that fancy apartment.

"At least the set's compact. Everything fits in one box. I can bring it over tomorrow afternoon."

Too quick. She needed more time than that to think through their situation before she saw him again. To seduce or not to seduce, that was the question. And every ordinary encounter they had lowered her chances of staging a seduction.

If she ended up deciding to seduce him, she'd need all the help she could get, including advice from Meg. However, this wasn't a topic to bring up during office hours. She hoped Meg and Tom didn't have big plans for tomorrow, because she needed to consult with Meg. Then she'd have to rent a maid's uniform, and she might not be able to get that until Monday.

She liked the fact that he was so eager to bring her the table, though. He might even be looking forward to seeing her again this weekend. Thwarting that wish might work to her advantage, or it might cause him to lose interest.

If she were in Virtue, she'd know which. The guys she'd dated had loved it when she played hard to get. But Linc wasn't from her hometown, and a sophisticated city man might not be into those kinds of games.

Still, she needed some time. She decided to try to buy some. "I would love to have the table that soon, but I have a lot of errands to do tomorrow and I probably won't be home."

"Oh." He looked disappointed, but he quickly covered his reaction and shrugged. "Whatever."

Damn. The hook wasn't set yet. If she wasn't careful, he would get away. Maybe she could manage this program by tomorrow night, one way or the other. The idea made her tummy tingle with nervousness because she still didn't feel ready, but the pace was fast in New York. You had to keep up or get left behind.

And because this *was* New York, a costume shop might be open on a Sunday. Meg might have a contact or ideas about creating the maid's costume. Meg was terrific at things like this.

Trudy was torn by indecision. In the cold light of morning she might want to back out. Reality would hit, and she'd realize this project was doomed before it ever started. In that case it wouldn't matter when he brought the table.

She decided on a compromise. "I'll probably be home by seven. Would that be too late to bring it over?"

"Uh, no. No, that would be okay. Or we could wait until next weekend." Either he'd lost interest or he was excellent at faking it.

Next weekend was way too late. If she let six days go by he'd have forgotten all about her connection with his former object of lust, Belinda of the short skirts and straining buttons.

She'd be a fool to let Linc get away. If she ignored the fact that Meg had practically thrown him at her, he fit perfectly into her grand scheme of becoming more worldly through sexual liaisons with different types of men. Once she'd experienced a sexual relationship with Linc, she could check *Wall Street Stud* off her list and move on to another kind of city guy.

Perhaps she'd investigate the possibilities of his polar opposite and look for a long-haired, unconventional artist from Greenwich Village. Or maybe she'd consider a man in uniform—either from the NYPD or the fire department. The possibilities for a girl to enrich her experience seemed endless in a city this size. She would be cosmopolitan in no time.

Yes, Linc was the perfect guy to help her launch this odyssey. From what Meg had said about him, he would be fine with a temporary affair. When the time came to move on, he'd totally understand.

"If you can make it at seven," she said, "we could order pizza or something."

His look of uncertainty faded and he smiled at her. "You're not going to offer to cook something to put on that table?"

"Nope. That would be a Virtue, Kansas, move. In New York, I'm ordering in." If she followed through with the maid's costume, she'd be too busy cooking up a fantasy to be bothered with food, anyway.

She shivered in anticipation. This was it. Her big-city fantasy life was about to begin.

7

ALL THROUGH DINNER Linc ate automatically and tasted nothing. Now that he'd made the connection between Trudy and Belinda, he couldn't let it go. In a way, he was relieved to discover that his sexual response to Trudy was all tied up with his teenage infatuation with Belinda. Knowing that, he should be able to control himself better.

He really *had* to control himself better. Staying out of bedrooms with Trudy would be a good start. He'd spent far too much time talking to this woman while a bed loomed invitingly nearby, especially considering that she looked like Belinda and she had at least one packing box full of sex books. No wonder he was so tempted.

During dinner, they cruised the safe topic of his work and hers while he covertly studied her across the intimate table for two and made comparisons between her and Belinda. Although his memories of Belinda were golden, he had to admit Trudy was prettier. Her mouth was fuller and her eyes a deeper green. The line of her chin was softer, and her voice more pleasant to his ear.

Watching Trudy eat felt familiar. He used to hang around the kitchen when Belinda took her lunch break and pretend the two of them were on a dinner date. Now that he thought about those days, Belinda probably knew about his crush all along. He hadn't been very subtle.

Everyone in the household had probably known, even his parents. There was an embarrassing thought. Fortunately he was better at hiding his reaction to women these days. Trudy knew there was chemistry between them, but he didn't think she had a clue how much she turned him on.

She voted to skip dessert. Because this was her special night, he had to go along with her decision, but he hated to leave the restaurant. Once they'd covered the first few items on his itinerary, they'd come to the part where he introduced her to some nightclubs. Undoubtedly she'd expect him to dance with her, and dancing could be hazardous in his current state of mind. Not only that, he'd be showing her clubs where she might find one of her big-city dream guys in the near future. Giving her a tour of Manhattan meat markets still seemed weird to him, but he'd promised Meg.

Outside the restaurant, Saturday night traffic was in full swing with horns blaring and cabs whizzing by. Because several other restaurants lined this two-block section of the Village, foot traffic was brisk, too. Competition for cabs would be stiff, which was the way Linc liked it.

Early in his dating career he'd discovered that women admired a guy who could commandeer a taxi when the odds looked hopeless. He'd decided it was the modern equivalent of slaying the woolly mammoth, and he'd perfected the technique several years ago. Phoning for a cab from inside the restaurant would be cheating, so he hadn't done that.

"Isn't this great?" Trudy said. "I *love* traffic jams."

He couldn't help grinning, because he'd come to love them, too. "Then you're going to be head-over-heels for New York. Now if you want to stay here by the doorway where it's a little warmer, I'll get us a cab." Adrenaline pumped through him as he started toward the curb. *Me, Tarzan, get Jane taxi.*

She hurried forward with him. "I want to do it."

"Get a cab? Listen, Trudy, at this hour it's very difficult to get a—"

"I've been practicing."

"On what? I can't believe they have taxicabs in Virtue."

"I've been practicing my whistle."

Before he could stop her, she'd stepped in front of him, put two fingers in her mouth and produced an eardrum-splitting sound. Sure enough, a cab swung over to the curb.

"See?" She turned toward him, her expression triumphant. "I got one!"

"That's good," he said, hiding his disappointment at not being able to show off his expertise. He should have known she'd be able to whistle like that. After all, she had her own toolbox. "Now you'd better get in before—" He hadn't even finished the sentence when a man ducked in behind Trudy and opened the cab's back door.

Linc quickly nudged Trudy aside and grabbed the door. "Sorry. Our cab."

The middle-aged guy scowled at Linc. "I don't think so."

Linc's adrenaline surged again. Trudy may have bagged the cab, but he was going to save it for her. He leveled his most intimidating stare at the guy. "Yes, it is. So if you'll just—"

"Which way are you headed?" Trudy asked, inserting herself between Linc and the cab-nabber.

"Times Square."

"I wouldn't mind going up there next," Trudy said. "We could share."

"Trudy, wait a minute." Linc wanted to vanquish the guy, not bring him along for the ride. Not only that, Times Square wasn't next on the itinerary he'd worked out. "We're not going to—"

"Your name's Trudy?" The man smiled. "That's my mother's name. Trudy Besselhoffer."

"Imagine that," Trudy said. "So is your last name Besselhoffer, too?"

"Yep. I'm Herman Besselhoffer."

Linc felt as if he'd been transported to an alternate universe. In his world people didn't strike up conversations with strangers who had tried to steal your cab out from under you. He was torn between irritation and fascination, and fascination was winning.

"I'm Trudy Baxter." She put out her hand. "Pleased to meet you. This is Linc Faulkner. We—"

"Hey, people!" the cabdriver called. "In or out!"

"In," Trudy said. She ducked down and slid all the way across the back seat. "Come on, Herman and Linc. There's plenty of room for all of us."

"Okay by me." Herman got in.

Linc had no choice but to follow. Things weren't going according to plan, and he hated when that happened. He'd thought they'd take a cab to Fifth Avenue and from there walk to Rockefeller Center to see the skaters. Times Square was supposed to come after that, and then they'd hit some nightclubs.

His mistake had been not telling Trudy about the itinerary, which was still in the pocket of the trench coat. He'd tell her the plan once they got rid of Herman. True, the guy made a good chaperone sitting between him and Trudy, but Linc wasn't crazy about having Trudy thigh-to-thigh with a strange man, even if he was old enough to be her father and wasn't even slightly hitting on her.

"Where to?" asked the driver.

"Times Square," Linc said. Then he sat back, arms folded and listened to Trudy make a new friend. That was all well and good, because he was right here to protect her if this Herman character turned out to be Jack the Ripper. But Linc planned to have a talk with her about striking up acquaintances like that. She wasn't in Virtue anymore.

The cab driver let them out about a block from the heart of Times Square, and they split the fare three ways. Linc tried to pay Trudy's share, but she was having none of it after he'd insisted on paying the huge bill they'd racked up keeping a taxi waiting outside both her apartment and his. Finally it was easier to let her pay so that they could bid Herman goodbye and get on with the evening.

Once Herman took off to meet a friend who worked at one of the souvenir shops, Linc was about to mention the itinerary when Trudy lifted her arms toward the lighted messages scrolling across the top border of the triangular Allied Tower building.

"Will you look at that!" Her breath made a little cloud of fog in the night air.

He was looking, all right. He'd been raised to avoid public displays of affection, but Trudy was so damned kissable that he had the insane desire to grab her right here, with dozens of people around. The lights reflected on her glossy curls and sparkled in her eyes. The sharp wind tousled her hair and brushed her cheeks with pink so that she appeared even more innocent and starry-eyed. He suspected she was far from innocent, that many farm boys had kissed those full lips that were parted in wonder. Yet none of them had kissed her in the middle of Times Square.

She seemed oblivious to him, though. She might not appreciate it if he kissed her, which would interfere with her view. Besides, he wasn't going to kiss her. Absolutely not.

"I keep having to pinch myself so that I know this isn't a dream," she said. "What I wouldn't have given to be here on New Year's Eve, but I couldn't get away from Virtue then. Were you down here for New Year's?"

"No." He'd gone to an elegant party with an equally elegant woman. Clarise would have invited him to spend the first few hours of the New Year in her bed if he'd felt so inclined. His response had been totally illogical and not like him at all. He'd decided that having sex with a woman who meant very little to him would be a bad way to start the year. Although he hadn't been quite that blunt with Clarise, she'd absorbed enough of his meaning to be insulted. They hadn't dated since.

"Well, next New Year's I'm going to be here," Trudy said. "And that's a promise."

"I'm sure you will be." He wondered who would be here

with her, and felt a jealous, possessive tug on his emotions. Not good.

He hated to sound a negative note when she was so obviously enchanted by her environment. But he had a job to do. "Trudy, there's something we have to talk about. You need to be very careful about who you talk to as you move around this town."

"I know." She continued to gaze in rapture at the lighted messages marching around the building. "Don't worry. If you hadn't been there to take care of me, I wouldn't have asked Herman to share a cab."

"Well, that's good." Linc stuffed his hands into his pockets because if he hadn't, he might have been tempted to reach for her hand. Holding her hand might lead to that kiss he couldn't seem to get out of his mind.

She craned her neck as she took in the glittering buildings towering above them. "I knew you wouldn't let anything happen to me."

"Yeah, but you should be aware of the danger," he said with more gruffness than he actually felt. Knowing that she trusted him that much was both scary and thrilling. In a way, he felt privileged to be her protector. Dumb reaction, but true, nevertheless. This assignment had started out as an obligation, but he'd begun to realize that Trudy was special, and the guy asked to watch out for her should consider himself lucky.

"I'll work on being more suspicious of people," she said. "Meg warned me about that, too." Then she brought her gaze to meet his and, at that moment, the wind died down. Even the traffic noise seemed quieter. "I liked the way you stepped in and tried to keep him from taking the cab away, though," she murmured. "You gave me chills when you did that."

He gulped as desire slammed into him again. "You were probably standing in a draft," he said, trying to make a joke out of it. But his heartbeat quickened at the idea that she'd been sexually aroused by his behavior. Of course, she was on sexual tenterhooks. The slightest little thing might stir her up. And that was exactly what was driving him crazy.

"There's no draft, now." Holding his gaze, she stepped closer and the lapels of her coat touched his. "And I'm still getting chills."

He looked into her eyes and a shudder of need ran through him.

"Are *you* getting chills?" she asked softly.

He didn't remember taking his hands out of his pockets, but all at once he was holding her, gathering her as close as he could considering the bulky leather trench coat. "Yes," he whispered, and lowered his head.

TRUDY MET LINC HALFWAY, throwing her arms around his neck and standing on tiptoe. She couldn't think of a better way to commemorate finally getting to New York than to kiss a man as gorgeous and worldly as Linc while standing smack-dab in the middle of Times Square. She could pretend it was midnight on New Year's Eve, because that's how she felt, as if a whole new beginning was opening up for her.

She wanted the kiss to be spectacular, so she put a lot of enthusiasm into it. She hadn't quite bargained for the result. With a groan Linc pulled her in closer and heat poured through her body.

In no time their tongues were involved, and it wasn't tentative involvement, either. No little licks and forays. Linc went straight for the deliberate thrust that signaled exactly what he wanted from her. She slackened her jaw, letting him know he could have it, not even caring if she was tipping her hand.

She told herself it was the excitement of being in Times Square that was making her head spin and her body throb. Any good-looking city man would have caused the same reaction in her, so there was no need to panic. She could relax and enjoy.

But enjoyment wasn't a strong enough word to describe what was happening to her. The deeper the kiss, the damper her panties. The honking horns and catcalls were minor background noise compared to the thudding of her heart and the rasp of his breathing.

He shoved his fingers into her hair and cupped her scalp so he could tip her head and try a new angle. She moaned and put her arms around his waist to cinch him up tighter. She wanted to feel the erection that she knew was there, but there were too many layers of material between them.

Somehow her trench coat must have loosened. She didn't know if he'd done it or she had, but when he slid his hand inside, she sighed with happiness. She didn't care if his fingers were cold when he found the hem of her sweater and reached underneath to stroke her skin. She wanted his touch, and she wanted it now. When he found the back catch of her bra, tremors of anticipation shook her.

He gasped against her mouth and pulled his hand free. Then he lifted his lips from hers and gazed down at her with a shocked expression. "What am I doing?"

She had a little trouble finding her voice. "Making a memory?"

Slowly he loosened his grip on her scalp and eased away so that he could pull the lapels of her coat together. All the while he stared at her in disbelief. "I...I forgot where we were."

"I didn't."

He swallowed. "Then you should have stopped me. I didn't mean to embarrass you like this. I—"

"Who's embarrassed? I thought it was awesome."

A flush climbed from under his collar. "The kiss was very nice, but I'm not in the habit of behaving like that in public." He retied the belt on her trench coat, pulling it tight.

"Me, either." She found his discomfort kind of fun. "That sort of thing is frowned on in Virtue, although I have to admit there was one incident in the town square. I thought we'd be okay to try it in the gazebo at one in the morning, but sure enough, we almost got busted."

"I shouldn't be kissing you in the first place." He looked extremely upset with himself. "Let alone putting my hand inside your coat like that."

"And under my sweater," she added, feeling rather proud of the way she'd made him lose it. Maybe it was the whole Belinda thing going on, but she could live with that. It wasn't as if she really cared why he'd reacted so strongly to her. Heck, she'd made it through her dating years in Virtue by pretending that those farm boys were gladiators. Fantasy was good.

His face got redder. "I'm really sorry, Trudy. I don't know what came over me."

"Lust."

"It won't happen again."

Wanna bet? After that spectacular kiss, she decided to revise her plans for the night. As Linc showed her Manhattan, she would look for opportunities to throw him into a sexual tizzy. This city seemed to inspire her to be creative. Maybe she wouldn't be totally smooth in her approach, but that was okay. Linc was the perfect guy to practice on.

FOLLOWING WHAT LINC THOUGHT OF as The Kiss Episode, he was very, very careful. That kiss had scared him straight, and now he knew that he couldn't risk getting into another kissing situation with Trudy. She suggested they walk to Fifth Avenue from Times Square, and Linc kept any necessary touching impersonal, like when he put his hand to her elbow as they crossed the street.

The exercise and chilly night air should have cooled his hot thoughts about Trudy. They didn't. And Trudy wasn't helping any by telling him the story of her gazebo rendezvous back in Virtue. He considered asking her not to describe that particular experience, but that seemed wimpy, as if he couldn't handle the thought of Trudy having sex outside on a warm summer night. So he spent several blocks of their journey trying to think himself out of getting an erection.

Finally the story ended, they reached Fifth Avenue and he looked forward to some relief. He'd never seen anything sexy about window-shopping.

But then, he'd never been window-shopping with Trudy. Now that they were strolling instead of striding, she linked her arm through his, which brought them close enough that he could smell her perfume. Smelling her perfume reminded him of The Kiss Episode. As he was fighting off that memory, she squeezed his arm against her body, and even through the trench coat he could feel the swell of her breast.

"Oh, look at that!" She pulled him to a halt in front of a large window display.

He might have known she'd pick out a display featuring nightwear. "Uh-huh," he said, trying to think of something else besides Trudy in a nightgown and then Trudy out of the nightgown and lying naked and available in that huge bed.

"That's exactly what I need."

He doubted she was talking about the granny gown on a tall mannequin near the window. No doubt she had her eye on the little shorty job in the back, the black one with satin trim that looked like an abbreviated tux. "Uh-huh," he said again, determined not to picture her in that black number.

She glanced up at him. "I'll bet you have no idea what I'm talking about."

He let his attention glide over her face without spending a lot of time looking into those green eyes of hers. Prolonged eye contact was a bad idea. "I figure you need a nightgown."

"Nope. Well, I do. I need several, as a matter of fact.

But what I *really* need is that folding screen. Or *a* folding screen. That one's part of the display, so I doubt if they'd sell it to me.''

''Oh.'' He'd become increasingly aware of the way she was holding his arm against the side of her breast. The breast he'd very nearly fondled in the middle of Times Square.

No woman had ever made him forget himself that way, and that alone should warn him to keep his distance from Trudy, because he cherished his self-control more than any trait he possessed. Yet here he was, standing close enough that he could lean down and bury his nose in her fragrant hair while he battled the urge to do exactly that. He didn't know why she had to smell so damned good.

''Aren't you going to ask me why I need a folding screen?''

He was afraid to ask, but he was trying to act cool and unaffected by her. ''Why?''

''Logistics. Now that I've turned my living room into my bedroom, I need a little private nook where I can change clothes.''

''Couldn't you do that in the real bedroom?''

''I could, but it wouldn't be very dramatic or sexy. I mean, picture me bringing someone home.''

He'd definitely rather not.

''So I tell him to mix himself a drink in the kitchen while I slip into something more comfortable,'' she continued. ''But if I have to change in the bedroom, then it would be awkward, because I have to walk past the kitchen to get back into the living room, where the bed is. It's clumsy. It lacks flair.''

''Maybe.'' He wasn't at all happy with the image of her slipping into something more comfortable while some bozo mixed himself a drink in her kitchen. He couldn't figure out why that should bother him, either. He should want her to have an exciting sex life if that was what she'd come to town for.

"The answer is a folding screen in a corner of the living room," she said. "I can have one of your folding chairs behind it and hang the lingerie I plan to wear over the chair, ready for the occasion."

"Uh-huh." He wondered where she came up with such outrageous ideas. Apparently she had the seductive instincts of Cleopatra.

"You don't sound very enthusiastic. Wouldn't that be sexy, to go behind the screen and change while I'm talking to my date? I could even drape a stocking over the screen after I've taken it off, for more effect." She peered up at him. "Is that a really bad idea? You're scowling something terrible."

He made an effort to neutralize his expression. "It's not a bad idea."

"Yes, but is it a *good* idea? You can be honest. If it sounds hokey and dumb, then maybe I shouldn't. Try imagining yourself in that scenario."

He'd been trying very hard *not* to imagine himself in that scenario. "Okay."

"So, do you think you'd be turned on by having your date undress behind a folding screen and carry on a conversation with you at the same time?"

Another twenty seconds of standing here and he really would kiss her again and then she'd know how little control he had when it came to her. "Yes, I would. Now, can we get going?" Damn, but it sounded as if he was begging. She did terrible things to his self-discipline, and he hated that.

She smiled at him. "Sure. Sure we can." She kept that little smile as they started off down the street.

If he was as smart as he liked to think, he'd ask her to haul out the itinerary so they could get this evening back on track. He suspected that she was creating her own itinerary in that sexually focused brain of hers, and it looked nothing like his. He was crazy to give her free rein. No telling what might happen tonight. Anything could happen. *Anything.*

8

TRUDY FELT QUITE PROUD of her ability to rattle Linc with her talk of folding screens and undressing behind them. Her triumph put a spring in her step as they continued down Fifth Avenue toward Rockefeller Center. Only three days into her New York adventure and she'd already tripped the switch on a Wall Street hunk's libido. Score!

Her sexual confidence lasted until Linc took her to her first honest-to-God New York nightclub. After ten minutes of watching super-trendy urban professionals dance to music she'd never heard before and drink concoctions she'd never known existed, she felt like a complete hayseed. With smooth efficiency Linc ordered them a bottle of champagne. Left to her own devices she could easily have made the mistake of asking for a rum and Coke.

Her hair was the wrong style and her nail polish the wrong color. Even the shape of her nails wasn't quite the same as the women who held stemmed glasses to their perfectly outlined lips. She remembered too late that she'd never repaired her lipstick from the kiss on Times Square, and she'd been walking in the wind so she probably looked like she'd stuck her finger in a light socket.

Linc leaned toward her. "Something must be wrong. You're not bubbling over with happiness at being in your first nightclub."

"That's because I'm bubbling over with insecurity."

He looked surprised. "*You?* Why?"

"I just—oh, never mind." She decided not to try and

explain. Being a guy, he wouldn't get the thing about nail polish and hairstyles. He'd try to talk her out of her conclusions, although on some level he must know that she didn't fit in.

She shouldn't kid herself that she was anything more than a curiosity to a man like Linc. When it came to sexual sophistication, she didn't play in his league and she knew it. That was why she needed to practice her skills on him before he became bored with her country ways.

"Would you rather try a different place?"

"No, this is fine! Great!" She doubted a different place would cure the problem unless he knew of a club that catered to recent transplants from Kansas. Besides, he'd ordered what was probably a very pricey bottle of champagne and she'd only had one glass. She couldn't imagine wasting something that tasted that good. With that thought, she asked him to pour her another glass.

"I brought you here because it's a favorite of people on the Street. Chances are most guys you'd meet at this club would be decent."

"Thank you." She drained her champagne flute, and like magic a waiter appeared to refill it. She noticed that Linc had used the term *the Street,* meaning Wall Street. Fortunately she'd watched enough TV to know what he meant, but she'd have to work on her speaking vocabulary if she expected to fit in. They'd eaten dinner in Greenwich Village, but he'd called it simply the Village. The more time she spent with him, the more she'd learn the terminology.

But she'd probably never pick up his accent. Even Meg and Tom didn't have his distinctive way of talking. She loved listening to him because his accent represented the city that she'd yearned for most of her life. The ultimate would be hearing that accent murmuring sweet nothings in bed.

Earlier in the evening she'd been sure that would happen, but looking around at the sleek women in this nightclub, she wondered if she'd been kidding herself. The champagne helped take the edge off her insecurities, so she had some more.

"I'm really surprised at how you're reacting to this place," Linc said. "I thought you'd have dragged me out on the dance floor by now."

"I guess I'm just thirsty." She reduced the level in her champagne flute by half. The way she looked at it, the sooner they finished the champagne, the sooner they could leave. No way was she going out on a dance floor until she'd spruced up her wardrobe and perfected her moves.

"Aren't you thirsty after all that walking?" she asked, glancing pointedly at his glass, which he'd barely touched. As good as it was, she couldn't very well drink the whole bottle by herself. She was already feeling a little fuzzy headed.

"Obviously I'm not as thirsty as you." He took another sip.

Then it hit her that swilling the champagne wasn't particularly sophisticated. She felt her cheeks grow warm as she wondered what he must think of her, tossing back the bubbly like that.

"*Now* what's wrong?" He looked genuinely concerned as he gazed at her. "Did I say something to upset you?"

She shook her head and noticed the room seemed to tilt a little. Blushing was such an inconvenient response. The more you tried not to, the more you did it.

"Maybe you're allergic to something in the champagne. You're really getting red."

"I'm fine. Really." How mortifying. Here she was sitting in this ultra-chic nightclub, her hair a mess, her makeup wearing off, halfway sloshed, and her face the color of a ripe tomato. So much for smooth and suave. She reached for her backpack. "Maybe I'll take a little trip to the ladies' room."

He pushed away from the table. "Are you feeling sick? I could run you over to an all-night clinic. They could—"

"No! I'll be right back." She got up so quickly that she bumped into him as he tried to help her with the chair. If he hadn't grabbed it, it would have clattered to the floor.

She had no idea where she was headed, so she guessed, and guessed wrong, ending up in the nightclub's tiny kitchen. A waiter glanced up and she mumbled her request.

"To your left and down the stairs," he said, his face expressionless.

He thinks I'm an idiot. She managed to find the narrow, carpeted stairs to the basement where the bathrooms were located and get down them without stumbling. She really had gone a little heavy on the champagne.

Of course the women's rest room was filled with a few of the same glamorous babes she'd seen upstairs, which did nothing for her shaky ego. Vowing never to go out in public again until she'd beefed up her image, she waited for a chance in front of the mirror and at last, miraculously, she was alone in the bathroom.

Once she looked in the mirror, she groaned. Her hair was windblown and her mouth was totally bare of lipstick. She repaired the damage as best she could, but there was no way she'd come out of there looking as sleek as the others. Maybe she should have her hair professionally straightened. Or shaved off. She'd seen one woman with hair about a quarter of an inch long and she'd looked amazing.

But she couldn't shave it now, so she finger-combed her hair and held it back from her face. That was the answer, to get all these curls away from her face to give her a more minimalist look. She remembered tossing a couple of small butterfly clips in her backpack two days ago. Because of the way her head was buzzing, it took her some time to find them. Ah. There they were, the little devils.

She used water to tame her hair as she smoothed it back and secured it with the clips. When a curl threatened to spoil the smooth look, she saturated it with more water. Then she studied herself in the mirror. Still not great, but better than all those cutesy curls she had going on.

Someone rapped on the outer door. "Trudy? Are you in there?"

Linc! "Be right there," she called.

"Not good enough."

She spun around in surprise as he opened the door.

His eyes widened. "What in hell happened to you?"

"Nothing! I only—"

"Of course something happened." He stepped inside, closed the door and leaned against it. "And you're not leaving until you tell me what it is. Meg asked me to watch out for you, and I can't do a good job if you're going to get sick and not tell me about it. Did you throw up and have to wash your hair? Is that why it's all wet?"

She considered pretending she *was* sick, just to get out of this humiliating situation.

Linc blew out a breath. "Damn. I should never have let you walk around in the cold wind like that. You're probably run-down from all the excitement of moving, and it's late, and the food tonight probably wasn't what you're used to. I'll bet they don't have Thai food in Virtue. And to top it all off I ordered you champagne without asking if you had an allergic reaction to it. Some watchdog I turned out to be."

Her heart squeezed. He was so conscientious, and absolutely adorable. "Linc, I'm fine."

And they were alone in a public rest room. She walked over and stood right in front of him, so that he could see for himself that she was okay. "I'm not sick. I never was sick. In fact, I'm a strong Kansas farm girl, and I'm hardly ever sick. You're probably used to more delicate types, but I'm not one of those, so please stop worrying. You didn't do anything wrong."

He didn't look convinced. "Then what's up with your hair?"

One of her books had mentioned a sexy interlude with a guy in a women's rest room, and it had sounded naughty and fun. She'd never have dared in Virtue, but New York City was a different story. Yet it was too soon for her to try that with Linc. Wasn't it?

She gazed into his eyes and decided the least she could do was explain her seemingly bizarre behavior with the hair. "I walked into this nightclub and realized I didn't have the New York nightlife look. So I was feeling insecure, and I came down here to see if I could make myself more presentable. I was going for something more sleek."

Confusion clouded his blue eyes. Then they gradually cleared and began to sparkle as the corners of his mouth twitched.

"And don't you *dare* laugh," she warned.

"Of course not." His voice sounded suspiciously hoarse.

"You are. You are laughing."

"I'm not laughing." He cleared his throat. "And for the record, I like the way you wear your hair."

"You do?"

"Yes. So, all things considered, what do you want to do next?"

His grin was a little too jolly to suit her. She wanted to wipe it right off his face. Maybe it wasn't too soon to try an interlude in a public rest room. Maybe it was the perfect time. The champagne would give her that extra ounce of courage she'd need. She might not stack up very well against all those pulled-together women in the club upstairs, but she was the only woman in the room at the moment.

She moved in close and wound her arms around his neck. "Ever made out in the women's bathroom?"

"No, I haven't." Excitement flared in his eyes, but he clasped her arms as if to pull them away. "And I don't think that's a good idea."

"Yes, you do." She nestled against him, lifting her pelvis enough to settle it right where it would do the most damage. "You want to and you know it."

"Someone could come along and want to get in here." His voice sounded tight, as if he was holding on to his control with difficulty. But instead of pulling her arms from around his neck, he began a light caress that gave her a great deal of encouragement.

"We'll figure that out if it happens." Watching the heat build in his eyes, she didn't care so much about her hayseed appearance anymore. She had one thing going for her that the others didn't. She looked like Belinda. "I dare you to kiss me," she murmured as she guided his head lower.

He allowed her to draw him down to her waiting mouth. His body was obviously ready, but his mind hadn't quite decided to follow. "We should just leave."

"We will. In a minute." Balancing on the balls of her feet, she slid upward to meet him, noting along the way that he had a great start on an erection. Knowing that brought a rush of moisture between her thighs.

When his mouth was close enough, she lapped at it playfully with her tongue. "You taste good," she whispered. "Like champagne." Her heart beat wildly. They were really, truly going to fool around in this New York nightclub rest room.

He swallowed. "Trudy, this is—"

"Fun." She brushed her lips over his and then licked him some more. "Naughty."

"Crazy." His breathing grew ragged.

"Come on," she taunted breathlessly as she nibbled at his mouth. "Kiss me back. I know you can."

With a groan of surrender he took the kiss she offered, delving deep into her mouth with his tongue. Need pulsed between them as she squirmed closer, wanting more. Yes, this had been an excellent idea. It was getting both of them very, very hot.

His grip on her arms tightened, and he lifted his mouth a fraction from hers. "Stop wiggling like that," he said, gasping for breath.

"Make me." She rotated her pelvis, massaging the bulge behind his fly.

He sucked in another breath. "Trudy...stop...please."

"I think you like it." She knew he did. New York or Kansas, men were the same in that regard. She could predict what he ultimately longed for, too, but a man like him would never ask. If she hadn't had a fair amount of champagne, she might not have offered, either.

She tried to tug her arms from his firm grasp. "Turn me loose," she murmured, feeling bolder by the minute.

"Then stop."

"I will." She eased her pelvis away and he loosened his grip. She slipped her arms free and smiled her most seductive smile. Oh, this would be a memory to last a lifetime.

He cleared his throat and adjusted the knot of his tie, but he didn't stop looking at her, not for a second. "We should go now," he said, but there was no force behind the suggestion.

"You don't want to. You're into this little fantasy."

He swallowed but didn't reply.

"I say we go for broke." Gazing into his eyes, flashing dark and hot with passion, she reached for the zipper on his slacks.

He covered her hand with his. *"Trudy."*

"You know you want me to." She ran her tongue over her lips.

"I—"

"I'll make you feel *so* good."

He shook his head, seemingly struck speechless.

"Yes. Let me." At last she read surrender in his eyes, and when she tugged the zipper down and sank to her knees, he didn't stop her.

Her heart pounded with excitement as she freed his penis

from the restriction of his navy cotton briefs. He was thick and hard in her grasp, his smooth skin hot to the touch, his veins pulsing with heat. Silken hair tickled her palm as she cupped the weight of his balls and breathed in the musky scent of aroused male. It had been a long time, but worth the wait.

His moans of pleasure as she slid her hand up and down thrilled her as much as the sensation of stroking him. Then she touched her tongue to the trembling tip and tasted a combination of salty and sweet, like the rim of a margarita glass with the first sip. His breathing grew labored. Circling the base of his shaft with her fingers, she slowly drew him into her mouth, inch by glorious inch.

A delicious ache throbbed between her legs as she took his measure and anticipated the pleasure of his thrust deep within her. She flicked her tongue against the underside of his shaft and he trembled. As much as she'd love to make this last, they were bound to be interrupted any minute. Hollowing her cheeks, she applied gentle suction while caressing him boldly with her tongue.

He came in a rush, his choking cry of release muted, as if he'd clenched his jaw against it.

The knob on the door jiggled. "It's locked," said a woman outside. "How can it be locked? There are three stalls in there."

Trudy swallowed the warm liquid and took her time sliding her mouth away.

"I think we should get the manager," said another woman. "This shouldn't be locked."

Sitting back on her heels, Trudy gazed upward. Linc's eyes were squeezed shut and he was struggling for breath. Gently she tucked him back inside his briefs and eased the zipper up over the still-substantial bulge.

"Pound on the door," said the first woman.

The door panel vibrated. Thump, thump, thump. "Anybody in there?" called the second woman.

Trudy was a little shaky herself as she stood. Shaky and very, very damp between her legs. She had come very close to having an orgasm, just from pleasuring Linc.

The knob rattled again. "Okay," said the first woman. "Let's go find somebody. This is ridiculous."

As their footsteps receded, Linc opened his eyes and gazed into Trudy's. He looked like a man who'd just had a near-death experience.

"We can slip out while they're getting the manager," she murmured.

He opened his mouth as if to say something, closed it again and nodded.

"You'll have to move aside."

"Oh." His voice sounded rusty. He edged away from the door.

Retrieving her backpack from the counter surrounding the double sink, Trudy opened the door cautiously and peered out. The short hallway and the stairs were empty. "The coast's clear. Let's go."

She slipped out the door and Linc followed her. They managed to get back to their table without incident, but Linc didn't sit down, so neither did she.

Studying him, she diagnosed a case of sensory overload. She smiled. "Maybe we'd better call it a night."

"Yeah."

Apparently she'd really blown his circuits, because she felt as if she were shepherding a sleepwalker as they retrieved their coats and took a cab back to her apartment. He was so quiet. Too damned quiet. As the champagne began to wear off, she wondered if she'd made a terrible mistake by following her impulses in the nightclub bathroom. Maybe she'd ruined everything.

As the cab pulled up in front of her building, she turned to him and spoke in a low voice. "Now I'm afraid you have a bad opinion of me."

He blinked. "You should have a bad opinion of *me.* I can't believe I let that happen."

Oh, no. She wasn't letting him shoulder the blame. "But I'm the one who started it." She was still proud of that, regardless of his reaction. "Besides, if I do say so myself, I'm very good at sedu—"

"And I'm very good at self-control. Usually." He paused and glanced toward the front seat. "Wait here," he said to the driver as he opened the cab door. A gust of cold air blew in. "I'll be right back."

"Linc, you don't have to walk me to my door."

"Yes, I do." He helped her out of the cab. "Every man you date should walk you to the door and make sure you're safe."

His take-charge attitude, considering their recent experience in the bathroom, rubbed her the wrong way. "Did anyone ever tell you that you're bossy?"

"Yeah, Tom says that all the time." He waited for her to use her key on the front door of the apartment building and then followed her in and over to the elevator.

"Well, he's right. You're very bossy. Maybe even bossier than Meg."

"Speaking of Meg..." Linc cleared his throat as they stood by the elevator. Then he rubbed the back of his neck. "Damn, Trudy, I feel like a sleaze for taking advantage of you tonight. Meg and Tom asked me—"

"Taking advantage?" Her voice rose along with her irritation. "How in hell did you take advantage of me?"

"You'd had too much champagne! Which I bought for you!"

"I hadn't had that much! I knew *exactly* what I was doing."

"But I'm the one who's supposed to make sure you're okay, and instead I go along with some wild stunt that could have gotten us both arrested!"

"But it didn't." She was glad he didn't think she was a

tramp, but she wasn't comfortable in the helpless victim role he was giving her, either.

"I shouldn't have allowed it."

She wondered where he'd gotten the idea that he was in total charge around here. The elevator arrived and she stepped in. "Look, I don't know how Meg portrayed me when she asked you to baby-sit, but I'm a big girl and I—"

"She warned me that you were impulsive, so therefore I should have been prepared for something like this. But was I? No, I was not."

Impulsive. Trudy decided to settle that score with Meg tomorrow. Labeling her as impulsive made her sound irresponsible, and she wasn't. "We wouldn't have been arrested, you know."

"Why not? I'm sure there's something on the books about having sex in public places."

"We wouldn't have been caught having sex."

"We damn sure could have been."

The elevator doors opened and she kept talking as they walked down the hall. "No way. You were leaning against the door. By the time someone came in, we would have been perfectly decent and I would have thought of a reasonable explanation." She got out her key and glanced up at him. "We weren't going to get caught."

A flush rose from his neck to his cheeks. "I can't imagine what you could have said to explain me being in there."

"That's easy. I fainted. You heard me fall and came to investigate. Or the water faucet wouldn't turn off and you came in to fix it. Or I saw a bug and screamed and you rushed in, thinking I had a problem. Or—"

"Okay, okay." He heaved a sigh. "Obviously you're better at this kind of thing than I am. It doesn't throw you for a loop to get carried away like that. But I'm not used to losing control, and it makes me...nervous."

Oh, he shouldn't have said that. He'd just presented her with a challenge, whether he realized it or not. Here was this yummy-looking guy with a movie star body, and losing control made him nervous. She could hardly wait to try and make him lose control again. And again, and again. He would be such good practice for her. In no time she'd be ready for big-city sex.

"But you're back in control now, I take it?" she asked innocently.

"Yeah."

She turned the key in the lock and opened the door. "Would you like to come in?" She didn't expect him to accept, but toying with him would be fun.

He took a step backward. "Uh, I'll take a rain check."

"You should be fine if you're back in control. I'd be glad to fix you a nightcap."

"Thanks, but the…uh…the *cab*." He gestured toward the street with a look of relief. "The cab's waiting."

She pretended to be disappointed. "All right." Rather than put her key into her backpack, she stuck it in the pocket of the trench coat he'd loaned her. A piece of paper crackled inside the pocket, and she pulled it out. "What's this?"

"Our itinerary for the night."

"Really?" She opened it up and glanced over the neatly printed list of activities. It was touching, if a little anal. "We didn't do them in order, did we?"

"No."

She glanced up at him with a coy smile. "At least one thing we did isn't even on here."

He grew even more flushed. "Trudy, could we forget about that? I mean, could we really, really forget about it, like it never happened?"

"We can try," she murmured, thinking of the list she planned to make. At the top would be French maid. "I'll see you tomorrow night, then?"

"Right. I'll bring the card table and chairs, and a pizza."

"Great."

He started to back toward the elevator. "What do you like on your pizza?"

"Surprise me," she said. "I know I'll love whatever you have to offer."

9

LINC SLEPT LIKE A DEAD MAN for four hours, and then he was wide-awake and ready for...something. Actually he knew exactly what he was ready for. The part of his body that had betrayed him the night before was clamoring for attention again, creating a tent under his designer sheets. It had been a long time since he'd awakened in this condition, feeling like a randy teenager whose every third conscious thought was about sex.

Or maybe it was every second thought. Right now he was imagining Trudy asleep naked on her black satin sheets. And he couldn't dwell on that too long in his present state or he'd be moved to some really juvenile behavior. He got out of bed, grateful that his gym was open twenty-four hours a day. Throwing on sweats and running shoes, he bumped into the card table more than once as he moved around the room. Good thing he was getting rid of that today.

In general, he had too much stuff, and mostly things someone else had chosen for him. Decorating interested him not at all, so he'd hired a professional to buy furniture for his apartment. For some reason they'd assumed he'd like antiques. Antiques were okay—he'd grown up with them—but this morning the furniture looked stodgy to him.

Hell, this morning his whole life looked stodgy in comparison to the hours he'd spent with Trudy. He was all status quo, while she was all new millennium. Being around her could be good for him, shake him up a little, so long as he kept control.

Except that he'd done a piss-poor job of that so far. If only he hadn't let things get out of hand. No, if only he hadn't let things get *into* hand, namely, Trudy's hand. He groaned as remorse and sexual frustration jockeyed for position in his fevered brain.

Frustration was liable to win if he didn't get a move on. He grabbed a heavy parka on the way out the door, then clambered down the fire stairs all the way to the building's underground garage. A parka was the only coat Trudy owned, but he, the man of means, an establishment type, had coats for every occasion and clothes to fit any event. He had a well-stocked liquor cabinet and the right type of crystal, silver and china for any conceivable delicacy. His designer linens matched his decorator-created color scheme.

Oh, yes, Linc Faulkner was prepared for every contingency except one—being closed into the women's bathroom with Trudy Baxter.

He'd asked her to forget it, and he knew *he* never would. As he walked through the musty, dank garage toward his Benz, he could still feel her warm fingers surrounding his penis, her lips closing over him....

He walked right past his car and had to retrace his steps. No woman had ever tried anything on him remotely like the stunt Trudy had pulled last night. He'd thought Tom's stories of back-seat sex were wild, but to have a woman on her knees in a public bathroom while he leaned against the door, fully clothed except for an open fly—the concept made him shake with desire, even now, hours later.

Nevertheless, it never should have happened. It might be the most explosive sexual experience of his life thus far, including losing his virginity, but the fact remained that he'd shirked his responsibility by going along with the program.

As he electronically unlocked his car and slid onto the cool leather upholstery, he tried to pinpoint the moment when he'd lost control of the situation. He'd thought trapping her in the bathroom was a good way to find out what was going on with her. While he'd been thinking mild intimidation, she'd been thinking sexual opportunity.

Then again, he wasn't being quite honest with himself, he conceded as the car's powerful engine turned over. She wouldn't have been able to seduce him if he hadn't had the idea in the back of his own mind.

He'd seen the way she was drinking the champagne, so when he'd gone down the long, narrow stairway to find her, he'd simply been thinking about taking her home and putting her to bed. But with the effect of their kiss in Times Square still messing with his head, he'd also been thinking about doing more than that, although his conscience had been conducting a lecture, warning him to keep his hands off her.

Well, he had kept his hands off her. She'd been the one with the roving hands, and apparently that kind of boldness really turned him on. Who knew? Well, now he was alert to the dangers of a spunky gal like Trudy. Next time, the minute his brain started down the wrong road, he would know what could happen and make a correction before it was too late. He'd underestimated her, but he wouldn't make that mistake again.

He realized he was sitting in the garage with the engine running, thinking about Trudy. She sure did affect his concentration. Forcing himself to pay attention to what he was doing, he backed the car out and drove toward the exit. He'd have to watch himself at the gym. At this rate he'd start daydreaming about Trudy and drop a barbell on his foot.

She was something, though. And it wasn't only her sexiness that got under his skin. When he'd found out that she'd slicked back her hair so that she'd fit in, he'd been amused, yet touched, too. Yes, he'd had to hide his laughter, but his heart had gone out to her at the same time. She had guts, sailing into New York without a clue. He admired her courage.

Maybe that's why he hadn't made a stronger stand when

she'd come on to him. Yet he should have, because when he'd allowed her to take an inch, she'd taken…several. Oh, God, how she'd used her tongue. He'd enjoyed the hell out of the experience and would have cherished the memory if only Trudy hadn't been the woman he'd shared it with. He was supposed to take care of her, damn it!

From now on, he would.

TRUDY WOKE UP disgustingly early, before any daylight showed in the sliver of sky wedged between two tall buildings. So, still wearing the silk tank top and tap pants she'd worn to bed, she made a pot of coffee and drank it while she unpacked her sex books. She needed her reference library if she expected to stage a coup tonight.

She also needed to consult with Meg, but she didn't dare call until at least nine, and nine-thirty was more like it. She wouldn't want Meg to think she was *impulsive*. Every time she thought of that, her jaw clenched. Meg had some explaining to do.

At eight she used her new phone book to find a bakery that delivered warm bagels with cream cheese in six flavors, and by eight-thirty she was considerably less grouchy and willing to forgive Meg for the "impulsive" label. Although the description still sounded patronizing, it wasn't entirely inaccurate. She did like to be spontaneous.

Her little stunt with Linc was a perfect example. She hadn't planned it, but once he was there, blocking the bathroom door with his gorgeous body, what was a girl to do? Meg would have leaped to the same conclusion, given those circumstances.

At nine-fifteen her phone rang. She leaped to answer her first-ever phone call as a bonafide resident of New York City. She wondered if it could be Linc, and her heart beat faster at the thought.

If it was Linc, she didn't want to sound too perky. She

didn't think New Yorkers tended to be perky in the morning. Instead she aimed for sounding sleepy and slightly annoyed.

"Were you asleep?" Meg asked.

"Oh, it's you!"

"Of course it's me! Linc and Tom just left to play a few games of racquetball, and you don't know anybody else in town, so it has to be me."

"Racquetball?" She preferred imagining Linc sitting in a dingy café drinking coffee and missing her. He couldn't possibly be giving her much thought while he was racing around the racquetball court.

"Yeah, they sometimes play on Sunday mornings."

"So how did Linc seem to you?" She balanced the cordless phone between her chin and shoulder while she picked up a tub of strawberry cream cheese and ran her finger around the bottom to get the last of it.

"That's why I'm calling," Meg said. "He seemed distracted. Spacey."

Trudy licked her finger and smiled. "Good."

"Why good? Aren't you guys getting along?"

"We're getting along okay, considering that you told him I'm the impulsive type." She managed to get another quarter teaspoon of cream cheese on her finger and sucked it off.

"What's wrong with that? You *are* the impulsive type."

She tossed the empty carton in the trash and picked up the tub of blueberry. "I'm *spontaneous*. There's a difference, Meg."

"If you say so. And what do you call *getting along okay?*"

Trudy laughed, unable to keep the juicy details to herself another minute. Meg was the only person in the world she could share this triumph with. "Do you remember that book of mine that gives suggestions on unusual places to have sex?" Holding the tub of cream cheese, she flopped back on her unmade bed.

Meg's voice blasted through the receiver. *"You had sex?"*

Trudy grinned as she pictured Meg's expression right now. She wished she could have waited to tell her in person, but this was too good to keep that long. "Remember the bathroom scene?"

"Oh...my...God. You didn't."

"I did." This was the best, lying on her new satin sheets, eating blueberry cream cheese and dishing with her best friend about sexual escapades. Virtue seemed a million miles away. "See, I went down to the rest room to fix my makeup, and I'd had a fair amount of champagne, so when I didn't come back right away, he came down looking for me."

Meg's voice quivered with excitement. "I can't believe this. You lured him in there?"

"No. He was sure I was sick and wouldn't say so. He came in and said I couldn't leave until I told him the truth. Instead..." She paused for dramatic effect. "I convinced him to let me twirl his baton."

"You *didn't.*"

"Meg, it was outrageous. You should try it with Tom sometime."

Meg whooped. "Unbelievable! You did Linc Faulkner in the ladies' bathroom! I'll bet Wall Street Wonder Boy never had that happen to him before."

"From the way he acted, I don't think so. He was all repentant."

Meg laughed in delight. "He would be. I think his ancestors came over on the *Mayflower* and he's never quite eliminated that Puritan streak. Trudy, does this mean what I think it does? Are you starting your adventures with Linc?"

"Unofficially, I guess so. It's just for practice, you know?"

"Oh, I do, I do. I'm loving this."

"See, I found out that I have this other thing working for me in his case. He had a crush on the maid when he was a teenager, and I look like her."

"French maid costume!" Meg said immediately.

"Bingo. Can I get one today?"

"Oh, you can so get one today."

That was when it finally began to sink in that she was really in New York City, a place where anything was possible, even on Sunday. Her fantasy of big-city sex was about to begin, and she could hardly wait. She popped out of bed and started pacing. "Okay, I also need a folding screen for the living room, as a changing place. Is there somewhere I could find one secondhand?"

"I know just the place," Meg said. "Oh, this will be awesome. They have big ostrich feather fans, too, if you decide to do a Gypsy Rose Lee thing some other time. And do you want some toys? Maybe we should get some—"

"Whoa! The company isn't paying me that much yet."

"Consider it an early birthday present."

"Three months early?"

"We'll haggle about it after you get here. How soon can you come over? We have places to go and people to see."

"Um, just a sec." Trudy hurried into her bathroom and peered into the mirror. Her hair was a mess but she could pull it back with a clip. A quick power-shower and she'd be good to go. "It's a ten-minute bus ride to your apartment, right?"

"Maybe nine, if the traffic cooperates."

She started stripping off her tap pants. "I'll be there in twenty minutes."

THREE HOURS LATER Meg, exhausted but triumphant, put Trudy on a bus laden down with her birthday and Christmas presents for the next two years. The folding screen would be delivered later in the afternoon. They'd found a lovely hand-painted one for next to nothing in a little secondhand shop that was going out of business.

Best of all, Meg was beginning to see signs that Trudy was falling for Linc. Her eyes lost focus when she talked about him, and she probably didn't realize that she wore a goofy smile whenever Meg mentioned his name. Meg had struggled to keep her glee to herself, but she'd managed. The time for gloating would come later. Trudy had been so sure that she could avoid such a thing. She was so wrong.

Clutching her own purchase in a plain plastic bag, Meg climbed aboard the bus that would take her back to her apartment. She couldn't go into a sex toys store and not come out with something to surprise Tom. Besides, if she kept him happy enough he might not interfere with her campaign.

If fate was kind, Linc would be there watching sports with Tom as he often did after a racquetball session. If they were there, they'd be drinking beer and eating Cheez Doodles, which usually drove her nuts because the Cheez Doodles got all over everything. Today she didn't care if they were knee-deep in Cheez Doodle crumbs. She needed to talk to Linc.

Maybe a talk with Linc was totally unnecessary, but with things going so well, she didn't want to take any chances. Trudy was exactly the woman for Linc, and she'd known it all along, but Trudy could be overwhelming at times. Although Meg approved of the French maid approach as Trudy's first move, there was the slightest possibility that Linc would be scared off by the thought of enacting one of his cherished fantasies.

Meg planned to give him a reason to stay.

Sure enough, when she opened the front door of the apartment, pro football was on the tube and the guys were sprawled on the furniture in the middle of orange crumbs. They were each on their second beer.

"Hey, guys. Who's winning?" She always asked, even

though she didn't know one team from another. Men seemed to care about professional sports, so she tried to seem interested. At a cocktail party last week she'd tried to sound knowledgeable by mentioning the Houston Oilers, only to discover they hadn't existed as a franchise for years.

"Hey, honey." Tom leaped up immediately and hurried over to her.

"Hi, Meg," Linc said. He stood, too. "Can I get you anything?"

"Yeah, we were just thinking about lunch." Tom reached for her package, even though it was small. "Let me take that."

"That's okay." She pulled it out of reach. "Have a seat, Linc. You, too, Tom. I'll just go in and take off these shoes and then we can talk about lunch."

"My treat," Linc said as he returned to the sofa.

"Let me have the package," Tom said. "You shouldn't be carrying things. What did you buy? Something for the baby?"

She stuck it behind her back. "Something for *you*, baby," she murmured. "We'll see about it later, okay?" She stood on tiptoe and kissed him, enjoying the taste of real beer, which she couldn't have for another three months.

"Oh, yeah?" He lowered his voice. "You took Trudy to that little place next to the tattoo parlor, didn't you?"

"Maybe." Meg gave him a mysterious smile.

"We need to talk. Something's going on." Very subtly he jerked his head in Linc's direction.

"Yes, I think something is. Now let me get comfy and put away your surprise. I'll be right back."

Tom looked as if he wanted to say something more, but fortunately for her one of the teams accomplished some feat that made Linc yell. Tom rushed over to see what had happened.

Once she'd escaped to the bedroom, she tucked her purchase away in the closet and slipped out of her shoes. She and Tom had been talking about wrist and ankle restraints for months, teasing each other with the possibility. When she'd seen these in the softest fake fur she'd ever touched, she hadn't been able to resist. Trudy had decided against those for now, but at least she knew where the goody store was when she was ready for more supplies.

Watching Trudy walk through that store had been a kick and a half. She'd start to go wild with delight over something, then immediately become blasé and disinterested, as if she saw cock rings and flavored body oil every day of the week. Meg had tried to convince her that she didn't need to become a jaded sophisticate to fit in, but Trudy was convinced that was the image she needed in order to counteract her country bumpkin tendencies.

Meg had decided to use that attitude to her advantage. Wearing her favorite slippers, she returned to the living room where the men were once again absorbed in the football game. "Tom?"

He scrambled to his feet. "What, honey?"

It was so cute the way he jumped up, ready to do whatever she asked. Tom was a really good guy, and he would be sweet to his wife regardless of what kind of sex life they had. But Meg happened to believe that outstanding sex could turn a good guy into a great guy. Once she'd convinced him that sex wouldn't hurt the baby, they'd continued with their bedroom adventures. The bigger she got, the more they had to adjust positions, but in the process they'd found some interesting ones they might not have tried otherwise.

"You know what I could go for right now?" she said.

"What's that?"

"Calzones. I just love the way you make them." She did, but whipping up three calzones would keep him busy in the kitchen for a while, and that was her primary goal.

"Sure," he said. "Halftime's in about three minutes. Can you wait?"

"I can wait." She settled into her favorite chair and picked up the January issue of *Cosmo* she'd been too busy to read. Now that she looked at it, she realized she should have given it to Trudy. It was chock-full of tips for making the man in your life drool.

Although Meg was always searching for hints to help keep her romance fresh, she could afford to turn the magazine over to Trudy. The way Meg figured it, if a woman was carrying a man's child and also had fake-fur wrist and ankle restraints hidden in the closet, that woman could relax and assume she had it going on.

Halftime arrived. "I can't believe they tied the score," Tom said as he stood.

"Boy, me, either." Meg smiled at him.

Tom gazed at her with tolerant fondness. "I'll bet you have no idea who's even playing today."

"Sure I do. Some very strong men with tight buns."

Linc groaned. "Sexist, sexist. Hey, want some help with the calzones, buddy?"

"Not this time, okay? Sunday emergency room visits aren't my favorite."

Linc pulled a long face. "Now, see, you've hurt my feelings and made me feel like a liability to the operation."

"Hey, you were awesome with the Allen wrench yesterday, dude."

"Stay here and keep me company, Linc," Meg said. She'd counted on the fact that Tom wouldn't want a repeat of the last time Linc had insisted on chopping veggies. As near as Tom and Meg could tell, Linc had zero experience with a kitchen knife and he'd nearly severed the tip of his forefinger.

"Yeah," Tom said. "See if you can get Meg to understand the difference between a tight end and tight buns. She seems to think the terms are synonymous."

"They are!" Meg said. "Any person with eyes can see that."

Tom grinned. "You have your work cut out for you, buddy. I'll be in the kitchen if you need reinforcements."

"I think I can handle this." Linc picked up his beer and took a swallow.

As Tom left the room, Meg glanced over at Linc. She didn't have much time, so she couldn't lead up to the subject gently. "I need to talk to you about Trudy."

He choked on his beer.

"There's something you need to know before you go over there tonight. She—"

"Meg, I'm—" He coughed as his face turned red. "I'm really sorry." He coughed again. "I feel like a jerk for how last night turned out, and I promise that kind of thing won't happen again."

She was *so* glad she'd decided to say something to him. The blood of his Puritan ancestors still flowed in his veins, giving him a conscience the size of the Empire State Building. Trudy could probably overcome that influence eventually, but she might become discouraged and give up. That would never do.

"I hope it does happen again," she said. "Or some variation of that activity."

He stared at her. "I thought you wanted me to make sure she didn't have sex right away?"

"With some stranger who could hurt her. You're the only one on the approved list, but I couldn't say that in the beginning. It would have sounded too weird."

Linc sat with his arms resting on his knees, his hands clasped. He dropped his gaze and studied his hands for several seconds. "It still sounds weird, Meg." He glanced up at her. "Believe me when I say I've never had this kind of conversation with anyone in my life."

"Oh, I believe you. I know this is an unusual situation, but here's what you need to know. Trudy desperately wants to try out some of her fantasies about sex in the big city, and…she wants to practice on you."

"What?"

"Please humor her first attempts, Linc. She pretends to be tough, but she's very vulnerable right now. If she sets up a seduction and you refuse to be a part of it, she'll be devastated. If you play along she'll be able to build her confidence. Then when she starts her sexual adventures for real, she'll be stronger, less likely to be taken advantage of."

"Whew." Linc scrubbed a hand over his face. "I don't know, Meg."

"I'd count it as a personal favor."

He gave her a wry smile. "Some favor."

"I know."

"Calzones coming up!" Tom announced as he walked into the room.

Meg glanced questioningly at Linc, hoping he'd indicate with a nod or a smile that he'd decided to do as she asked. But his gaze gave nothing away.

10

A LIGHT SNOW DRIFTED past Trudy's uncurtained windows, random flakes that reflected the light shining from other windows. Very little light came from hers. The only way she could imagine getting through the first few nerve-racking moments of Linc's arrival was to cloak her apartment in semidarkness.

She hadn't expected the French maid's outfit to be quite so skimpy, and she definitely hadn't expected to become sexually excited just by putting it on. But the ensemble was the most provocative thing she'd ever worn, and knowing that she was wearing something designed to incite a man to lust was doing the same for her. Her black lace panties were already damp.

The dress, what there was of it, was more like a lace-trimmed black bathing suit with a miniskirt attached. The salesclerk had raved about the underwired, fiberfill cups set into the bodice, and Trudy had to admit she suddenly had an impressive amount of cleavage. She could hold a wallet and a set of keys in there, no problem.

The outfit also included a frilly white apron, a lace cap and lace wristbands. The feather duster had been Meg's idea, and the salesclerk had suggested fishnet stockings. Trudy had bought those stockings in a New York minute, along with a garter belt. She'd waited her entire adult life for a chance to wear fishnet stockings.

Her final touch was a pair of five-inch black stilettos, bad-girl shoes she'd ordered from a catalog two years ago and never worn. There wasn't much call for five-inch heels in Virtue, but maybe she should have tried them out before in private. She hadn't realized how tough it was to walk in shoes that put the entire weight of her body on the balls of her feet. But she had to stick with the shoes. This was not the occasion for sensible little pumps.

Meg had advised her about the music. Smoky jazz was perfect for a guy like Linc, Meg had said, so Trudy had saxophones and clarinets going on in the background. She didn't want to meet Linc at the door, because he'd be lugging a big box with the folding table in it and balancing a pizza besides. She'd hate for him to drop everything in the hall and make a mess.

So she'd worked out her plan. She'd already unlocked the door, but she'd left the security chain in place. That could be moved without making any noise. Once he rang the doorbell, she'd check the peephole, a habit she was trying to get into, and then she'd carefully remove the security chain. But she wouldn't open the door.

After that she'd retreat halfway across the room and call to him, telling him to come on in. She'd have time before he opened the door to scurry around her bed and behind her new folding screen. While he set up the card table and chairs she could pretend to finish dressing while she talked to him. When she figured he'd accomplished that and had his hands free, she'd appear.

She wasn't sure what she should do after that. Meg didn't seem to think she needed to plan her moves beyond appearing in the French maid outfit. Once he got over his initial shock, according to Meg, he'd know exactly what to do. He was a normal male, she'd said, and the bed was right there.

Fate had stepped in yesterday, forcing Trudy to put the bed in the living room, and now she couldn't imagine it anywhere else. She'd turned down the covers to make it even more inviting, and she'd slipped condom packages under the pillow. Her voice-activated tape recorder was under the bed. She became even more aroused looking at that bed and imagining Linc in it with her and both of them being recorded having sex.

Her first big-city seduction was upon her, if she didn't count the incident in the women's rest room. That was more like a prologue, anyway, because there was no way it could have lasted very long. But tonight's episode could last as long as either of them wanted it to. She felt really glad Linc was the man of the hour, now that all was said and done.

A glance at the stove's digital clock told her that the time was a mere one minute away from seven o'clock. Her pulse raced as she pictured him getting into the elevator about now. She wondered what he'd be wearing tonight, and how quickly it would come off. In an effort to calm down, she took several deep breaths, which nearly caused her breasts to pop out of the tight bodice.

At exactly seven, the doorbell chimed. She tiptoed slowly over to the door and peered out through the peephole. Pizza delivery had never looked this good. Even elongated by the lens of the peephole, he was breathtaking. He wore jeans, a collarless knit shirt and a black leather jacket.

The snow had dampened his dark hair, making it glisten in the light from the hallway and fall in spiky little bangs across his forehead. He balanced the pizza box in one hand and grasped the handle of the packing box with the other. He looked so smooth, so suave. She had a moment of unease wondering if she could really pull off this seduction. But it was too late to reconsider now. He rang the bell again as she carefully eased the chain from its slot.

LINC STILL HADN'T MADE a decision. Here he was at Trudy's door, and if Meg's information was correct, Trudy was planning to seduce him tonight. Of course he should go along with her, as Meg had asked. Only an idiot would turn down a chance like this.

The trouble was, he might be that kind of idiot. On the surface he'd spent the afternoon at Tom and Meg's eating calzones and intently watching football, but it had been a cover. Most of that time he'd been thinking about his love life in general and Trudy in particular.

Up to now he'd followed a predictable pattern with women, a pattern he'd never recognized. Thanks to Trudy, he understood what he'd been doing, and he wasn't happy about that insight. Because he was so afraid of marriage, he'd unconsciously gravitated to cool, unemotional women, which kept him safe from entanglements.

Then along came Trudy, with her bed in the living room and her arms spread wide, ready for all that New York had to offer, all he had to offer. There was nothing cool and unemotional about Trudy, although she imagined eventually she'd perfect that attitude. No way. She was too vibrant ever to be toned down, and he was captivated by her infectious energy.

Meg had made it seem so easy—go along with Trudy's seduction schemes, help her build her sexual confidence, and then they'd both walk away. Maybe Trudy would be able to walk away. As she'd made clear, she had a lot of living to do. But for the first time in his life he wondered if he'd be able to walk away. Trudy was seriously close to being the woman to get past his defenses and make him question his whole approach to relationships.

He didn't want to have to question anything. He wanted life to rock along exactly the way it had been before this nymph sailed in from Kansas with her sex books and her impulsive behavior. If he became sexually involved with Trudy, there was a chance she'd engage him emotionally, too. Then he could end up standing in the middle of the road watching her run off to new adventures while he nursed a broken heart.

But he didn't want to be responsible for wrecking her self-confidence, either. Meg seemed to think if he didn't go along with her planned seduction he'd crush her. Maybe he could work out a compromise and let her know how tempted he was, which would be true, but that he…that he what? Thought he might be coming down with the flu? Had suddenly been called away on business? Was allergic to black satin sheets?

For a reasonably bright guy he sure was coming up with lame excuses. Maybe something would occur to him once he saw what she'd planned in order to lure him into her bed. When she didn't open the door on the first ring of the doorbell, he began to wonder how elaborate this fantasy of hers might be.

He rang again and thought he heard some activity on the other side of the door. Bracing himself for whatever she had in store, he waited for the door to open.

The door remained closed, but her voice drifted through it. "Come on in, Linc. I'm not quite finished dressing."

That was enough to put him on alert. Something strange was going on, but he had no choice except to walk right into the trap she'd obviously set for him. Leaning the card table box against the wall, he started to open the door at the same moment he heard her cry out. A soft thud followed.

He was through the door in no time, pizza box raised like a weapon. And there was Trudy, sprawled facedown on her bed, fishnet-covered legs splayed to give him a tantalizing view up her short black skirt. It didn't look like the seductive pose she'd planned on, but he grew hard immediately.

"Damn shoes!" Gasping, she flopped right side up and sagged inelegantly against the edge of the bed.

It was his turn to gasp. He nearly dropped the pizza box, but he grabbed it before it tumbled to the floor. "What the hell are you wearing?"

Her chin lifted and she adjusted the lace cap knocked sideways by her fall. Her cheeks were pink with embarrassment, but she met his gaze defiantly. "What does it look like?"

A wet dream. She'd taken his teenaged fantasy and amplified it a hundred times. He stared at her heaving breasts threatening to escape from their tenuous confinement, the lace bands circling her slender wrists, the snow-white apron defining her pelvis and the fishnet stockings drawing attention to her spectacular legs.

He could see exactly how she'd fallen. She was still wearing one of her do-me shoes, but the other one lay beside the bed where she'd obviously tripped on her way across the room. Saliva pooled in his mouth. He wanted her so much he began to quiver. Desperately he tried to marshal all the arguments against having sex with her.

"You can go ahead and laugh if you want," she said. "This was supposed to be a fun little surprise for you. I thought it would remind you of Belinda, and we could have a good time with it."

"Oh." His blood had drained from his head to his groin, leaving him with a very limited vocabulary. He'd been kidding himself to think that he could resist her. Messing up her routine had made her even more appealing. He was putty in her hands.

Apparently she didn't realize that fact. "Since I've totally ruined the effect I was going for, we might as well relax and have that pizza. I'm sure I look ridiculous."

"No, you don't." If only he thought so. Instead he was battling a red haze of lust that was in danger of wiping out all rational thought. Seeing her propped against that fantasy bed in her fantasy outfit was more than he could handle. Between the candlelight and the saxophone wailing in the background, he felt as if he'd stepped into an adult video. And he knew his role.

"You're just being nice. I should have prepared better and spent time practicing in these killer heels." She pushed away from the bed and picked up the fallen shoe. "To think that they dance in these things on Broadway." Bracing one hand on the bed, she leaned down and put the shoe on.

He stifled a groan. From the matter-of-fact way she engineered the move, she must have no clue how sexy she looked doing it. She really believed she'd failed in her attempt to seduce him with the maid's uniform. With every motion of her body, she was succeeding more than she could possibly know.

"You can put the pizza on the counter over there." She waved in the direction of the tiny kitchen as she teetered over toward the door he'd left open. "I assume the table and chairs are still out here?"

"Yes." He'd forgotten all about them. Moving woodenly into the kitchen, he set down the warm pizza carton. By the time he'd turned around and walked into the living room again, she was dragging the table and chair box through the door.

A gentleman would help a lady in such circumstances. A rogue would hang back and watch how her short skirt rode up over her bottom when she leaned forward to tug the box into the room. A rogue would forget courtesy in favor of checking out her black garter belt and black lace panties. Faced with a French maid's costume, Linc crossed the line from gentleman to rogue.

She closed and locked the door before turning back to him. "I guess we should set this up and eat the pizza, huh? Before it gets cold."

He coughed and cleared his throat. "Okay."

"You really are trying hard not to laugh, aren't you?"

"No, I—"

"Believe me, if I'd made it behind that screen before you came in, and then I'd eventually come prancing out with feather duster in hand, I'll bet I'd have blown your circuits."

"You have a feather duster?" Oh, God, he'd watched Belinda wield a feather duster as she'd sashayed through his parents' mansion. He'd also figured out from the dialogue he'd taped of her making it with the butler that she'd used the feather duster in an entirely different way in private.

"Yeah. Is that too clichéd? It's still behind the folding screen."

"Um…"

"You're right, it's probably too overdone. In fact, is the outfit a bit much? You can tell me if you think so. Maybe I should have tried to find a real maid's uniform instead. That might be classier."

She really had no idea of the effect she'd created. He didn't give a damn about class right now. All he could think of was raw, raunchy sex. "It looks—"

"I know. Like a hooker. Well, how I imagine a hooker might look. I've never actually seen one. Have you?"

"Yes."

"Cool! Did you actually…I mean, not to get too personal, but I've never known a man who really hired…what I'm trying to ask is, have you ever paid anyone for—"

"No. And for the record, you don't look like a hooker." Wow, he'd actually strung a few words together. She might even think his brain was in working order.

Instead of being pleased with his remark, she looked disappointed. "Well, if I don't look like a hooker, and I don't look like a classic French maid, then this outfit is probably a total washout for exciting a man."

"I wouldn't say that."

She brightened. "Then you think I could eventually make it work?"

"Uh-huh."

"You're a good sport, Linc. Tell you what. Humor me and let me wear this getup for a while and practice walking on the heels. The effect may be lost on you after that graceless flop onto the bed, but I spent money for this stuff and someday I might be able to knock a guy's socks off with it." She wobbled over to the kitchen. "Now if you'll set up the table and chairs, I'll get out plates and napkins. Do you want the same brand of beer you drank when we had lunch here on Saturday?"

"Sure." This might be the strangest situation he'd ever encountered. She'd set out to seduce him, but after screwing up her grand entrance she'd abandoned the plan completely. Now it appeared she wasn't going to seduce him, after all.

Of course now he wanted her to more than life itself.

But she apparently planned to eat pizza instead, so he took off his leather jacket and hung it on her doorknob. Then he opened the packing box and pulled out the table and chairs. "Where do you want the table set up?" he asked.

"I think in the far corner by the window. Do you want your beer in a glass or a bottle?"

"Bottle's fine." He hauled the table and chairs over to the corner of the room, past that amazing bed. He'd never eaten pizza in a woman's bedroom before. The way things were going, he'd eat the pizza, drink the beer and leave. All his agonizing over whether to allow her to seduce him had been unnecessary.

He was arranging the chairs around the table when she came up behind him.

"Here's your beer, sir," she said.

The *sir* part sent a shiver of anticipation up his spine, but she was probably only kidding around. He turned, figuring he'd imagined a husky, provocative note in her voice. Then his eyes widened.

In both hands she held a large plate loaded with pizza slices. She'd also brought his bottle of beer. She'd opened it and tucked it down between her breasts. The material had strained to cover her before, but with the addition of the beer bottle, she looked ready to pop out at any moment.

Fluttering her eyelashes, she gazed up at him. Her green eyes sparkled with invitation as she dropped a demure curtsy. "Dinner is served, sir."

His throat went dry. "More...practice?"

"Please play along with me, kind sir," she murmured.

"I botched up the opener, but maybe I can save the evening."

He began to quiver with excitement and gratitude. She was going to try to seduce him, after all. He had a feeling she'd accomplish it. "What do you want me to do?"

She glanced at the folding table. "Will that table hold me, sir?"

His heart thundered in his ears as he tried to imagine what she had in mind. Whatever it was, he didn't care if she broke the damn table, but he didn't want her getting hurt. "For what?"

"As the lord of the manor, you might find some pleasure in having me feed you, sir."

Oh, God, this was going to be awesome. He'd never play-acted with a woman in his life, and he could hardly wait. "It'll hold you," he said, his voice rough with anticipation.

"Very good, sir." She set the plate on the far side of the table. Then she scooted carefully up on it and slowly spread her legs, dangling her feet and those sexy shoes off the edge. Turning, she retrieved the plate and settled it between her stocking-clad thighs.

A plate of pizza surrounded by creamy thighs sheathed in fishnet. He'd never be able to eat pizza again without thinking of this moment.

She motioned him to the chair in front of her. "The table is prepared, sir. Please be seated."

He eased down in front of her and wished he'd worn something more forgiving than denim tonight. The scent of yeasty pizza dough and melted cheese blended with the musky scent of arousal, his and hers. The fly of his jeans pinched ferociously.

She leaned forward. "Some beer, sir?"

"Thanks." Holding her gaze, he slid his hand between one breast and the bottle. One little nudge with his wrist, and the material over her left breast slipped down an inch, exposing her nipple, pebbled and erect.

"Oh, my *goodness,* sir."

"Is there a problem?" Heat surged through him, but he managed to keep his tone neutral, as if she really were the maid and he the master of the house, as if she had no choice but to tolerate whatever he chose to do. He couldn't believe the rush of excitement as he pulled the bottle free and stroked the cool, moist surface over her nipple, making her gasp. Then he absently plucked at the tip of her breast as he took a long swallow from the bottle.

"Is…the beer to your liking, sir?" She sounded a little breathless.

"It will do." He settled the bottle between her breasts again and made sure in the process he exposed her other nipple. The bottle tucked between her breasts was decidedly phallic, making him imagine positions he'd never tried, sensations he'd never experienced—Trudy's full breasts, several drops of scented oil, and him astride, cupping her oiled breasts…thrusting slowly…

"Pizza, sir?"

He glanced up to discover her holding out a slice of pizza, cheese oozing from the tip. He'd slipped past some boundary in the last few seconds, and his imagination was overrun with X-rated ideas. Pizza no longer interested him at all. He wanted something else.

Leaning forward, he flicked his tongue over the dangling end of the pizza slice, but he didn't take a bite. Then he gazed into her eyes. "It's not hot enough."

She moistened her lips and her breathing became more agitated. "It's not?"

"No. Put it back on the plate." He waited until she'd set it down before he reached for the beer bottle again, carelessly fondling her breasts in the process. "In fact, you can take that plate away."

"As you wish, sir." She placed the plate behind her.

He took a swig of beer, faking nonchalance. He'd never realized a game like this could turn him on like nothing he'd ever tried before. ''What can you do for me?'' he asked.

''What would you...like?''

He brushed the bottle over each of her breasts, watching her nipples tighten and grow darker. ''I want something hot to eat, Trudy.'' For the first time he used her name as part of the charade, and he was rewarded with her shiver of recognition. He looked into her eyes. ''As the master of the house, I demand you give me that.''

She swallowed. ''Do you mean what I think?''

''Sir,'' he prompted.

''Do you mean what I think, sir?''

''Yes.'' He gave her no quarter, daring her to break eye contact.

She didn't. ''Where, sir?''

''Right here.'' He set the bottle on the floor beside his chair and nearly knocked it over, he was trembling so much. ''Lift your skirt and apron.''

She did, presenting him with a black triangle of lace covering his impending feast.

''Pull that aside.''

She reached down between her thighs, and the lace encircling her wrist seemed like a symbol of her submission, making the gesture even more erotic. Her fingernails were painted red, the perfect color for what was happening. Breathing rapidly, she drew the black lace aside.

His moan of pleasure blended with the muted wail of a saxophone. Damp brown curls quivered with each breath she took. Beneath them, only partially hidden, was the moist treasure he sought.

He cupped her bottom in both hands and guided her closer to the edge of the table. Then he pushed his chair away just a little, just enough. There.

''Looks delicious,'' he murmured, his heart racing as he lowered his head. ''And very, very hot.''

11

EXTREMELY HOT. Trudy was so churned up she could scarcely breathe. She gripped the side of the folding table with her free hand, and as Linc drew nearer to his goal, she became so light-headed that she wondered if she'd pass out from excitement. Back-seat sex, even gazebo sex, hadn't prepared her for a candlelit view of Linc's head between her thighs.

Then she felt the first practiced flick of his tongue and gasped. Sweet heaven, at last a man who knew what he was doing, a man who knew the territory and could navigate without a guide. She'd never been so wet in her life, and she had a feeling she was about to get much wetter.

His murmur of appreciation nearly made her come. Then he settled in, pressing his mouth against her with obvious enjoyment. And talent. Oh, the man had a clever tongue, and he wasn't afraid to use it. He explored and caressed, nibbled and licked. The sound of him doing that mingled with smoky jazz and took her to places she'd never been. She lost all inhibition—leaning back and spreading her thighs even more, breathing hard, panting, gasping. And so, so ready.

He obviously knew. He had to know from the way she quaked whenever he returned to slide his tongue where it had maximum effect. But he seemed to be in no hurry. Ah, the novelty of that. The maddening, thrilling, aching novelty of that!

She'd never been held on the brink so long, never known

a man who took such pleasure in giving pleasure to her. It was so good. It was beyond good...and if he didn't finish the job *right now,* she would fly apart like a windmill in a tornado.

"Please make me come," she begged.

He lifted his head and gazed up at her, his blue eyes dark with lust, his lips moist. His voice was thick with desire. "Please make me come, *sir.*"

Those words alone nearly took her over the edge. She gulped. "Please, sir," she murmured, trembling and holding on to the table for dear life. "Oh, please make me come, sir."

Heat flashed like lightning in his eyes and his breathing was as labored as hers. "What if I'm not quite finished with you? What if I like toying with you and making you wait for what you want?"

"I—"

"You need to say *Do as you wish with me, sir.*"

"Do...as you...wish with me, sir," she whispered, drowning in the depths of those eyes. The way he was looking at her might be all she'd need to take her where she wanted to go.

"That's better." Then he slowly lowered his head again.

But he honored her request. Did he ever. Her moans of ecstasy mingled with the rhythmic sound of his tongue, and in seconds she tumbled into the most spectacular climax of her life, her cry rich with a kind of satisfaction she'd only dreamed about.

While she was still shaking and gulping for air, he shifted his hold, sliding one arm under her and bracing the other across her back.

His breath tickled her ear as she heard the scrape of his chair. "Wrap those sexy legs around me, Trudy, and put your arms around my neck. I'm taking you to bed."

And that's how her uncovered breasts and her hot, damp center became pressed tight against the soft shirt covering his flat belly. The waistband of his jeans brushed the underside of her thighs as he stood and turned, kicking the chair aside. It clattered to the floor.

She nestled her head against his shoulder and hung on while her world continued to vibrate from the aftershocks of her release.

"Do you have condoms?" he asked, carrying her the short distance to the bed.

"Yes, sir." Her heart hammered. This was it. Big-city sex.

"Where?"

"Under the pillow...sir."

"You're insolent, you know that?" He nipped at the curve of her neck. "I should make you undress me, but I don't know if you'd do it fast enough to suit me."

As she began to recover from her mind-shattering experience, she thought of how much she'd love to undress him. That was part of her fantasy, too. She lifted her head to look into his eyes. "Please let me undress you, sir."

"If you do it wrong, there will be penalties to pay."

Anticipation shot through her. He'd obviously immersed himself in this game and she loved the way his imagination was working. "I understand, sir," she said meekly.

"Good." He sat her on the bed with her legs dangling over the sides.

She liked the fact that her feet didn't touch the floor when she sat on the mattress. She felt as if she'd boarded a fantasy ship where anything could happen. Looking up at him standing there beside the bed, his erection creating a promising bulge in his jeans, she knew she'd found the right person to take on the bed's maiden voyage.

"You can start with my shirt." He stepped close enough that she could reach him.

"Yes, sir." She gathered the soft jersey in both hands and tugged it from the waistband of his jeans. He was a little too far away to do it easily.

He moved between her legs, crowding her now. "You're already too slow."

She could feel him shaking. "I'll try to do better, sir." She pulled the shirt up, admiring his taut abs and his well-rounded pecs. A smattering of dark hair swirled around his nipples. She leaned forward and touched her tongue to the nipple centered over his heart.

He shuddered. "I didn't say you could...do that."

"No, sir." Bunching the shirt at his collarbone, she licked the areola and bit the tip gently.

His breathing grew quick and shallow. "You're incurring penalties."

"Yes, sir." She treated his right nipple to the same caress.

With a groan he stepped away and pulled off his shirt, throwing it on the floor. "Many penalties. I might as well take care of the shoes." He toed off his loafers. "Let's see if you can do any better with my jeans."

He was so beautiful. A fine sheen of perspiration covered his chest, and she could hardly wait to have him. Her hands shook as she unfastened the metal button at his waist and drew the zipper down. She remembered the shape and size of his penis, and saliva dampened her tongue, as if preparing her to repeat the caress she'd given him the night before.

"Way too slow, wench." He moved back again and shoved his jeans to the floor, stepping out of them.

Wench. She quivered with delight. Not every man would know how to play the game. Linc did. She could barely believe her good fortune that she had him standing there almost naked. She couldn't stop looking at him, from his muscled calves and strong thighs to the prominent jut of his penis under the black briefs.

"I'll finish this myself," he said with a show of disgust. He pulled off his socks, and then the briefs were history, too.

She stared in open admiration. Her sneak preview the

night before hadn't allowed her to savor what he had to offer. He had a great deal to offer.

He came toward her, his gaze intense. "And now for the penalties you must pay for being so slow at your task."

Her pulse drummed rapidly as desire claimed her, stroking her with unseen hands into hot readiness again.

"You must do as I say while I use you for my pleasure."

"Yes, sir." She lowered her gaze as if to show humility and submission. In fact, lowering her gaze allowed her to check him out at close range. His thick penis was fully erect, springing forth from the dark hair covering his groin. His balls hung heavy with promise between his thighs. Oh, baby.

"Kick off your shoes."

She had no trouble with that. The damn things had been a problem all night long.

"Get on your knees facing me." He glanced up at the canopy. "And hang on to that railing."

She did, and realized that positioned her breasts directly in front of his face.

Apparently that's what he'd had in mind, because he wrenched the bodice down until it was bunched under her breasts, displaying them even more prominently. "Perfect," he murmured. "Don't move."

He crossed to the table and came back with his bottle of beer. Pouring a golden pool about the size of a quarter into his cupped hand, he put down the bottle and rubbed his palms together. Then he stroked them over her breasts.

He repeated the process several times, massaging and stroking until her skin was wet and fragrant with the yeasty smell of beer. She'd never realized before how much the scent of beer reminded her of the aroma of sex.

"And now I'll lick you clean." He circled her breasts with his tongue, lapping at her soft skin but carefully avoiding her nipples, as if he knew that was what she wanted most.

She thrust her nipples forward and whimpered.

His soft laughter feathered her damp skin. "As *I* wish, wench." Then with a groan he cupped her left breast. "And I wish it now." He sucked greedily while he massaged her other breast with strong fingers.

Amazingly she felt a climax building. She hadn't known such a thing could be possible. Her breathing quickened and she closed her eyes to concentrate on that miraculous tightening. Oh, yes.

He lifted his mouth from her breast and she moaned in frustration. Then he cradled her right breast and began to suck. The tightening began again, and she started to pant. She was close, so close, but she needed the barest of touches to go over.

Letting go of the railing with one hand, she reached between her legs.

He released her breast and grasped her wrist, catching her where the lace band circled it.

Her eyes flew open.

"At my pleasure," he said, his voice a deep growl of command. "Hold the rail until I have had my fill of your breasts."

She gazed at him with a silent plea.

He swallowed. "You're incredible," he whispered, dropping his mask of arrogance for a moment. Then he cleared his throat and frowned at her. "I will have my way with you," he said sternly.

"Yes, sir."

"My way," he muttered, lifting her breast, drawing it into his mouth, sucking rhythmically. Only this time, he also reached between her legs, insinuating his fingers under the elastic circling her thigh. Several firm, rapid strokes later she erupted, bucking against the pressure of his fingers and drenching her panties all over again.

Leaving her breast, he reached up and circled her wrists

with his fingers. Then he sought her mouth with his as he drew her wrists down and put them behind her back.

She leaned against his solid chest for support and took his stiff penis between her thighs. Rocking her hips gently to set up a light friction against his shaft, she drank in his kiss, flavored with imported beer. From this moment on she'd associate the taste of it with wild loving and Linc. In the guise of seeking only his own pleasure, he'd given her two fantastic orgasms. She suspected that had been his plan all along.

He lifted his lips a fraction from hers. "On your hands and knees, wench," he said, gasping for air. "Facing away from me."

A new wave of passion rolled over her, leaving her quivering and ready for more. This man knew how to play.

He put a small distance between them and guided her around until her backside was toward him. "Lower that saucy bottom until I tell you to stop."

She'd never felt so deliciously vulnerable as she eased slowly down.

"More. No, stop." The tip of his penis brushed the delicate folds. "Raise a little. There. Stay right there." His voice shook slightly, but he maintained that arrogant tone that sent shivers of delight down her spine.

In real life she'd never tolerate that tone from a man, but in fantasy it was incredibly sexy. The pillows sailed to the floor as he uncovered the condom packets.

A delicate rip, the snap of latex, and his hands, fingers splayed, cupped her bottom. His fingers pressed harder, urging her to open to him. "Wider," he commanded.

"Yes, sir." Heat coursed through her as she obeyed him.

"You are here to serve me." He pulled aside the thin strip of lace blocking his way.

"Yes, sir." She closed her eyes with pleasure as he eased forward, parting her, filling her.

"And I'll take what I want. I am in control of your pleasure." With one smooth movement, he buried himself deep.

"Oh, *yes.*" Like a guided missile, he'd honed right in on her G-spot.

He drew back and thrust forward crisply again. "Yes, what, wench?"

"Yes, sir!"

"That's better." He clutched her hips and groaned as he began a steady rhythm. "So much better. Better…and better…"

She was speechless, swimming in ecstasy as he stroked that elusive spot over and over, carrying her along on a tide of indescribable feeling. He had the perfect angle, creating a miracle with each thrust.

Tiny, breathless cries flew from her as he increased the pace, slapping his thighs against her bottom. She gathered the satin sheet in both hands, needing to grab something, have some purchase on the whirlwind that was building within her.

And he did have control of her pleasure. The movement, the pressure, the rhythm were all up to him. She could only stay motionless, the sheet fisted in her hands, and allow him to bring her the gift of another orgasm.

He pumped faster, and she gasped as her climax hovered nearer. There. His rhythm became frenzied as thighs slick with sweat pounded against her bottom. Now. *Yes.* Her world exploded with color, light and sensation. Incredible sensation. Her loud moan of gratitude came at the same moment that he cried out and surged deep, his penis pulsing within her.

LINC STOOD WITH HIS KNEES BRACED against the bed and struggled to breathe as the force of his climax gradually ebbed. He'd never had sex like this, never played a fantasy role, or had the woman play one for him. And now he knew he'd been missing something amazing.

He eased away from her, knowing that the position might be difficult for her and he should allow her to relax onto the bed. But he didn't want to let her go. He'd loved the game they'd played with each other, and he didn't want it to be over yet.

"Trudy," he murmured, guiding her down onto the mattress. "I'll be...I'll be right back." Then somehow he found the strength to stumble past her kitchen, through the place that was supposed to be her bedroom and into her little bathroom. Candles lighted his way, as if she'd known he'd eventually need to make that trip.

He dispensed with the condom and washed his hands. Then he stood there, his hands braced against the sink, his head down, as he wondered what in hell he'd gotten himself into.

In only two nights, she'd wrapped him around her little finger. Here he was supposed to be doing *her* a big favor, and he felt like a little kid waiting in line for the Tilt-A-Whirl. She was the most exciting thing to happen to him in years, and he was pathetically eager for her. That wasn't the balance of power he was accustomed to, and it scared the devil out of him.

Two days ago he would never have imagined he'd be standing naked in her apartment—naked and unwilling to leave. He wanted to crawl into that big bed with her and tease and play until dawn.

That could be dangerous, though. Spend that much time in bed with a woman and it started to look like emotional entanglement time. He'd be far better off getting dressed and going home, putting some distance between them. He didn't want distance. He wanted more of her lush, responsive body. He wanted more surprises, more fantasy, more, more, more.

With a sigh of surrender, he walked out of the bathroom. He didn't have the discipline to walk out of this apartment now, and he might as well face that humbling fact. Whatever Trudy had in mind, he was happy to go along.

He expected her to be lying in the big bed waiting for him. But she wasn't there. She didn't appear to be anywhere, not in the kitchen and not over by the table. "Trudy?"

"I'm changing." Her voice floated from behind the folding screen. Just then a fishnet stocking flipped over the screen to dangle there, reminding him of the wild ride he'd just had. Then the second stocking joined it.

His penis grew thick and solid again as he gazed at those stockings and thought of her naked behind the screen. Saliva pooled in his mouth. If he hadn't closed it, he literally might have drooled. "Changing into what?"

"It's not important."

With Trudy, it was *always* important. His anticipation grew.

Her garter belt flopped over the edge of the screen. "Linc…"

"Yes." He was shaking.

"I think maybe you should leave, now."

"Leave?" He couldn't have been more shocked. "Are you upset? Did I overdo the—"

"Oh, no. You were *wonderful.* I adored what we did together."

"Then why—"

"Because I want to maintain a sense of mystery."

He almost laughed, but instinct made him stifle the impulse. She was serious, and she wouldn't appreciate his laughter. Mystery had nothing to do with how he'd reacted to her. That outfit might have reminded him a little of his fantasies about Belinda, but Trudy's sexuality had quickly overridden any dusty old memories of the former maid.

No, it wasn't mystery causing him to get as hard as one of Tom's steel wrenches. That happened thinking of Trudy's full breasts and that wondrous place between her thighs. The costume had been intriguing, and he knew that their game had added excitement, but he was hooked on Trudy, and she wouldn't have to add a thing to make him pant for her.

That wasn't a speech he'd be making tonight, however. Speeches like that could get a guy into big trouble. So the alternative was to leave as she'd suggested and go home to his boring luxury apartment.

"Okay." He walked over and started retrieving his clothes. "I should probably get some sleep, anyway. Tomorrow's a work day." As if he cared. He needed to remember it was a work day for her, too, though. She was starting a new job, and she couldn't afford to come into the office groggy from a night of too much sex and not enough sleep.

"Will you think of me while you're working tomorrow?"

The entire day. "I suppose I will," he said casually. "It's not every day I spend quality time with a French maid."

"Except in France."

He smiled as he pulled on his clothes. She had some endearingly crazy ideas about his lifestyle. "Sorry to disappoint you, but I've never had sex with a French maid."

"That's a relief." Her costume joined the row of tempting items hanging over the folding screen. "I thought about trying to do a French accent, but I'm not very good at languages, and I thought it would come out like a cross between Pepe le Peu and Bugs Bunny. So you ended up with a French maid from Kansas, I guess."

"Trudy, I had a great time," he said softly. "Really great." He couldn't leave without letting her know that much.

Her voice was more tentative. "You seemed to be enjoying yourself. I'm glad you really did."

"I did." What a gigantic understatement. But if he laid it on too thick, he'd give himself away. He'd been afraid in the heat of the moment, when he was having the orgasm of his life, that he'd already given himself away. But she had no basis of comparison where he was concerned. She might not know he'd been delirious with joy. She might think he hollered like that every time he came. Hardly.

"Then you might want to...do something like this again?"

Oh, thank God. The fun wasn't over. "I might."

"When?"

Now. And if not now, then at your earliest convenience. "When's good for you?"

"Tomorrow night?"

Yes. "I'm pretty sure I'm free. Let's say tentatively I can come by, and if there's a problem, I'll let you know."

"Okay. Same time?"

"That's fine." He couldn't believe they were making an appointment so unemotionally, as if they'd be getting together over coffee for a casual chat instead of planning to screw each other's brains out. "I'll see you then."

"See you then. Oh, and Linc, I really appreciate you giving me a chance to practice my big-city sex."

"Not a problem." He was all heart, accommodating her this way.

"You know, I was afraid you might be bothered with us doing it with no curtains on the windows tonight, but I guess that didn't faze a sophisticated man like you."

He blinked and stared at the uncurtained windows. Ye gods and little fishes, he'd never given a single thought to those windows! He felt a blush rise to his cheeks as he gazed across the street to the apartment windows on the opposite side. Had they seen anything?

"With the candlelight, it wouldn't have been real obvious, but I thought the uncurtained windows made things a little more risqué and exciting," she said.

And so it did, he realized as he began getting hot all over again. So it did. That was another thing he'd discovered about himself, thanks to her. He had a trace of exhibitionist in him. He'd be wise to break off this liaison before he uncovered more unsettling parts of his personality.

Of course he no longer cared about being wise. "The bare windows are fine," he said. "I'll see you tomorrow night at seven."

"For sure? You don't have to check your calendar?"

"For sure."

12

ALL MORNING Meg was in a lather wanting to know how Trudy's big night with Linc had worked out. But Trudy was so busy learning the routine at Babcock and Trimball that Meg didn't dare interrupt her. No matter how much Meg looked forward to sweet revenge, she was here to help Trudy succeed at the PR firm, not sabotage her on her first full day on the job.

Meg forced herself to wait until lunch, when she would spirit Trudy away to a little diner that the other employees avoided because they said it served "truck driver food." Maybe so, but the mashed potatoes and gravy on the menu reminded Meg of home, and she and Trudy could talk there without fear of being overheard by someone from Babcock and Trimball.

Finally Trudy was ready to break for lunch, and Meg hustled her out of the building and down the snowy street to the diner. She got such a kick out of watching Trudy walk along in Linc's leather trench coat. If Meg had her way, that coat would be the first of many things Trudy and Linc would share.

Meg ushered Trudy through the door of the little diner. "I know this place isn't fancy," she said as they settled onto the vinyl-covered seats in one of the booths lining the wall opposite the counter. "But I absolutely have to hear about last night, and nobody from the office will come in here, so you can say whatever you want."

"Why won't anybody come here?" Trudy looked around with suspicion. "Did somebody get food poisoning?"

"No. The food is too Midwestern for them." She handed Trudy a menu. "Take a look. It's like being back home."

Trudy scanned the menu and laughed. "Wow, you're right. I could be sitting at Hanson's in Virtue. The place even smells the same, like fried onions and strong coffee." She pointed to the menu. "Look at this. Meat loaf. I thought once I hit the big time I'd never eat meat loaf again."

"You don't have to, now. The turkey club is good. Listen, Trudy, did you and Linc—"

"And how are you ladies doing today?" asked the waitress, coming up with order pad in hand.

"Great," Trudy said with a smile. "I'll have the meat loaf special and a cup of coffee."

Meg was glad Trudy sounded perky. She'd *seemed* perky this morning, but that might have been for show, to impress the brass at Babcock and Trimball. Here in the diner she didn't have to impress anyone, so she must actually be feeling perky.

"And for you, ma'am?" The waitress turned to Meg.

"I'll take the same, except herbal tea instead of coffee." She actually liked meat loaf, and these days she was always hungry. Besides, she didn't want to take time to order something different. She had things to discuss and she wanted the waitress gone.

Once the waitress left, Meg tucked her menu into its aluminum holder and leaned forward again. She kept her voice low because there was no point in shocking the white-haired couple in the next booth. "So, did he like the maid's outfit?"

Trudy folded her hands on the Formica-topped table. Her green eyes sparkled. "Uh-huh."

"Excellent. Tell me all." She sat and listened with great satisfaction while Trudy described the proceedings, starting with her pratfall in the high heels. Vintage Trudy, she thought, and just what Linc needed, a sexy goofball.

As the narration continued, Meg suspected she wasn't being told *all* that had happened, but Trudy was revealing enough for Meg to know that there had been one hot time going on in that apartment last night. The plan was succeeding.

"Did he stay over?" Meg asked. The minute the words were out of her mouth, she realized that question had sounded too eager. She didn't want to tip her hand. "I mean, you weren't really set up for that, is all I'm saying. It's nice to have an extra toothbrush and a razor handy for those times."

"Oh, I didn't want him to stay over," Trudy said. "I was so glad when he disappeared into the bathroom so that I could—" She paused as their order arrived. "Mmm. Smells delicious."

"Be careful. It's extremely hot," the waitress said.

"Okay," Trudy said, and for some reason blushed a bright red.

Meg had sense enough not to ask why. She didn't need to know every little detail that had taken place between Linc and Trudy. Even with best friends, there could be such a thing as too much information. But she was very disappointed that Linc hadn't stayed all night. Staying until morning signified that some real bonding had taken place.

Once the waitress had refilled Trudy's coffee mug and left them alone again, Meg prompted her friend to continue. "What did you do when he left the room, then?"

"I got right out of that bed and hid behind my new folding screen."

Meg's cup clattered into the saucer. "You did *what?*"

"I didn't want him to come back to the bed and find me there."

"Why not, for heaven's sake?" She was imagining how Linc must have reacted, to stroll back into the room and find Trudy missing. By now he might think she was really strange.

Trudy's expression was earnest. "I wanted to keep the mystery in our relationship." She dug a fork into her mashed potatoes.

"By making him think you'd jumped out the window? What's that all about?"

"Think about it, Meg." She gestured with a forkful of potatoes. "We were involved in a fantasy world, but that fantasy had played itself out. If he'd come back to find the French maid still there, the game would get a little old and tired." She popped the mashed potatoes in her mouth.

"So you could have slipped out of the French maid outfit and slid under the sheets. What's the problem?"

She swallowed the potatoes. "Then it would just be *me*."

"So?"

"That's the whole point of this. I had more than enough time to be just me in Virtue, in the back seat of somebody's car. Now that I'm here, I want to try out all the fantasies I can think of. I want to be someone new and exciting each time, and I want the man I'm with—in this case, Linc—to think of me in those terms. The veil of mystery must remain in place, or it won't be as thrilling and different."

"Oh." Meg wondered how well this veil of mystery had stayed in place when Trudy tripped over her own shoes and landed fanny up on the bed. But Meg couldn't bear to bring that to her friend's attention. If Trudy believed that she'd created a veil of mystery, then Meg would support that belief. "I see."

"So getting behind the screen was the only solution. I am *so* glad we found that screen. It'll be the perfect prop. Hey, are you going to eat anything? You haven't touched your plate."

Meg glanced down in surprise and promptly picked up a fork. It was a measure of how much she cared about the outcome of this scheme that she'd forgotten about food. As her pregnancy approached the last trimester, eating was beginning to edge out sex as her favorite activity. "Okay, you ducked behind the screen, and Linc came out. What then?"

"He called out my name."

"I'll just bet. Another few seconds and he might have dialed 911."

"Well, he didn't, because I answered right away, and I used that screen exactly the way I'd planned to at the beginning of the evening, only it was even more effective, because I stripped off what I'd been wearing, the fishnet stockings and so on, and hung them over the screen while I talked to him."

The meat loaf was wonderful, Meg decided. She'd have to start making it at home. "And he didn't go behind the screen and pull you back out?"

"No, because I told him I thought he should go home."

Meg tried to hide her dismay. Too much mystery could alienate a guy, especially somebody like Linc, who'd apparently never had much love in his life. "Wasn't that a blow to his ego?"

"I don't think so. I told him I'd had a wonderful time. We're seeing each other again tonight."

Meg grabbed her napkin and covered her mouth to disguise her grin of triumph. He was coming back for more. This was very good. "That's nice," she said. "I assume you're cooking up another fantasy?"

"I am." Trudy looked smug. "But before I tell you, I want to hear about those fake-fur wrist and ankle restraints. Did you and Tom try them out?"

"We did." Meg realized the white-haired couple in the booth behind Trudy had stopped talking and the man was mopping something up with his napkin. She leaned forward and mouthed her words. "There are a couple of senior citizens in the booth behind you. I think they're listening in."

Trudy's smile was mischievous. "Oh. So are you gonna tell me, or not?"

"You're a bad influence on me."

"Oh, *sure.*"

Meg laughed, feeling sixteen again as she flicked a glance to the next booth. The older couple looked nailed to their seats. Maybe she and Trudy would give them a few ideas to take home. Then again, maybe the couple was more advanced than they looked.

"Well, I guess he'd always imagined he'd use the restraints on me," Meg said, "but I talked him into being first, and he was *very* nervous."

"But you got him to do it, right?"

"Of course. I promised him I'd take them off anytime he wanted me to. Funny thing, he never did ask."

Trudy's eyes twinkled. "Was it awesome?"

"He said it was the best orgasm of his life. I think it's a fantasy that scares guys, because they're so used to being in charge, but deep down I think they really want to be a woman's love slave." She paused. "If it works that well for a mild-mannered guy like Tom, imagine how it might affect a more take-charge type like Linc." And Trudy was just the woman to do it, Meg thought. Linc had always had too much control over his relationships and over himself, in her opinion.

Trudy nodded, her expression eager. "You're absolutely right. I need to go back to that store."

The woman in the next booth turned in her seat. "Excuse me, dear, but what would be the name of that store?"

After Meg and Trudy exchanged a grin, Trudy swiveled to talk to the woman and Meg returned to her meal.

So the couple hadn't been shocked at all, Meg thought, or at least the wife hadn't. Her husband was sort of red in the face.

Meg watched in amusement as Trudy proceeded to give the woman the name and location of the adult novelties store along with precise directions for getting there. Then, typical of Trudy, she went on to recommend a few items, and before Meg realized it, the lunch hour was gone and they had to leave and race back to the office.

"I didn't get to hear what you had in mind for Linc tonight," Meg said as they walked quickly through the slush covering the sidewalk.

"I think I've changed my mind now that you've brought up this love-slave thing. But I still plan to use my tape."

"You bought a sexy video?"

"No. I had my voice-activated tape recorder under the bed last night."

"Cool!" Meg laughed with delight. She'd bet her best silk G-string that Linc had never been recorded *en flagrante delicto*. And it was about damned time, too.

As LINC WALKED DOWN the hall to Trudy's door at one minute to seven, his pulse hammered and his penis began to stiffen. They hadn't talked about dinner, so he'd brought a bottle of red wine, a cheese spread he liked and some crackers. He didn't care about food, but she might, and he didn't want her to think he was only interested in…oh, hell, no matter what he brought to her door, she'd know he was there for the sex.

But the wine and cheese made him feel a little more civilized about it. Not a lot, considering that he was already picturing how they might make use of the cheese spread and how her special juices would taste flavored with red wine. He shocked himself with the direction of his thoughts, and he'd been on that track ever since leaving here the night before.

Tom had figured out something was going on and had wanted to talk about it, but Linc had managed to keep himself busy and unavailable for any private conversation. He didn't want to talk about this until he had some control over what was happening. At the moment he felt as if he'd been thrown into the rapids without a paddle. Yet he didn't want to make for shore, either, not when he didn't know what amazing sexual exploit Trudy would come up with next.

He rang her doorbell and took a deep breath. That didn't do any good. He was still a quivering mass of need.

The door opened, but the chain remained in place. The music drifting from the apartment was in a minor, exotic key, and incense perfumed the air.

He looked through the narrow opening into her eyes, dramatically outlined with dark pencil and plenty of mascara. Across her nose and mouth she wore a lavender veil. Below that he could make out a sequined bra and filmy lavender harem pants. He grew very hard.

"Who goes there?" she asked, making the veil quiver with her breath.

He made a guess, thinking that she was to be his slave girl tonight. "Your master."

She lowered her darkened lashes. Then she lifted them again, and her green gaze was bold. "I have no master. But I have many slaves ready to obey me."

Excitement tightened his chest, affecting his breathing. Yet he wondered if he could really let her have that much control over him.

"Are you ready to obey me?" she asked with an imperious tilt of her head.

A realization slammed into him. He would do anything to satisfy this craving that had kept him awake most of the night and distracted him all through the day. Anything. "Yes," he said.

"Good." Her gaze swept downward and settled on his crotch. "You've made a wise choice, slave." She looked up at him again. "I will unfasten the latch, but you must wait one minute before entering. Lock the door after you come in. Your instructions will be on the table."

"As you wish."

"Lower your eyes when speaking to me!"

At her command, the ache in his groin intensified. Did he

secretly want to be her love slave and give over all control? That was an unnerving thought.

She waited, challenging him with those green eyes.

Slowly he dropped his gaze. He could see one bare foot through the small opening. She'd painted her toenails red, and a small gold chain circled her ankle. He began to quiver. Would she want to tie him up? Could he handle that? He had no choice. He had to have her, on any terms.

The door closed, blocking his view. In one minute, he would find out what she had in mind.

It was a very long minute. At last he opened the door and stepped inside. He quickly turned and locked the door, afraid that if he didn't do it right away, he'd forget completely. Then he surveyed the room, heart pounding, half-expecting to see some version of whips and chains.

Nothing like that was lying around, so perhaps he was letting his imagination run away with him. Trudy was nowhere to be seen, but that didn't surprise him. Barefoot, she'd been able to make it to her hiding place without falling down.

She could be behind the screen again, but the enormous canopy bed was draped with sheets so that he couldn't look inside. He suspected she was there, stretched out like Cleopatra on her barge, waiting for him. But he was supposed to do something first. His passion-fogged mind searched for what it was.

Oh, yes. His instructions were on the table. On the way over he took off his leather jacket. As he hung it on the back of a chair, he looked at the table and remembered what had happened there the night before. He'd have to give her the furniture, because he'd never be able to use it again without thinking of Trudy spreading her thighs for him.

He found a note beside a small tape recorder. Setting down his small bag containing the wine, cheese and crackers, he picked up the note. *Turn me on,* it read, *while you take off all your clothes. When you are fully prepared to*

*become a slave, you may part the curtains on the bed and
request entrance.*

Even her wording was drenched with sex. He didn't think
it was an accident that she'd written about turning on and
parting curtains and requesting entrance. All of it was designed to make him think of burying himself in her sweet
body.

He wouldn't be allowed to do that until she said so, of
course. Tonight it was her call. No doubt she wanted to
watch him squirm first and she'd probably expect him to
beg. He was damned close to begging now.

The tape recorder baffled him, though. He couldn't imagine why she wanted him to listen to something, when the
breathy sound of a flute already provided mood music.
Pushing the button on the tape recorder, he started to pull
off his shirt.

He paused mid-motion, totally confused by what he was
hearing on the tape. It seemed to be someone breathing hard
interspersed by a lapping sound. Then came a soft moan.
At first he wondered if it was some sort of *Blair Witch
Project* joke. Then he heard Trudy's voice pleading with
him. *Please make me come.*

Dear Lord in heaven, she'd recorded him giving her oral
sex. As her cries mingled with the sound of his mouth pleasuring her, he began to shake.

That made it tougher to get out of his clothes, and he
really wanted out of his clothes. He couldn't seem to rip
them off fast enough. It was way past time to set his throb-
bing penis free.

He was impressed that she'd remembered about the re-
cordings of Belinda and the butler. She'd not only remembered, she'd decided to use that knowledge to drive him
straight out of his mind. He tossed his shirt on a chair.

As he fumbled with his shoes and socks, hopping around
in his eagerness, the scenario on the tape moved to the bed.
Oh, yes, he remembered that part. His shoelace became one

impossible knot and he cursed himself for not wearing loafers again. The running shoes had seemed like a good idea at the time.

Swearing under his breath, he yanked off the shoe while it was still tied. Then he did the same with the other shoe as he listened to himself sucking on her breasts. Man, this was erotic, especially knowing that she was lying in that curtained bed listening, too. He wondered if she'd listened before now. Sure, she had. Maybe several times. He whipped off both socks.

Finally he went to work on his jeans, and damned if he wasn't all thumbs. At this rate, he'd be lucky if he didn't come before he crawled into that bed with her. The tape was wild, even wilder than the one with Belinda, because he'd been there, experiencing everything. He was experiencing it all again, and he'd never been so hot in his life.

He nearly tripped as he tried to get out of his jeans, and he made a grab for the table, getting a grip on it and the tape recorder at the same time. Then he righted himself. But as he scrambled out of his pants and shoved down his briefs, the moans from the tape changed. Suddenly high-pitched squeals and gibberish filled the room. It sounded...like chipmunks mating.

In his agitated state it took him a second to realize he'd hit the fast forward button by accident.

A groan came from within the tented canopy bed. "Damn it!" Trudy muttered. "Foiled again!"

He couldn't help himself. He started to laugh. The longer the tape played, the harder he laughed. Too bad she hadn't caught them on video, too.

Even without a video, he could still listen to the audio and picture them going at it like speed demons, which is exactly how he'd been getting undressed and probably how he would have wanted to make love once he'd dived headfirst through those curtains. He'd been so frantic.

She poked her head out through a break in the curtains,

closing them under her chin so only her head appeared. "Excuse me." Her breath fluttered the violet veil.

With great effort he controlled his laughter. Then he grinned at her. "I didn't mean to. I stumbled and grabbed the recorder by accident. Incidentally, dynamite idea." The tape whirled to the end and clicked off.

She sighed. "And now that the mood is completely ruined, what next?"

"Oh, I wouldn't say it's completely ruined." He glanced down and, sure enough, he was still ready for action. He looked at her, thought about that harem outfit and was even more ready. "Want me to rewind the tape?"

13

TRUDY GAZED at him in all his magnificence and tried to think about how gorgeous he looked instead of dwelling on the failure of her perfect plan. She'd never imagined he'd punch the wrong button on the recorder. And the recorder had been such a brainstorm, too. She wasn't sure if the effect would be the same, now that he knew what was on the tape.

"We started over last night," he said gently. "That worked out pretty well."

"Oh, okay. Rewind the tape. It'd be a shame to waste a naked man."

With a grin, he turned to pick up the recorder.

Oh, yum. She'd never had a clear view of his buns before. Maybe this Laurel and Hardy routine with the tape was worth it, just for this unobstructed view of his tight, sexy behind. The light wasn't very good inside the makeshift tent she'd created, and she might have missed how absolutely megalicious his backside was, especially since she'd planned to enjoy him sunny-side up tonight.

He turned back to her, the recorder in his hand whirring away on rewind. "Where was this last night?"

"Under the bed. It's voice-activated."

"Or moan-activated."

She met his gaze and the smoldering fire in his blue eyes began to erase her disappointment. Allowing her attention to drift lower to his prominent erection helped a lot, too. But she needed to know that her plan had worked the way she'd intended. "Before you hit the wrong button, was listening to the tape really a turn-on for you?"

"Uh-huh. In fact, that was the problem." The rewind clicked off and he pushed play. "I was so desperate to get out of my pants that I almost fell. When I reached out for support, that's when I accidentally hit the button."

He held out the recorder as the erotic sounds spilled from it once again. "How many times have you listened to it?"

She'd lost track. "Several."

"So you're sick of it by now?"

"No." If anything, she'd become more aroused each time she heard it. The words *Please make me come* nearly did make her come, every time.

"I've told you how the tape affected me." He paused, and his voice softened. "What was going on with you inside your harem tent?"

She met his gaze and a seductive smile came naturally. "What do you think I would be doing while listening to something like that?"

He swallowed.

"Use your imagination," she said in a sultry voice. "The tape gets me hot, Linc."

He cleared his throat. "Then let's keep playing it."

She considered how it would sound, the combination of their recorded cries with the real thing. "It'll seem like an orgy's going on."

Heat flashed in his eyes. "Is that a problem?"

"No," she murmured. "Not a problem."

He walked up to the bed and handed her the recorder. "A gift...from your slave." Then he dropped to one knee in front of her and lowered his gaze.

He'd returned to the game! She found that endearing, and sexy as hell. She held the recorder and looked down upon the man who had helped her create the sounds on the tape. Now he was hers to command. Hot damn.

"When I call for you, arise and approach me, slave." She

still hadn't picked out a title for herself. Not *your highness* and certainly not *madam*.

"I will."

Then it came to her. "I will, *mistress*."

"I will, mistress."

Hearing him say that made her tingle in all her special places. She'd never had a love slave before. She had a feeling she was going to adore it.

Ducking back into the twilight of her sheet-draped canopy, she tucked the recorder in among the pillows stacked against the headboard. Then she lounged against the pillows, making sure that her sequined bra was adjusted to provide Linc with a view of maximum cleavage. She'd been lucky to find the outfit on sale when she'd made a quick trip to the novelties store after work. The harem pants were crotchless, but the billowing material would conceal that convenient feature until she was ready to make use of it.

She'd allowed Linc to believe that she'd been having a good time all by herself while he undressed. In fact she'd been worried that once she started she might never stop, and she'd wanted to be in control of herself when he appeared. She had to make sure he was properly settled. The fake-fur restraints were already attached to the four posts of the bed.

She hadn't decided exactly what she'd do once she had him secured in those restraints, but the sight of him spread-eagled on her fantasy bed should inspire all sorts of ideas. As she'd told Meg, she wasn't impulsive, but she loved spontaneity.

"Enter!" she called out in her most commanding tone.

"Yes, mistress." Linc crawled in.

His stare was too bold, too hot. She should order him to lower his eyes again, but first she wanted him to take a gander at her outfit and the restraints hanging from the bed-posts.

The tape played the sounds of her first climax. As her cries of ecstasy filled the cozy little tented area, Linc looked at her as if he'd love to repeat the taped activity. But tonight she would call the shots. She reached up and fingered one of the wrist restraints.

She could tell he hadn't noticed them until that moment by his startled glance. Then he turned his head as if to confirm that there were four.

"Your gaze is far too presumptuous, slave," she said. "Therefore you must be punished. Come here."

He hesitated, and the tape played on, teasing him with what he'd done the night before, when he'd been in charge.

"Now."

He crawled to where she lay, and from his expression she figured he might be considering rebellion. That could be exciting in its own way, but she really wanted to have him under her power, just to see how he'd react.

"Lie on your back," she commanded.

Once again he hesitated.

"Do it!"

Defiance mingled with passion in his eyes. "Yes, mistress." Slowly he did as she'd demanded until he lay flat on his back, his erection jutting firmly upward.

"Good. Now, for your transgressions, you must be bound."

His whole body stiffened.

Her veil covered her smile. The poor guy was really worried. She decided he needed some reassurance. "Although you are my slave, I will not harm you. If at any time you need to be released, you have only to ask. Now give me your right hand."

Staring up at the ceiling, he held out his hand.

She took hold of his wrist, the first contact between them. She marveled at how hot they'd made each other without even touching. His skin was very warm, and when she placed her lips against his pulse she felt it beating wildly.

The furry restraints fastened with Velcro. Moving around the bed on her hands and knees, she soon had him exactly the way she'd envisioned, his legs spread and his arms angled away from his body.

He watched her with hungry eyes, and as she tightened the last restraint, she looked into those eyes and knew how she wanted to tease him. The tape was doing a fine job, but she could add to the assault on his senses. She propped two pillows under his head so that he wouldn't miss a thing.

Kneeling between his outstretched legs, she had an impressive view of his male equipment. She looked her fill, and enjoyed the way his penis twitched and his balls tightened under her scrutiny. She was careful not to touch him.

"And now you must pay for your disobedience and clumsiness," she said, reaching behind her back to unclasp her sequined bra.

His hot gaze settled on her breasts. As she slowly removed the bra, his breathing grew ragged.

Tossing the bra aside, she lifted her arms above her head and arched her back. Then she held her arms out at her sides and began a slow shimmy. She and Meg used to practice this for hours back in high school. She'd never found a use for the skill until now.

Her shimmy was having excellent results. Linc was in a bad way, judging by the tight muscles in his jaw. After a few moments of that, accompanied by the moans and rhythmic slap of bodies coming from the tape recorder, he looked desperate.

Cupping her breasts in both hands, she kneaded them gently. "Remember how you enjoyed stroking my breasts?"

His voice was a harsh croak. "Yes."

"Yes, *mistress*."

"Yes, mistress."

"Tonight you may only watch." She moistened her finger and drew it carefully around her nipple, all the while holding his gaze.

His muscles bunched and his lips parted.

She treated her other nipple to the same caress. Moisture dampened her thighs, and she wondered if she could keep this charade going without jumping him. She was going to try.

"This feels good," she murmured. "So good." Plucking both nipples until they were hard and tight, she felt the tension of an impending orgasm coil within her. "But I know something that will feel even better. Can you guess?"

Linc groaned.

"I'm afraid it doesn't involve you." Massaging her breast with her left hand, she moved her knees further apart and pulled aside the filmy material covering her sex. "Just me." Then she slid her fingers through her damp curls and into her wet heat. Oh, yes. She closed her eyes as the sounds from the recorder grew more intense.

With a strangled cry, Linc pulled against the restraints.

Stroking herself rapidly and breathing hard, she opened her eyes. "You can't take the punishment, slave?"

Gasping, he sank back to the bed, his gaze riveted on her. "I can, mistress."

"Good." Her heart thundered from the excitement of having him watch while they both listened to the tape. It *was* like an orgy. She would have liked to torture him even longer, but she couldn't wait. She was too close. So very close. She pinched her nipple and increased the tempo. "I'm coming, slave," she whispered as her legs began to tremble.

Linc writhed against the bed, but he didn't ask to be freed, and he never pulled his gaze away. He just watched and quivered.

Her vision blurred as the climax hit, wrenching soft cries from her. She tumbled into a heap in the vee of his legs, her fingers pressed deep.

LINC WAS SURE he would climax right along with her, which he didn't want to do. Somehow he managed to avoid coming, which amazed him. He deserved an award for getting through the episode without turning into Old Faithful.

He hoped she didn't have too many tests like that in store for him. And yet—damn, it had been incredible to be lashed to the bed and forced to be a voyeur while she got it on with herself. If anybody had asked if he wanted to try that he would have said hell, no. But now that he'd experienced it, he wouldn't have missed it for the world.

No woman had ever let him in on a solo performance before, not even Giselle, the sculptor. She might have if he'd hung around a little longer, but he'd sensed she might move him out of his comfort zone and so he'd left.

Trudy had dragged him so far out of his comfort zone he'd lost track of where it was. She'd talked him into letting her stake him out in the most vulnerable position he could imagine. And strange as it seemed, the longer he stayed like this, the harder he seemed to get. He was beginning to wonder if he'd ever deflate.

Maybe the incense had something to do with his state, too. He could swear he was in some exotic pleasure palace, where the scent of incense mingled with the unmistakable scent of sex. The air was thick with sensuality, and he drew it in, a glutton for punishment.

The recorder behind his head clicked off. She'd timed her performance to coincide with what was happening on the tape, and with her at his feet and the tape at his head, he'd listened to orgasms in stereo. She was a devil woman. She was also the sexiest lover he'd ever had, bar none.

She took a deep breath, rose to a sitting position and straightened her veil. Taking stock of his still-rigid penis, she nodded. "Awesome staying power, slave."

His vocal cords were tight from the strain of trying to control himself, but he managed to answer. "Thank you, mistress."

"Of course, we have ways of breaking slaves like you." She fondled his balls.

He gasped.

"You realize I could end your misery in no time?" She circled his shaft with her fingers.

Oh, she absolutely could. He clenched his jaw. "Yes, mistress."

She leaned over him, and her veil tickled his hot skin. Then she tried a maneuver that nearly did him in. Flipping the veil in front of his penis, she slid her mouth over the tip. He could feel the pressure of her lips and tongue, but the veil hid what was happening. The erotic quotient was huge.

His lusty groan filled the tented canopy. "No fair...*mistress*."

She drew back a fraction, and her breath fanned the moist skin she'd licked. "Will doing that make you come, slave?"

He struggled to breathe. "Most...definitely, mistress."

"Then perhaps I won't do that again. Because I don't want you to come. At least not yet."

She was very perky, he thought. But then she'd had her first orgasm, so she would be perky. He was stretched so tight he felt like an overinflated helium balloon.

"I like you naked," she said. "But perhaps you're a bit too naked." She crawled over him and reached beneath a pillow to the left of his head.

He was sure she'd deliberately nudged him with her breast in the process. She was obviously enjoying his helplessness. It was having a tremendous effect on him, too. Now that he had so little control, his world narrowed to sexual pleasure. It was all that mattered, all he wanted.

She took a condom out of the package. "I'm going to saddle you up, slave, and take a little ride."

He felt light-headed with the anticipation. At last he'd be able to drive his aching penis into her. "It might be a short ride, mistress."

"Maybe not." She rolled the condom on with merciful quickness.

Despite that, he had to clench his muscles and fight to keep from erupting. "You're...good at that, mistress."

"I've practiced." She glanced at him, mischief in her eyes. "On cucumbers." Running her tongue over her full lips, she laughed. "A girl can practice all sorts of techniques with a cucumber." She straddled his thighs. "Good girls don't have vibrators in Virtue." She slipped her fingers into her soft triangle of curls and gazed at him as she caressed herself. "But cucumbers grow everywhere there."

He watched her through a red haze. She sure knew how to taunt a man until he couldn't see straight.

"Is there something you're needing, slave?" She continued to hold his gaze, her eyes sultry, her fingers sliding slowly in and out of that spot where he longed to be. "You're looking a bit...eager."

His voice was hoarse with tension. "You know what I want, mistress."

"Do you know what *I* want?"

Mesmerized by the action of her fingers, he could only shake his head.

"I want you to beg me."

Now that was easy. "Please, mistress." The words rasped from his tight throat.

"Please what? What is it you want me to do?"

"Ride me..." His body was rigid and slick with sweat. "Please ride me, mistress."

"Yes, perhaps I will." Bracing her hands on his heaving chest, she edged closer and rose above him until she was balanced directly over his waiting shaft. Her fingers were moist against his skin and her breasts swayed seductively.

The urge to bury himself in her overwhelmed everything else. Pulling against the fur restraints, he lifted his hips, seeking her heat.

"Now, now, now," she scolded, moving away again. "I'm in charge, not you."

Sweat beaded on his skin and he began to pant.

"Poor baby. I guess I need to put you out of your misery." This time when she moved over him, she eased down over the tip of his penis. Then she stopped. "Is that good?"

Speech was beyond him. He groaned.

"I'll take that as a yes. Okay, slave. You have suffered enough." She moved away from him again.

"Trudy!"

"Hold on," she murmured, becoming very busy with the restraints. "They warned me not to leave you like this too long."

He thought she meant he shouldn't be left in a state of arousal too long. He was so busy trying not to climax that he didn't realize she'd let him loose until she returned to her position poised above him.

"You're free," she whispered. Then she lowered herself in one smooth motion.

He gasped and grabbed her bottom. *"Hold still!"*

"No." She resisted him, trying to wiggle out of his grip.

"Trudy, if you don't hold still, I'm going to—"

"I know! Me, too! Me, too, Linc!"

He released her and she rocked once, twice…and it was all over, with both of them laughing and moaning and coming at the same time.

Incredible. Closing his eyes, he pumped into her again and again, unable to give up the sensation of being inside her, even when the orgasm was over.

She leaned down and brushed her mouth against his. "Very nice, slave."

"My pleasure…mistress." Sighing, he kept his eyes closed and reveled in the warm shivers running through him. The aftermath of a climax had never lasted this long and he wanted to savor it. He started to wrap his arms around her, wanting to feel her body against his. Before he had a good grip, she slipped away. He was so sated that he didn't have the strength to grab her and pull her back down.

"Just rest," she murmured.

As the exotic music played softly, he drifted on the edge of consciousness. Just as his sweat-covered body began to feel a little too cool, a warm washcloth slid over his chest. "Mmm, nice," he mumbled. Trudy was first-class all the way, including the moist, heated cloth treatment when he needed to freshen up.

She washed him slowly, following the washcloth with a soft towel. He relaxed totally, and his sexual satisfaction was so complete that she could even move the washcloth over his penis without arousing him. Then he vaguely sensed her leaving again, but he was too whipped to question anything.

Sometime later she came back and gently placed something on his chest. The material felt vaguely familiar.

"I brought you your clothes," she said softly. "When you're dressed, you're free to leave."

His eyes snapped open. *Leave?* Who the hell wanted to do that? Certainly not yours truly. He turned his head to object to the plan, but she'd already slipped through the curtain surrounding the bed.

"Trudy?" Much as he hated to move and disturb the bliss he had going on, he sat up, which caused his clothes to slide off to one side. "Trudy, don't do that behind-the-screen thing again, okay? Couldn't we cuddle for a while?"

No answer.

He pulled back the curtain surrounding the bed, gathered up his clothes and climbed out. "Trudy, come on out from behind that screen. This is silly."

Holding his bundle of clothes against his chest, he walked around the bed toward the screen to find her and convince her to come back to bed. He hadn't realized the importance of cuddling after sex until now, when he wasn't getting any. Men's magazines always advised guys to do it to make women happy, and the assumption seemed to be that men didn't need it.

Linc needed it.

He peered behind the screen, expecting to see Trudy back there changing out of her harem outfit. She wasn't there. Damn.

It was the weirdest thing. Physically he was totally satisfied, but emotionally he was frustrated as hell. He wanted to hold Trudy, just hold her. No big deal, really, except that it was becoming a bigger deal the longer he didn't get to do it. Prowling around in search of her, he finally arrived at her closed bathroom door. Hearing splashing noises, he called her name again.

"I'm in the tub," she called back.

In the tub. Now that presented some interesting options. His body began to stir at the prospect of Trudy in the tub. Maybe he wasn't as physically satisfied as he thought. He turned the doorknob and discovered she'd locked him out.

Maybe she was upset with him because he'd let her wash him and hadn't offered to do something like that for her. "Are you mad at me?" he asked.

"Goodness, no." She sounded amused. "You've been fantastic."

"Then why did you lock the door?"

"I'm preserving the mystery. As time goes by, you'll thank me for that."

He leaned his forehead against the door. He felt like banging it against the wood a couple of times, too. Oh, well. Meg had asked him to go along with Trudy's sexual schemes in order to build her confidence. If he told her this mystery stuff was highly overrated, he might cause her to doubt her approach.

Her approach was beyond excellent, except for this one little part at the end where she disappeared. But now wasn't the time to talk about that. In fact, before they talked about it he might do well to examine why it bothered him so much. Maybe she was right. Maybe he should be thanking her.

However, he couldn't leave the apartment while she was

still in the tub. "Okay, I'll go, but not until you're finished and ready to come out and lock up after me."

"You're right. Give me five more minutes."

He used the time to get dressed. All the while he wondered if asking to see her again tomorrow night would make him sound too eager. Probably. He should let her suggest their next date. By the time he'd untangled the knot in his shoelace, she called through the door and told him she was ready.

Quickly putting on the shoe and tying the lace, he grabbed his jacket on the way over to the door. "Good night," he called.

"Good night." Her voice was so, so sexy. But she didn't ask about seeing him again.

He waited a couple of seconds. She wasn't going to bring it up. Finally he couldn't stand it any longer. "Are you free tomorrow night?"

"Unfortunately, no."

For a few seconds he went through hell wondering if she'd met another guy already.

Then she spoke again. "One of the women at Babcock and Trimball is retiring and they're having a dinner for her. It's kind of a roast. According to Meg, it'll run late." She paused. "But I'm free Wednesday night."

He didn't even hesitate. "What time?"

"The same? Seven?"

"I'll be here."

"Good." Her voice was rich with delight.

He carried that sound with him as he left the apartment, clung to it as evidence that she was having as good a time as he was. Riding down in the elevator, he realized that he also needed to examine the reasons why that was so important to him.

14

TRUDY WAITED until she heard the apartment door close before she came out wrapped in her terry robe and went over to lock up. She missed Linc already, and it was all she could do not to open the door and call him back. But that would be a mistake for many reasons.

She had to be careful not to become too attached to this man. He was her first big-city lover, and a practice run at that. She had many more sexual adventures ahead of her with men she hadn't even met.

Things were going too well to chance messing everything up now. She was handling this first big-city affair exactly the way she'd always planned to do it. First she'd give the guy amazing sex, and then she'd withdraw, keeping him off balance so that he'd never become sure of her.

Once a man became sure of a woman, boredom could so easily set in. With Linc's varied experience, boredom might take hold sooner than with most men. Linc was still eager, and she wanted to keep it that way.

Still, she hadn't wanted to send him home.

That was only natural, though, because she'd never had her own place, never had the option of asking a guy to linger after the main event. Maybe she was just curious about how that would feel. Instinctively she knew it might feel a little *too* comfortable. Before she knew it Linc might decide to leave his toothbrush in her bathroom. Then he'd bring over some spare underwear, and maybe even a change of clothes.

She'd worked too hard to get a space that was all hers to

want to share it with anyone. Pulling the tie of her robe a little tighter, she walked around the room blowing out candles. When she was finished, the only light in the room came from the checkered glow of windows in the many tall buildings surrounding hers.

Perched on the windowsill, she leaned against the cold glass and gazed toward her little sliver of Central Park, a shadowy thicket of bare branches that also happened to be close to where Linc lived. He'd be at the building by now, maybe going through the front door and saying hello to the doorman. She pictured him taking the smooth ride up to his luxury apartment, unlocking his door and walking past the small statue in his foyer. Then he'd head into his bedroom.

There he'd be, all alone in his sleigh bed, and here she was, alone in her big canopied bed. In some ways that seemed silly. They'd been having a good time, and they could have had more of those good times if she'd been willing to spend the whole night with him.

But that was heading in a direction that made her nervous. No, this was the better option. And she was not lonesome. Definitely not. After all, this was exactly what she'd always wanted.

LINC DECIDED not to fight the routine that Trudy preferred. If she wanted him to leave after treating him to the kind of sex he'd only dreamed about, then he would leave. If that became more difficult with each subsequent night he spent in her apartment, he took it as a warning sign that he was letting himself get too involved with her. She knew what was best for both of them, even if he didn't always remember.

The pattern of their nights together had become predictable, but the fantasies she introduced him to were anything but predictable. She kept him guessing, both about the type of fantasy she'd cook up and what sort of glitch it would have. Trudy was not a smooth operator, and he found that way too appealing.

The ostrich-feather fan she'd used to cover herself in her striptease routine made her sneeze. Another time she'd tried to make a dramatic entrance from behind the screen and had knocked it completely over. One night she brought out some flavored oil she'd found on sale and they'd quickly discovered it was rancid. Fortunately chocolate syrup had worked even better, and he was proud of himself for being the one who thought of it. Her impulsive behavior was rubbing off on him, and he'd discovered he liked that, too.

Trudy made him hot, hotter than any woman ever had, but she also made him laugh, and that made her extremely special. His favorite memory was of the life-size blow-up doll she'd bought to simulate a sexual threesome. It had sprung a leak and circled the room several times before running out of air.

She'd been so disappointed he'd spent the next two hours convincing her that she was more than enough woman for him. The truth of that was beginning to dawn on him. Trudy was everything he could ever want.

The blow-up doll told him more about her than she might have realized, and it was all good news. Although she'd wanted to give him a kinky experience, she hadn't been willing to bring a flesh-and-blood woman into the apartment, and he cherished that about her. Trudy wanted to play, but she'd never suggest anything dangerous or manipulative, and he grew to trust her more than he had any other woman in his life.

No, there was no danger in having sex with Trudy. The danger was in his growing tendency to think of it as making love. It was a good thing she kicked him out of her apartment every night. A very good thing. At least one of them remembered the rules of the game.

Another warning signal was his reluctance to discuss

Trudy with Tom. Linc had always discussed his girlfriends with Tom. And Tom obviously wanted to discuss this one.

When Tom walked into Linc's office on Monday of the second week of Trudy's Manhattan adventure, he looked ready for deep conversation, exactly what Linc had tried to avoid by canceling Sunday's racquetball game. He'd needed time alone to think about things, and he hadn't felt ready to be questioned by either Tom or Meg.

Tom started out the conversation with some rigamarole about a stock they'd both been considering, but soon he came to his real reason for being there. "I'm worried about you, buddy," he said.

Linc pretended to misunderstand as he walked around the desk and leaned his hip against it. "Okay, that tech stock move of mine wasn't brilliant, but I—"

"Not in the business sense. You know what I'm talking about." Tom rubbed the back of his neck and looked embarrassed. "I know Meg said this wasn't a fix-up, exactly, but I have to tell you, even Meg's acting like it's a fix-up. And if it goes south, I feel responsible, like it's my fault that you got mixed up with Trudy."

Linc had suspected from the beginning that Meg was trying to play Cupid. Funny how that concept didn't bother him now as much as it should. "Nothing's your fault," he said. "And nothing can go south, either. No matter what Meg had in mind, Trudy doesn't want anything serious and neither do I."

He was positive Trudy didn't. If he was having second thoughts about marriage for the first time in his life, that was his problem. Once this affair was over, he'd get himself straightened out.

Tom glanced at Linc as if wanting to say something. Then he seemed to change his mind and looked out the window behind Linc's desk instead. "More clouds coming in."

Linc turned, relieved that Tom had thought better of

whatever he'd been about to say. "Yeah. It'll probably snow again tonight."

"You sure have a good view of the Statue of Liberty from here."

"Maybe I should face the desk the other way, so I can see it more often." He could almost hear the turmoil in Tom's head as his friend tried to decide how much to say. Linc would rather he didn't say anything. He gave Tom a broad hint. "Well, I suppose we should both get back to work, huh? The market waits for no man."

"I just want to say something."

Linc groaned. "And maybe I don't want to hear it."

"It's just that you're acting different with this one."

"That's your imagination."

"I don't think so, buddy. I hate to say this, but—"

"Then don't say it." Linc clapped Tom on the shoulder. "I'll be fine. Trudy's a great gal, and we're having fun." What a pale word for what happened when he was in her apartment. "Eventually we'll part ways, and that'll be fine, too."

Tom's forehead remained creased with worry. "The thing is, I recognize the way you're acting, and if Trudy's ready to play the field like she says, then you could be in big trouble, because you're acting exactly like I did when I first met Meg."

Linc's stomach churned, but he managed a laugh of disbelief. "Not this guy. I'm bulletproof."

"I used to think that about you, but there's a certain look in your eyes these days that—"

"You worry too much. Must be that impending fatherhood thing. Your hormones are out of balance." He searched for something, anything, to switch them away from this disturbing topic. "Listen, speaking of sexual adventure, have you guys scheduled that limo ride yet?"

"Funny you should ask." Tom grinned. "We're going

tomorrow night. It's a slow time for them, so we got a cheaper rate.''

"Well, have fun.''

"Oh, we will.'' Tom started out of the office. "You're sure you're cool with the Trudy situation?''

"Totally.''

"Okay, then.'' Tom gave him a little salute and walked back down the hall.

Deciding that Tom was overreacting, Linc convinced himself that he wasn't behaving anything like Tom had with Meg. Tom had been totally snowed—out every night with Meg, walking around in a fog during the day, uninterested in any of the guy things they usually did. *Like a game of racquetball?*

That didn't count. He'd opted out yesterday because he'd wanted to avoid a long discussion of Trudy, not because he'd planned to be with her. Then again, maybe that had been Tom's motivation a year ago when he'd missed some scheduled events. Tom might have needed thinking time, too.

Still, Linc's situation wasn't anything like Tom's. Tom had known all along that he'd get married someday, whereas Linc had decided that a wedding wasn't in his future, period. Even as he thought that, he recognized that a subtle shift had taken place in the bedrock of his beliefs. A crack had opened.

A rap on the door frame interrupted his tortured thoughts. He glanced toward the door and saw Michelle, the firm's curvy blond receptionist, standing there.

"Your mother's on the line,'' she said. "I buzzed you, and when you didn't pick up I asked to take a message, but she was very insistent that she had to talk with you now. Do you want to take it?''

He straightened his vest, as if that would make him feel more in command of the situation. Wow. He'd been so out of it he hadn't heard the buzzer on his telephone. "Sure.

Thanks, Michelle. Sorry you had to walk all the way down here.''

''No problem, Linc.'' She smiled at him and walked away.

Michelle was new in the office, and she obviously liked him. He'd sensed for a month or two that she would accept an invitation if he asked her out. He'd been thinking about doing that before Trudy arrived in town. Now the idea of dating Michelle didn't appeal to him at all. That in itself was an unsettling thought.

Well, a talk with his mother should reestablish his priorities and take the stars from his eyes. Crossing to the desk, he punched a button and picked up the cordless phone. ''Hi, Mom.''

''I was beginning to wonder if you'd become too important to talk to your own mother.''

''Sorry about that. You know how it is.'' He still marveled at how clear the connection was between New York and Paris.

''I certainly do. When your father was in that line of work, I could never get him on the phone, either. Anyway, I'll cut to the chase. I'm in town for a few days and your father and I would like to take you to dinner tonight. You know, the annual gathering of the clan.''

Linc grimaced. She always put it like that, as if the three of them constituted a clan. The invitation was usually last-minute, too, as if they were a spontaneous little group that enjoyed spur-of-the-moment encounters.

He'd always accepted the invitations, figuring that he could spare one evening a year to play this little charade and pretend they were a family. Maybe deep down he was clinging to a scrap of hope that they might become a family again. If so, he should kill that hope. His mother had been living in Paris for twelve years, which made it highly unlikely that she planned to return to the Faulkner estate.

''Shall we say about eightish?'' After all these years his

mother could rightly assume he'd agree to have dinner, so she continued on as if he'd already said yes. "I'd forgotten it was Monday night, so I had a devil of a time finding a good place that would be open, but I finally settled on that new Lebanese place in the Village. I'm sure you know it."

He knew it. The restaurant was usually jammed with celebrities, and that would suit his mother. But he was scheduled to see Trudy tonight. He didn't want to give that up, and he didn't want to work Trudy in after dinner, either. These occasions with his parents sometimes ran long.

"How about if I bring someone?" he asked. Good Lord, he could hardly believe he'd said that. Talk about a crazy impulse.

After a second of shocked silence, his mother recovered herself. "Of course! That would be lovely. Who is she?"

"Her name is Trudy Baxter."

"Baxter, Baxter. Is she one of the Long Island Baxters? I remember your father went to prep school with—"

"No, she's one of the Virtue, Kansas, Baxters."

"Kansas?" His mother sounded as if she hadn't heard of the place. "What's out there?"

He couldn't help laughing. "Cucumbers," he said. "They raise a lot of cucumbers in Kansas."

"Is that what her family...does?"

"I'm not sure. You can ask her." Linc decided his impulse had been a good one, after all. He wasn't sure if Trudy would even agree to go to this dinner, but if she would come, he might make it through the evening without getting a raging headache.

"I will ask her," his mother said. "It's good to know a person's background. Well, I must run. I have an appointment at Elizabeth Arden. See you around eight."

"See you then." Linc hung up and punched in the number for Babcock and Trimball. He'd never called that number, although he might have looked it up a time or two. Or forty.

Several times last week he'd considered calling Trudy and asking her to lunch, but he'd always discarded the idea as ridiculous. They didn't have that kind of relationship. He hadn't meant to memorize the number, either, but there it was, right at his fingertips.

"Babcock and Trimball. How may I direct your call?" chirped the receptionist.

He had to clear his throat before he could answer. Surely he wasn't nervous. Surely not. He'd done things with this woman that belonged in an adult video, so a simple dinner date request shouldn't throw him like this. But his heart was hammering, anyway. He was afraid she'd turn him down. "Trudy Baxter, please," he said.

TRUDY WAS THRILLED to get a phone call. She had made tons of them since coming to Babcock and Trimball, but the calls hadn't started going the other way that much. Maybe some of her earnest prospecting had finally paid off and she'd begin to build her client list, get promoted, move to a bigger apartment…no, maybe not move. She was growing fond of the place. Linc probably had something to do with that, if she could be totally honest with herself.

"This is Trudy Baxter," she said in her most professional yet perky telephone voice. "How may I help you?"

"You can come to dinner with me and my parents tonight."

She almost dropped the phone. "Linc?"

"Hey, Trudy. I'll bet you're surprised to hear from me in the middle of the day."

"Um, yeah." His voice on the other end of the line was having the most interesting effect on her. Her tiny cubicle created from portable walls gave a little privacy but not much. The voices, ringing phones and clicking keyboards filtered over and under the movable walls. Yet Linc's voice in her ear made that all fade away and she was transported to the magic world they'd created together. In a matter of seconds, she was aroused.

"My mother just called, and she wants me to have dinner with her and my dad. It's something she sets up once a year, and I never know when the mood is going to strike her."

Trudy had trouble focusing on the meaning of his words. All she seemed to absorb was that familiar masculine timbre that signaled sexual adventure. She managed to decipher enough to realize that she should turn down his invitation. It sounded like a private get-together. "Linc, don't worry about our date tonight," she said. "You're certainly free to have dinner with your parents. Maybe if you don't get home too late, we can—"

"I didn't say this right. I'd like you to go, too, as a favor to me. The whole concept of my parents pretending that they're a normal married couple is exhausting, and having you there would be like a breath of fresh air. I could sure understand if you don't want to, though. You'd probably be bored out of your mind."

She'd never be bored if she could be with Linc, and she was very curious about his parents. "Don't be silly. I'd love to go. How should I dress?" Now there was a loaded topic. She'd dressed and undressed for him in various imaginative ways in the past week. Memories of that made her quiver. She pressed her thighs together.

His reply was a little deeper, a shade richer. "What you wore last Saturday would be fine."

She laughed softly and decided to risk teasing him, to see if he was on her wave length. "So I guess the French maid outfit wouldn't be appropriate."

There was a little pause on the other end. "We've never really talked on the phone, have we?"

"No." She slipped her hand under her short skirt. "Would you like to talk a little longer? And have a little…fun?"

His voice grew husky. "I'm not sure what you mean."

"I think you know exactly what I mean."

"God, Trudy."

"Nobody can see what I do under my desk," she murmured. "I have a little cubicle here."

He drew in a sharp breath. "But someone could come in."

"Yes. It's a risk. How about you?"

"I just closed my office door." He took another breath. "Now tell me what you're doing."

Her heart beat faster as she lowered her voice. "I have my fingers inside my panties. My panties are wet, Linc."

He moaned softly.

"Now you," she said. "Your turn."

"I...I've unzipped my pants."

"Are you hard?"

"Like a rock. I have been ever since I heard your voice on the phone."

"You had that reaction, too?" She slipped two fingers inside. How she ached for him.

"You...did, too?"

"I heard your voice and suddenly all I could think of was having sex with you. And now I will."

His laugh was ragged. "I'm not sure this counts."

"It does if we come together." Delicious currents swirled through her.

"Are you going to come, Trudy?" he asked softly.

"Yes." She stroked faster. "Oh, yes. Are you?"

He gasped. "Yes."

"Now?" There. That was the spot.

"*Yes.*" He groaned.

Her contractions began, and she gripped the phone hard, pressing it against her ear. "Ooh. Me, too. Me, *too.*" She clamped her teeth together to stifle a cry of release.

His breathing was heavy and harsh, but gradually it evened out again. "Ah, Trudy." His voice was so close, so intimate as he heaved a contented sigh. "There's no one like you, Trudy."

"You're—" She gulped for air. "You're pretty special yourself."

He sounded weary but happy. "Dinner's at eight, so I'll pick you up fifteen minutes before that."

"No earlier?"

His laughter seemed cozy, the kind people share who know each other well. "If I show up earlier than that, we'll never make it to the restaurant. And thanks for saying you'd come."

"To dinner?" She smiled into the phone. "Or just now?"

He laughed again. "Both. See you then."

15

TRUDY WASN'T SURE if she and Linc would be able to spend
time together in her apartment after dinner, but she rigged
up her latest surprise for him, just in case. Meg had told her
about a closeout on cheap door mirrors, the lightweight kind
with a plastic frame and a slightly skewed image. The image
was good enough for what Trudy had in mind.

After lugging three mirrors home on the bus, she'd wired
them to the underside of the canopy.

Linc wouldn't be able to see them when he first came
into the apartment, but she'd decided to take no chances
that he might wander over to the bed and accidentally catch
a glimpse. The minute he rang her doorbell, she snatched
up her backpack, slipped her arms into the leather trench
coat he'd insisted she keep for as long as she needed it, and
stepped outside the door.

Linc seemed a little surprised by her sudden appearance.
"You're not letting me come in at all?"

"You told me it would be dangerous if you showed up
early, so I decided we'd better not take any chances." She
smiled at him and started down the hall toward the elevator.
He looked fabulous, all decked out in a suit and tie under
his expensive wool overcoat. Wall Street meets Madison
Avenue. With the way he looked, she'd been wise not to
let him into the apartment. No doubt she wouldn't have been
able to resist kissing him, and she had a good idea how that
would have ended up.

He hurried to catch up with her. "Yeah, but I—"

"Here's the elevator. You have to get right in, or it smacks shut and you have to wait for another cycle." She stepped inside and automatically reached for the button to hold the doors open so they wouldn't close on Linc.

"I know. I battle this elevator all the time." He held her gaze as he walked into the elevator. "Almost every night."

The way he was looking at her, like she was the ice cream sundae he'd ordered for dessert, made her tummy quiver with excitement. "You're right, almost every night. I guess we only missed Tuesday, when I had the thing with Babcock and Trimball, and then Friday."

He drew closer, his aftershave wafting around her, his blue eyes darkening. "I should have canceled that deal on Friday."

She shook her head. "No. When the CEO invites you to a hockey game, you go to the hockey game." He sure looked delicious to her right now. She'd never seen him in a three-piece suit and tie. Taking it off item by item would be fun, assuming the evening ended up that way. She hoped it would.

His hungry glance roamed her face. "I want to kiss you."

"Can't." She loved the idea that he wanted to, though. "You'll smear my makeup, and I don't want to look frazzled when I meet your parents." For the first time she wondered what significance his parents would place on Linc bringing her to dinner. "You only do this once a year?"

"That's right. Usually in the first six months." He reached up and tucked a curl behind her ear. "Today on the phone with you was…wild."

She closed her eyes as his light touch ignited sparks of pleasure all through her body. "Yes."

"It feels so strange, to be with you like this and not be able to…do anything."

She opened her eyes and allowed herself to bask in the sensual light of his gaze. "I know."

"We don't have to go." He slipped a hand under her

coat and massaged her breast. "I could call the restaurant and leave a message that we can't make it."

"Linc, this is once a year. You need to go." She believed that, but his touch was weakening her resolve. "Do you usually bring a date to these things?"

He looked a little startled by the question and his hand stilled. He hesitated before answering. "No," he said at last.

She had a funny feeling in the pit of her stomach. Not a bad feeling, just a feeling that she was receiving significant information, here. She asked the next logical question. "Have you ever?"

Tension lines bracketed his eyes and mouth. "No, but—"

"It's okay," she said quickly. "No big deal. I was just wondering." Now that she'd received the significant information, she didn't want to make him uncomfortable by dissecting it. He would probably hate that.

"My mother's never asked me for a night when I already had a date," he said, as if to offer an excuse.

"Makes sense to me." She wanted to put him at ease. Actually she liked being the first woman he'd ever taken to dinner with his parents. That was a real coup, considering that he had no intention of settling down with anyone. But obviously he wasn't crazy about the implication that he was serious enough about her to want her to meet his parents.

"I'll bet you just want to shock them by bringing a girl fresh off the farm," she said.

The tension lines began to disappear and a small smile took their place. "Yeah, that's it." He squeezed her breast through her sweater. "I need to warn you that I told my mother you raised a lot of cucumbers in Kansas."

Trudy laughed, enjoying the sparkle of amusement and desire in his eyes, the warmth of his hand under her coat. "Did you, now? I hope you didn't describe how the local girls make use of them."

"Not yet, but there's no telling what I might say during dinner. You've totally corrupted me."

"It wasn't hard."

"But now it is." With a chuckle he grabbed her hand and started to unbutton his coat. "Want to feel?"

"Yes." As lust swept through her, she began to wonder if they could be a little late to dinner, after all.

"You said you wanted to try elevator sex." He loosened the belt of her coat. "No time like the present."

One look in his eyes, and she was ready. "But we can't kiss."

His voice was rough with desire. "That'll be tough, but I'll try. Pull up your skirt, so I can—"

"First we need to press the Stop button so nobody—"

The clunk of the elevator reaching the ground floor interrupted her, and before she could reach for the button to keep the doors shut, they slid open. An elderly woman stood there, waiting to get on.

As Linc released Trudy abruptly and closed his coat, she quickly backed away from him. "Hi!" she said to the woman as she started out of the elevator. "I'm Trudy Baxter in 406. This is Linc Faulkner."

Linc stepped out and braced his arm against the door to hold it open. "Go right on in, ma'am."

"Why thank you, young man." The woman toddled into the elevator.

"And you are?" Trudy asked.

The woman turned, looking a little surprised by the question. "Millicent Hightower. I'm in 306. Did you say you're in 406?"

That was the moment Trudy realized she shouldn't have mentioned her apartment number. She glanced at Linc, who took his arm away from the door.

"Because if you're in 406," Millicent said, "then maybe you can tell me about those strange noises at night, starting about—" The doors snapped shut, cutting off the conversation.

Trudy started to giggle. "I'm not used to apartment living," she said as they hurried through the lobby.

"So I noticed."

"But I'm really not into traumatizing little old ladies. I was so excited about having a place of my own with a door that locked, that I didn't stop to think of sounds leaking out, but I should have, because sometimes my neighbor on the far side plays loud music and I can hear it perfectly." She turned to him. "Did you realize people could hear us?"

He glanced down at her. "To tell you the truth, when we're in the midst of...everything, I completely forget where I am."

"Me, too. That's the idea of fantasy." Her body was still moist from their near-miss. "We almost did it in the elevator," she murmured.

His eyes flashed with heat. "Tell me about it."

"How long's the cab ride?"

He opened the outside door and held it for her. "Not long enough. Unfortunately."

"Okay, then. I'll be good."

"You're always good. Very good." He looked down and smiled at her. "Now, do you want to hail the cab or will you let me?"

The fact that he'd remembered how much she loved doing it touched her. This was the first taxi they'd shared since they'd seen the town together, and he hadn't forgotten how excited she'd been about the cab-hailing process. But the way he'd worded the end of his question—*or will you let me?*—meant that Meg was right.

Recently she'd told Trudy that Linc was a vulnerable guy under all that suave success. Meg suspected he wanted to be able to do things for her, even little things like hailing a cab. Trudy found that incredibly sweet.

Until now, she'd only acknowledged to herself how he affected her sexually. Her body responded to him so eagerly it was embarrassing. But as she looked into his eyes tonight and heard the hint of vulnerability in his question, she realized that the bond between them had gone beyond sex. Like it or not, her heart was involved. Very involved. Shoot, Meg would have a field day if she ever found that out. Trudy had been so sure such a thing couldn't happen to her.

But it had, and she couldn't change it now. "I'd love for you to get the cab," she said, and took ridiculous pleasure in the way he smiled happily and turned to flag one down.

She decided right then that the nicest thing she could do for him tonight would be to help him get through this obviously awkward dinner with his parents. Because of that, she'd use the cab ride to find out more about them instead of trading sexual innuendos with Linc.

With that in mind, she started by asking for his mother's and father's names the minute they were tucked into the cab.

"She's Glenda and he's Lincoln, the Third, but everybody calls him L.C.," Linc said.

"So you're Lincoln, the Fourth?"

"Afraid so."

"I've never known anybody with Roman numerals after his name." She wondered if his parents had put any pressure on him to come up with Lincoln, the Fifth. "What does the *C* stand for?"

"Carlyle."

The upscale sound of that gave her shivers. "So you're Lincoln Carlyle Faulkner, the Fourth?"

He grimaced. "That sounds pompous as hell, doesn't it?"

"Don't make that face. I think it's a sexy name."

"You do? You don't think it sounds incredibly stuffy and boring?"

"Nope. If you want boring, try mine. Trudy Louise Baxter. Now *that's* boring."

"No, it's not." He took her hand and turned it palm up to trace the lines. "Your name sounds as if you'd be fun and perky. Which you are."

"I want to be sultry and sexy."

He raised her palm to his mouth and ran his tongue over the creases. "Which you are," he murmured.

"Stop that," she said, her voice husky. She pulled her hand away. "I promised myself we'd talk about your parents on this ride."

"I don't want to talk about my parents." He lowered his voice. "I'd rather get you hot." He reached for her hand again.

She drew it out of reach. "Too easy. Challenge yourself. Tell me about your parents."

He leaned against the seat with a sigh. "If you insist. Let's see. Dad took the family fortune and tripled it. Mom spends as much of it as she can, but even a power shopper like her couldn't go through it in a lifetime. So far as I know, they only see each other once a year, during this dinner with me. I don't think they communicate much beyond that, either. I assume they don't get divorced because they both know it would be a long, messy fight with the lawyers getting a big chunk of the estate."

Although he delivered the words in a matter-of-fact tone, she heard the disappointment underneath his cavalier attitude. "They must love you very much, to schedule this dinner once a year, even when they'd rather not."

"I can't believe that's why they do it."

"You can't? Why else, then?"

"Duty. Some twisted idea that a dinner once a year indicates we still have a family going."

"You do," she said gently. "No matter what the living arrangements are, they're still married, and they're still your parents. All three of you are still linked together." She thought of his nickname and wondered if his mother and father ever thought of him as literally the link holding them together. "If they hated the idea of staying married, they'd have followed through with a divorce, no matter how much it cost."

He gazed straight ahead for several seconds. Finally he turned to her and took her face in both hands. "Listen, my incurable optimist, please don't think that a little nudge in the right direction will get my parents back together. It isn't going to happen."

She looked deep into his eyes. "If you really believe that, why do you have the picture of the three of you sitting on your dresser?"

He stared at her for a long time, and his throat moved in a swallow. "Sometimes you get too close, Trudy."

"I'm sorry." And she was. "I didn't mean to probe into things that are none of my business." She glanced away, full of regret. She wanted to ease his pain, not press on the wound.

"Hey, it's okay." He caught her chin and gently turned her face back to his. "I guess I asked for it, inviting you tonight."

"Linc, I don't have to go. It's not too late. I'll take the cab back to the apartment."

He shook his head, and a faint smile teased his mouth. "It is too late," he said as the cab pulled over to the curb. "Come on. I want you to meet my mom and dad."

FOR THE NEXT TWO HOURS Linc watched in fascination as Trudy charmed his parents. He couldn't remember the last time he'd seen his father laugh until the tears came, but that's what happened when Trudy described her participation in the annual Fourth of July pie-eating contest. His mother, however, didn't seem to find that story nearly as funny.

But Trudy found his mother's soft spot when she uncovered the fact that Glenda was painting. Trudy expressed great interest, and soon Glenda was animatedly describing her work, which she'd been doing for years. Linc hadn't known that his mother had become an artist. Damn, she'd even had some gallery shows and had sold some paintings.

L.C. apparently hadn't known about the painting, either. For the first time in years, he seemed to be paying some attention to what his wife said. Linc realized that in the past, when he'd faced these two alone, he'd been afraid to ask very much about what either of them was doing, for fear he'd hit a sore point. Therefore the conversation had revolved mostly around a safe topic—him.

Trudy wasn't afraid to ask anything, and her presence at the dinner had a galvanizing effect on everyone. To Linc's amazement, he began to enjoy himself. If he could have Trudy around for these events every year, they might become halfway bearable.

But he couldn't have Trudy around every year. And he'd already crossed some sort of line, because he was wishing he could. Ever since Tom had accused him of behaving like a guy who was in too deep, he'd tried to refute that accusation. Refuting it was tough. With every minute that passed, he was more captivated by this curly-haired, green-eyed sprite from Virtue, Kansas.

Near the end of the meal, Trudy excused herself to go to the rest room. Linc remembered immediately what had happened the last time she'd done that when they'd been out on the town, and he grew hungry to have her to himself again. Yes, he'd had more fun at dinner than he'd planned on, but now he wanted to end this social event and get her home and into bed.

His mother waited until Trudy was out of sight before leaning toward Linc. "Is this serious?"

He glanced at her and pretended not to understand the question. "What do you mean?"

"I mean, are you serious about her? As in marriage kind of serious?"

It was an easy question to answer because no matter what he felt, Trudy wasn't in the market. "Mom, I told you a long time ago that marriage doesn't interest me in the slightest."

"I know, but you've never brought a date to one of these dinners in all the years we've been doing this. Besides that, I've been watching you. You care about her."

"Of course I do, but we're not—"

"Listen, son," his father said. "A girl like that, who comes from Nowhereville, U.S.A., only sees one thing with a man like you. Dollar signs."

Linc felt heat rise from his snug white collar. "Excuse me?"

"Your father's right, for once," his mother said. "She's very charming, and I can see how you'd be taken in, but—"

"I am not being taken in." Linc realized he'd become too loud, and he lowered his voice, but not the level of his anger. "How dare you accuse Trudy of going after my money? She only came to this dinner as a favor to me, and she's knocked herself out being gracious to both of you. Then, the minute her back is turned, you're ready to shred her to bits."

"Hey, I'm not saying she's a bad person," his father said. "It's only natural, when you've been raised without certain advantages, to want those advantages if you can see a way to have them."

Linc rose. "You'll have to excuse us, both of you. Trudy and I need to leave." He had to get out of there before he said something he'd regret. He knew his parents were snobs and he thought he'd accepted that about them. But he couldn't sit there and let them insult Trudy.

"Oh, Linc, don't go," his mother said. "We're not trying to cast aspersions on your little friend. We're only thinking of your welfare."

"Trudy's the best thing that's happened to me in years," he said. "If I ever did marry, she'd be the perfect choice. But you two don't have to worry your aristocratic heads about that, because Trudy has no intention of getting tied down to anyone."

His father frowned and shook his head. "She may say

that, but I've been watching her, too. From her expression when she looks at you, I'd have to say she has wedding bells on her mind, son.''

Linc knew it wasn't wedding bells on Trudy's mind. She might look at him with eagerness, but she was thinking of French maid outfits and chocolate syrup, not white lace and promises. "I'm not going to debate it with you." He saw Trudy coming back from the rest room. "Here she is, so we'll say our goodbyes now."

Trudy looked startled to see him standing by the table. "Is something wrong?"

"I feel the need for some air," he said. "Let's go."

Her jaw dropped, and she glanced at each of his parents. "You all must have had one whale of a fight while I was gone. Was it about me?"

Linc took her elbow. "Come on, Trudy. Let's just leave, okay?"

"Not yet." She pulled her elbow away. "I want to know what the problem is, first."

"No, you don't." Once again he tried to get her out of there. No good would come of her spending more time with his highly prejudiced parents.

Once again she resisted. "Glenda, what was said that caused Linc to decide we should leave?"

His mother cleared her throat. "Linc's father and I are concerned that the difference between your background and Linc's might cause problems if the two of you were to get seriously involved."

Trudy stiffened but maintained her composure. "What makes you think that we would get seriously involved?"

Linc got a firmer hold on her upper arm. There was no avoiding the issue now, but he didn't want to let the scene drag on indefinitely. "That's not the point, Trudy. The point is that my parents are convinced you're a gold digger. Can we go, now?"

To his amazement, Trudy laughed. "A gold digger? Really?"

"Linc," his mother said, "you know that's not what we meant."

"It's exactly what you meant. Come on, Trudy."

"Wait a sec. This is too astounding. I'm still assimilating." She cocked a hip to one side and pretended to be chewing a big wad of gum as she faced his parents. "Let me tell you folks a little somethin'." She pointed a manicured finger at them. "I ain't no gold digger."

His father leaned forward. "See here. We didn't say—"

"All I want from your boy, here—" she paused to hitch a thumb in Linc's direction "—is good, old-fashioned, foot-stompin', hollerin', barn-burnin' *sex,* which is precisely what he's been giving me. So that's the real reason we have to be leaving. It's past our bedtime. See y'all later."

As Linc reeled from her little speech, she took advantage of his disorientation to shake off his hold on her arm.

Then she pranced away toward the coat-check room, swinging her hips provocatively. After about six steps she turned and sent him a challenging glance. "Are you coming, big boy?"

He took quick inventory of his totally shell-shocked parents. It was the first time he ever remembered them wearing exactly the same expression of speechless amazement. "You bet," he said, and followed her.

16

WHAT FANTASTIC BUNS. Trudy couldn't imagine a bigger treat than feeling Linc's practiced stroke at the same time she watched that gorgeous backside flex with each plunge. She'd positioned a couple of lamps on the floor on either side of the bed so they'd have enough light to enjoy the mirrors. And they had *really* enjoyed the mirrors.

She'd insisted that Linc, who'd just been through a trying ordeal, take the first turn. Lying on his back, he'd caught the show when she climbed on top. She'd remained sitting upright, allowing him to watch her play with her nipples as she slid up and down on his rigid shaft.

When he'd claimed he couldn't take any more without coming, they'd switched places. She could see why he'd quickly run out of track on the orgasm express. This mirror business would make short work of her, too.

"Nice?" he murmured in her ear.

She struggled for breath as she clutched that muscular bottom of his. "You have…no idea."

"Yes, I do." His breathing grew heavy. "I love the mirrors. I even love knowing you're watching me."

She gasped as the first tremor caught her. "Linc…I'm—"

"I know." He pumped faster, making the bed shake. "Me, too."

"Oh, Linc…Linc…" Whether it was the tension of the evening being released, or the effect of the mirrors on her libido, the impending climax felt like a stampede approaching.

"Give me all you've got," he murmured. "Open for me. That's it." He groaned. "That's it. Oh, Trudy...come for me...come for me!"

And she certainly did—yelling her head off and bucking wildly, arching upward, taking every inch deep inside.

His voice rasped in her ear. "My turn...yes...oh, *Trudy*..." He surged forward with a loud cry, making the bedposts bang against the wall.

Through the swirling haze of her own climax, she looked upward to watch him shudder through his.

Fortunately.

At that moment the mooring gave way on one end of the mirror directly over his sculpted behind. Just in time, Trudy lifted her foot and caught it before it came down on him.

He moaned and stirred in her arms. "Trudy?"

"One of the—um—mirrors is falling. I'm holding it with my foot."

He gave a snort of muffled laughter, and soon his whole body began to shake with merriment.

She used to be annoyed when her schemes went awry and he thought it was so damn funny. But she was beginning to realize that he liked the goofy parts of her routine almost as much as the extremely sexy parts, so she wasn't annoyed anymore. "You know, it's the oddest sensation, having a man laugh while he's still inside you," she said.

He lifted his head and gazed down at her, still chuckling. "You might as well get used to it. I have a feeling this won't be the last time."

"This plan was almost flawless. You rocked the bed too hard."

His eyebrows lifted. "Is that a complaint?"

"Guess not, all things considered." She grinned at him. "Poor Millicent."

He groaned. "Once again, I forgot about Millicent. And

every other person on the planet, actually. What we need is a soundproof room or a house out in the wilderness.''

She wondered if he realized how that sounded, as if the two of them might go looking for a love nest together. He probably hadn't meant it that way, but that's how it hit her. She was intrigued that he seemed to be getting quite involved with her for a guy who never planned to commit.

Nothing would come of it, even if he did want to commit, because she certainly wasn't into that. Not at all. She'd have to keep watch over him, though, and make sure she didn't give him the wrong signals and make him think she was changing *her* mind about the commitment thing. Because she wouldn't. Couldn't. She'd just arrived in town, for heaven's sake. Besides, she couldn't give Meg the satisfaction.

She shifted slightly. ''I'm gonna need to move my foot.''

''Oh, yeah?'' He propped himself on his elbows and glanced around. ''Interesting position. I didn't know you could hold your foot like that. Maybe we should try doing it with you in that position.''

''I vote no. I'm cramping up.''

''Okay. Let's fix this.''

''Yes, let's.'' As he eased away from her, she sat up and grabbed the edge of the mirror. ''Got it.''

''Could you just hold it for a minute while I take care of things in the bathroom?''

''I can do that.'' Actually she figured she could fix it while he was in there. One of the wires had come untwisted, so it would be an easy repair.

He started to climb out of the bed. Then he glanced back at her. ''Don't disappear, okay?''

She met his gaze. They hadn't talked about his parents, hadn't taken the time because they'd both been so hot for each other. One glance at the mirrors and Linc had been throwing clothes everywhere.

But she knew he'd probably want to talk about his parents. Any person would, after a scene like that. Maybe she needed to apologize for what she'd said, although she didn't much feel like it. But maybe she would, anyway.

So this one time, she'd change the pattern. Just this once. "Okay, I'll stay here."

"Good." He headed toward the bathroom.

She was standing naked on the bed, her arms over her head as she twisted the wire around the canopy support, when he returned.

"Now there's a scene right out of *Playboy*," he said.

She glanced over at him. "And there's a scene right out of *Playgirl*." He looked yummy in a three-piece suit, but this was the outfit she liked the best. Here was a guy who didn't need shoulder pads in his Italian suits. The sprinkling of hair on his chest was just enough to make him all man, and below the waist he was Superman. Not bad for her first catch.

He approached the bed. "Need any help?"

She started to say no, but then she remembered the look in his eyes when he'd asked to hail a cab. "Sure," she said. "Longer arms would be nice."

He climbed up on the bed with her, and as they worked to secure all the wires tighter, the inevitable happened. Soon they were writhing on the tangled sheets again. Linc was the one who suggested trying it spoon fashion so they could both watch.

Another outstanding orgasm and another trip to the bathroom for Linc, and they were at last cuddling beneath the black satin sheets. Trudy pillowed her head on his chest and listened to his heart beat while he combed his fingers through her hair. It was nice. Maybe a little too nice.

She couldn't go soft on her program. She'd worked too many years to get to this point, and she wasn't about to stop with one man. But they needed to talk about his parents, so she'd hang in for that. Then she definitely needed to get him outta there, before they segued into an overnighter.

"We've never done it twice in one night," he said.

"Guess not."

"The second time was different. I liked being able to hold out longer without giving myself lockjaw in the process. And I had the presence of mind to think of more interesting things to do."

"Uh-huh. Nice things." She'd actually loved this second go-round, too. And if they kept talking about sex, they'd be in for round three. All things considered, that could be a bad idea. Barriers were coming down, and that worried her.

She decided it might be up to her to introduce the topic of his parents before they ended up in another horizontal hula. "Linc, I'm sure I offended your parents tonight, and I hope that doesn't cause a problem for you. When you talk to either of them again, feel free to tell them anything you want. Tell them I was taking happy pills. Whatever gets you off the hook."

He drew her a notch closer. "If we talk again, they're going to have to be the ones to initiate it. I would apologize for them, except that's the way they are, and I was a fool to believe they'd behave themselves the whole night. So I apologize to you, instead, for putting you through that."

"No problem." She repositioned her cheek so she could feel the steady thud of his heart. "Their accusation was so preposterous it slid right off my back. And besides, I had fun with the comeback."

"I loved your comeback." He stroked her hair silently for a while. "If they had their way I'd be married to some-body from the right family—a business liaison like in Me-dieval times—and my wife and I would probably end up living apart the way my parents do."

"You don't have to give them their way. We're not in Medieval times anymore."

He sighed. "You're right. But even if I did the choosing, she and I would still live the privileged life. So would any kids we had. I've seen how money isolates and separates people, and I'll be damned if I'll make another kid go through that crushing loneliness. For a guy like me, marriage is full of land mines. If you'd grown up the way I did, you'd understand why I've decided to stay far away from the whole concept.''

She propped herself up on one elbow to look into his face. ''You think you had trauma connected with wedded bliss? Try living in a small house with parents who are determined to have as many children as they can cram into it.''

''I'd take that over living virtually alone in a twenty-five-room mansion.''

''That's because you have no idea what you're talking about. My parents never had a chance to have fun. I was born that first year. Then there was a break because my dad was a traveling salesman, but the minute they'd saved enough for the farm and he was home again, the babies started coming, bing, bing, bing.'' She tapped on his chest for emphasis.

His gaze was unreadable. ''At least you weren't lonely.''

''I would have given *anything* to be lonely. This little apartment all to myself is heaven, and I plan to sow my wild oats for *years* before I even consider getting into that marriage stuff. It ties you down something awful.''

''It didn't tie my parents down, as you can see. They had the money to hire nannies and tutors so they could do whatever they wanted. They weren't forced to spend time with me or each other. I think too much money has the power to kill love.''

''And too little has the power to kill your spirit! I'm sorry, but you have no concept. You'd have to go to Virtue and stay in my parents' house before you'd even begin to get what I'm saying.'' She shuddered. ''You'd go nuts.''

Talking about this was good for her, she realized, because it impressed her goals more firmly on her mind. Cuddling with Linc tended to blur her focus, but thinking of Virtue sharpened it right up again.

"I wouldn't go nuts," he said.

"Oh, yes, you would. You lie here in safety and claim you could handle it, but that's because you won't ever have to."

"Now, wait a minute." He bunched a pillow behind his head so he could look at her. "I want you to know I'm not some kind of spoiled rich kid who throws a tantrum when he runs out of caviar."

"Ha! I don't think you could even *get* caviar in Virtue, let alone run out of what you had."

"You think I'm a wuss, don't you? A city guy who can't cut it out in the boondocks."

"This is the silliest argument I've had in a while." She propped her fist on his chest and rested her chin there. "But, trust me, you would run screaming out of Virtue if you were forced to spend any time there at all."

"Would not."

"Would so."

He gazed into her eyes for a long moment. "What are you doing this weekend?"

She blinked. "I...I hadn't figured that out. I need to set up some bookshelves, and I—"

"Nothing critical, right?"

"Not really, no."

"Then let's go to Virtue."

She grinned, figuring he was teasing her. "You're a hoot, you know that?"

He didn't return her smile. "I mean it."

"Of course you don't mean it. We can't just up and go to Virtue."

"Why not? That's what money does for you, and I'm willing to put my money where my mouth is. We'll spend the weekend in Virtue, staying right in your parents' house. It won't even cost me much more than the plane tickets, anyway, and I can prove to you that I could survive there just fine.''

She was thrown completely off course by his outrageous suggestion. ''I still think you're pulling my leg.''

''No.'' He smiled at her as he reached down to stroke her bare hip. ''I have other ideas for what to do with your leg.''

Of course she reacted to that sensuous touch, which was the problem with cuddling and talking after sex. It led to more sex, and sleepovers, and complications.

''So, are we going to Virtue?'' He slipped his hand between her thighs.

''You're crazy.''

''Yeah, I am. Come on, Trudy. You claim to be spontaneous. Prove it.''

The way she was giving in to all his wonderful fondling, they would make love again tonight, which meant they were venturing into dangerous territory, crossing the boundary from casual sex to serious involvement. She had to stay on track. If talking about Virtue helped keep her focused on her goal, a trip there would mean a whole rededication to her quest for freedom and adventure.

And it might turn Linc off, too. That would probably be a good thing. He was getting entirely too chummy.

She sighed and rolled to her back to give him better access. ''Okay, we'll go to Virtue.''

''Great.'' Then he slid down between her thighs, kissed her in a most wonderful spot and made her forget everything but their fantasy world for the third time that night.

''THAT WAS UNREAL,'' Tom whispered in Meg's ear late the following night after they'd rearranged their clothing and settled back against the leather seats of the limo. ''Are you sure you're okay?''

''Perfect. Pregnant ladies can do all sorts of fun things.'' She grinned at him in the darkness as the limo glided through the streets of New York. The window between the driver and his passengers was tightly closed and the chauffeur had been paid well to drive them around the city and keep his eyes firmly on the road.

Tom squeezed her knee. "We should do this again some time."

"It'll be more expensive when we have to hire a babysitter." She could hardly wait for the baby to be born, but she was realistic about how much their lifestyle would change. "Even if Trudy says she'll do it for free, I would want to pay her. She needs the money."

"Speaking of Trudy, what's up with this trip she and Linc are taking back to Virtue? Isn't that kind of weird?"

Meg relaxed against the plush seat with a sigh. Between a fabulous orgasm and the excellent prospect of her plans working out with Trudy and Linc, she was one satisfied woman. She'd tried to keep her influence subtle—a suggestion about mirrors here, a word about Linc's vulnerability there—and she was succeeding beyond her wildest dreams. Trudy was such a goner.

"I don't think the trip's weird," she said. It had been scheduled more quickly than she'd dared hope, but that didn't make it weird.

"Well, I think it is. Linc claims this is a short-term affair they're having, so it makes no sense for him to go there, right?"

"He's probably curious after the way we've all talked about the place."

"I don't buy it. Something's going on." He glanced over at his wife. "And you look like the cat who swallowed the canary."

She laughed. "Or the cat who swallowed the watermelon."

"You know what I mean. You look all smug, like you have about six really good secrets I don't know about."

"Why shouldn't I look smug? I just enjoyed limousine sex for the first time."

He blew out a breath. "Come on, Meg. You think Trudy and Linc are getting serious, don't you?"

She decided the trip to Virtue was enough progress to confess her plan to Tom. "Speaking of secrets, can you keep one?"

"Sure."

"I mean from everyone. Especially from Linc." She watched him wrestle with the idea. He hated not being able to tell Linc things.

Finally he nodded. "Yeah. Yeah, I can. But I hope you're not going to tell me that Trudy came here looking for a husband, after all, and the two of you decided to nab Linc."

"No. Trudy still thinks she doesn't want a husband."

Tom sighed with relief. "That's a load off my mind."

"As for Linc, I think he's weakening on the marriage thing."

"You and me, both. He doesn't want to admit it, especially since Trudy's all into her independence, but I think he's got it bad." He gazed at Meg. "Do you think he's going to Virtue because he thinks that might change Trudy's mind?"

Meg shook her head. "Linc doesn't know why he's going there. He thinks it's to settle some silly bet about who had the rougher upbringing, him or Trudy. But I think, subconsciously, he's going there to meet the parents of the woman he wants to marry."

"See, I do, too, but Trudy isn't into it, so I'm worried that he'll get hurt."

Meg rubbed her hand along his knee. "I'll handle Trudy when the time comes. Right now it's going better than I even imagined when I decided to get them together."

"I see you're pretty pleased about this fix-up of yours."

"It's more than a fix-up." Meg moved her hand a little higher and, sure enough, her husband was rebounding from their first encounter in this rolling pleasure palace. She'd hoped they could get in two sessions before their time was up.

"What do you mean? It's either a fix-up or it's not."

"To me, a fix-up means a blind date." She stroked the bulge under his fly. "My plan is much bigger than that. I wanted to save Trudy a lot of time and heartache by giving her exactly who she needed in a husband."

"Omigod. You really are trying to get them married off."

"Why not? The single life is not all it's cracked up to be. Am I right?" She gave him an affectionate squeeze.

"You know I'll agree with you when you've got me by the balls."

"And you love it."

"I'm pussy-whipped, is what I am."

"Oh, Tommy, why don't you admit that I'm brilliant for getting those two together. They're perfect for each other." And she would have her sweet, sweet revenge for all Trudy's teasing.

"Damn it, Meg, you're taking a hell of a chance. What if Trudy breaks his heart? Or worse, what if they get married, like you want, and it doesn't work out? You'll be to blame. And me, because I'm married to you."

"Don't worry, Tommy." She unzipped his fly. "It will all work out. You'll see."

"You're always so doggone sure of yourself, Megs. You could get your comeuppance one of these days."

She urged his stiff penis out of confinement. "Right now I'd like to get something else."

"So I figured."

"Ready for limo sex, part two?"

He groaned softly. "Apparently I am. But, about this other matter, someday you're going to go too far."

"For the moment I was thinking of only going as far as your lap."

"Then come on, you wild, bossy woman. Climb aboard."

She grinned at him. "Why, thank you. I think I'll do that."

17

OF ALL THE UNFAMILIAR SIGHTS and sounds that bombarded Linc when he arrived in Virtue on Friday afternoon, he knew he'd never forget two things—the flat, snow-covered farmland that stretched unbroken to the horizon, and the tears in Sarah Baxter's eyes when she ran down the snowy walk, coatless and arms open, to meet her daughter. A black Lab, obviously stiff with age, followed, tail wagging.

Trudy had only been gone for two weeks, and yet Sarah hugged her as if they'd been apart for a year. Trudy, Linc noticed, hugged her mother back just as fiercely. Afterward Trudy crouched down and put both arms around the aging dog. He licked her hand and she buried her face in his fur.

A lump formed in Linc's throat. Trudy might like to talk tough, but she'd been homesick.

Sarah wiped her eyes as she watched Trudy pet the dog. Then she glanced apologetically at Linc. "You'll have to forgive me. She's never lived away from home. I didn't realize how much I'd miss her. Prince has been grieving, too."

"I understand," Linc said, although all this emotion at a simple homecoming was like a foreign language to him. His parents would never act this way.

When Trudy stood and turned to him, her eyes were a little teary, too. "Linc, this is my mother, Sarah, and our dog, Prince. Mom, this is Linc Faulkner."

"Pleased to meet you." Linc transferred both his and Trudy's small bags to his left hand and held out his right.

"Tom's friend." Sarah clasped his hand in both of hers. Her smile was warm, even as her breath made clouds in the chill air. "I'm so sorry you didn't make it to the wedding."

"So am I." When Sarah released his hand he noticed that Prince had come forward to sniff his wool coat. "Hey, Prince." He hunkered down and scratched behind the dog's ears, which gave him a rush of pleasure. He couldn't remember the last time he'd had a chance to pet a dog, and he loved it.

"But you've more than made up for missing the wedding by bringing Trudy home this weekend." Sarah glanced at her daughter. "I still can't believe you got Friday off when you've barely started working at Babcock and Trimball."

"Meg did some sort of hocus-pocus," Trudy said. "She said she promised our boss her firstborn, but that might have been a slight exaggeration."

Sarah laughed. "It'll be a miracle if Meg lets anyone hold that baby, let alone steal it away. Well, whatever Meg did, I owe her. Coming in on Saturday would have given you no time at all. Well, let's get you in the house."

Linc gave Prince one final scratch and stood. He liked Sarah Baxter. A woman with six children still at home didn't have time for makeup or a fussy hairdo, but Linc couldn't imagine Sarah with either. She looked fine the way she was. The hair she'd pulled back in a ponytail was streaked with gray, and laughter had drawn gentle lines in her cheeks and set crinkles into the corners of her eyes. She was dressed in jeans and a sweatshirt, and Linc had the distinct impression she was content with who and what she was.

If being married and having all those children had broken her spirit, Linc couldn't see it. Her eyes were the same green as Trudy's, and they held the same sparkle, as if she could hardly wait to see what the next moment would bring. Now Linc knew where Trudy's infectious optimism came from.

"I'm the only one home right now." Sarah put an arm

around Trudy's waist as they all started toward the front door. "Everybody has after-school things going on. Your father took Sue Ellen to get a new pair of snow boots. Those old red ones we've handed down for years finally gave out, and Sue Ellen is just sure you're going to take her out in the snow while you're here."

"Of course I will."

"We both will," Linc said. And that was a perfect example of what he'd missed growing up. Getting someone, anyone, to help him build a snowman had been a major undertaking. When Belinda had first arrived she'd agreed to do it, and that might have been the beginning of his crush on her. She'd only helped him once, though. After that she'd been too busy. Everyone had always been too busy.

Sarah ushered them straight into a cozy living room with a fire blazing in the brick fireplace. As if that weren't welcoming enough, the air was fragrant with the scent of good things cooking. If he wasn't mistaken that was the smell of pot roast in the oven, with an overlay of baked apple pie. His mouth watered.

"Linc, I'm bunking you in with Kenny and Josh," Sarah said. "Trudy, you'll be in your old room with Linda, Marcie and Deena. Let's get both of your bags in where they belong, and then we'll have coffee by the fire." Excitement laced her words as she bustled down a hallway lined with family pictures.

"Didn't you put Sue Ellen in with the girls after I left?" Trudy asked.

"We did, but she can move back in with us for the weekend. We're so thrilled to have you that I think your father would sleep in the barn if we needed the extra room."

And that was the other thing Linc had missed—a love so great that parents would put their own welfare aside for their child. He realized Trudy had made sacrifices, too. She'd put her dreams on hold an extra few years to help her mother with the seventh kid. But how could she not? This hallway was lined with laughing, smiling people who stole your heart.

He could understand why Trudy had needed to get away to the big city to create her own identity. Nobody could share a room with three sisters and eat mom's pot roast forever. But as a place to come home to, this little farmhouse in Kansas was picture-perfect. He envied her so much it hurt.

His sleeping accommodations turned out to be the bottom of a bunk bed in a smallish room. It was Kenny's bed, to be exact. Josh, age twelve, slept on the top bunk. Kenny would roll out a sleeping bag on the floor for two nights, Sarah said. Linc glanced around at walls covered with sports posters and shelves filled with books and plastic models of planes, ships and cars. The teenaged room of his dreams. His room had been designer-created—a showroom piece that had no appeal for a boy.

"You may be a little cramped on that bed," Sarah said. "Even Kenny's starting to complain, and he's not as tall as you. But I wasn't sure—"

"The bed will be perfect, Mrs. Baxter."

"Oh, call me Sarah."

He felt as if he'd been handed a privilege. "Thank you for putting me up on such short notice, Sarah."

She flushed with pleasure. "Like I said, we're tickled pink to have both of you. It's no trouble at all." She gestured across the hall. "That's the nearest bathroom. We only have two for all of us, so it's first come, first served. Stan—that's my husband—threatened to put in one of those number machines like they have at the post office."

Trudy glanced at Linc as if to gauge how he was taking all of this. "The best strategy is to get up ahead of everyone else," she said. "But that's tricky, because the boys usually help Dad in the barn first thing, around five-thirty. And Sue Ellen's an early riser."

Linc smiled at her. "Maybe I'll challenge Kenny and

Josh to a friendly game of cards. Winner gets to use the bathroom first in the morning.''

"Oh, the boys would *love* to play cards with you," Sarah said. "They're so excited to meet a man who's been to Madison Square Garden. I hope you're up on the Knicks."

"I'm up on the Knicks." Linc held Trudy's gaze, letting her know that he was getting along fine in her world.

She pursed her lips as if to say *Just you wait.*

He wanted to kiss those pursed lips. In fact, except for the day they'd met, this was the longest he'd been in Trudy's company without having sex. He could feel the desire simmering there, ready to boil over at the least opportunity. With their sleeping arrangements, there wouldn't be much opportunity. Tom had warned him about that.

"I'll let you get settled, then," Sarah said. "Come on out to the living room when you're finished and we'll visit."

"Great."

Sarah and Trudy left and continued down the hall to the girls' room, followed by the slow-moving dog. All the while the two women talked animatedly about people Linc didn't know, catching up.

Linc thought of his once-a-year dinner with his parents. A whole year had passed each time, and yet there never seemed to be much for them to say to each other. Catching up took about five minutes, and then they were left with politics and the current state of the economy.

Yet once he'd introduced Trudy to the occasion, there suddenly had been plenty to say. She'd been a very positive influence on the gathering, until his mother had decided to accuse her of being a scheming money-grabber. Linc still boiled when he thought of that.

Still, he wasn't sure how matters had progressed from defending Trudy's honor to suggesting that they make the trip to Virtue. He had no clue where that impulse had come from.

Maybe it had stemmed from plain old competitiveness.

She'd moved with little effort into his world. She'd even handled his parents without breaking a sweat. But she'd been so sure he couldn't hack it in the wilds of Kansas, and maybe he just wanted to prove her wrong.

Yet he didn't think that was all of it. As he stashed his small suitcase in a corner of the room and laid his coat over the end of the bed, he admitted that coming here might have been an instinctive attempt to get to know her better.

He was desperate to know her better, in fact. Tom was right. Linc Faulkner was getting serious about a woman for the first time in his life, and it scared the hell out of him.

TRUDY HAD EXPECTED Linc to stick out like a sore thumb in her parents' tiny, crowded house with the beat-up furniture and the inevitable clutter created by eight busy lives. He didn't.

Oh, there was no doubt that he was the main attraction at the dinner table. Everybody except Sue Ellen pelted him with questions about New York. They bypassed Trudy, rightly assuming that she hadn't lived there long enough to know the place well.

Because he was the center of attention, Linc did stand out, but not like a sore thumb. More like a beloved celebrity. Linc appeared to be eating it up. He didn't seem to notice the chipped plates or the paper napkins. Instead he raved about her mother's pot roast and apple pie.

Trudy had to admit the meal tasted delicious. She was still enamored of the delis near her apartment, but nothing beat her mother's cooking.

With Linc claiming center stage she was free to gaze around the table, and she was a little surprised to notice how attractive her family was. At fourteen, Deena was becoming a real beauty, and the other girls were showing signs of turning into heartbreakers, too. Kenny had a new girlfriend, according to her mother, and Josh was starting to get calls from girls already, even though he was only twelve.

It made sense that her brothers and sisters would be good-looking. Trudy had always thought her mother was pretty, and her father wore his fifty years well. He was still broad shouldered and solid, plus the gray in his hair made him look even more handsome, in her opinion.

Linc would be the sort of man who would look good as he went gray, too. Not that she would know him then, of course. A sudden pang gripped her, a pang that spelled trouble. Being with her family was supposed to renew her dedication to the single life, not make her yearn for a family of her own. She hoped this trip didn't backfire on her.

After dinner, Linda, who was ten and very into games, excused herself from the table and came back with the old Chinese checkers set. "Let's have a tournament!" she suggested, eyes alight with excitement.

"Dishes, first," Linc said.

Trudy's mother beamed at him, but she insisted that she'd handle the dishes if they wanted to play games.

"Nope," Linc said. "You made the meal. The kids and I will get the dishes out of the way. Who wants to help me?"

All of them did, of course, and as Trudy stared at him, openmouthed, he led a parade of enthusiastic dishwashers into the kitchen, everyone carrying plates and glasses.

"Oh, I *like* him," Sarah said to Trudy.

"Nice guy," added her father. He took another sip of his coffee and smiled at Trudy. "I didn't expect you to find somebody special this quick, but I guess considering he's Tom's friend, it's perfectly natural."

Trudy rushed to set the record straight. "We're just friends," she said. "Linc's heard so much about Virtue from me, Meg and Tom, and he had the weekend free, so he suggested—"

"He's more than just your friend," Sarah said gently. "He didn't come to see Virtue. He came to meet us."

Trudy tried to think of a graceful way to get out of this

conversation. Of course her mother was wrong, but Trudy didn't know how to explain that they'd come here so that Linc could find out what a terribly deprived life she'd led in Virtue. Worst of all, he didn't seem to be getting the picture. He seemed to be having a wonderful time.

"No, really," Trudy said at last. "We're just friends. And to be honest, Linc felt sorry for me because I had a bout of homesickness. He's very well-off, so he wanted to treat me to this weekend."

Her mother smiled, obviously not believing a word of it. "You don't have to admit to anything yet if you're not ready," she said.

"That's right," her father said. "It's none of our business, really. But I don't care if the guy's King Midas himself, I can't see him spending the kind of money he did on those plane tickets unless he had a stake in coming here."

"Mom!" yelled eight-year-old Marcie. "We need more dish towels in here!"

Trudy leaped up. "Let me get them," she said, and practically ran toward the linen closet. Grabbing up a fresh stack of dish towels, she hurried into the ancient kitchen and was treated to the sight of Linc, the studmuffin of Wall Street, up to his elbows in suds. Next to him, standing on a chair so she could hand him dishes, was Sue Ellen.

Kenny was directing the drying brigade, while Deena was in charge of putting away.

"The sooner we get done, the sooner we play Chinese checkers," Linc hollered over the general hubbub.

Trudy was so mesmerized by the amazing sight of Linc doing dishes in a country kitchen that she barely realized that Marcie had snatched the towels from her and tossed one to Linda.

"But don't break anything!" Kenny yelled.

"Right," Linc agreed. "If you do, then we'll have to take time out for cleanup and everybody will have to ante up to buy your mother a new whatever."

"I have a piggy bank!" Sue Ellen announced.

"That's good." Linc nodded. "When you have enough saved, I'll help you invest it."

That brought a clamor of voices, as each of Trudy's brothers and sisters tried to be the one with the best savings plan, to impress Linc.

Shaking her head, Trudy backed out of the kitchen. She'd thought she knew this man. He was supposed to be an urban, sophisticated, swinging bachelor, not Mr. Rogers.

Yet as the evening progressed, he seemed to become even more involved in the homey doings of her family. In between rounds of the Chinese checker tournament he was surrounded by Beanie Babies, Pokémon cards, Hot Wheels and even Barbies as everyone rushed to show him their precious belongings.

Later on, Trudy's mother tried valiantly to get the younger ones to bed, but they were having none of it.

"Tell you what," Linc said. "Trudy and I need to go out for a little while, anyway. I want her to take me for a drive through town."

"Nothing's open," Kenny volunteered. "Except the show, and it'll be closed soon, too. The movie's nearly over by now."

"I know," Linc said. "But I've never been here, so I want to look around, get my bearings. We'll continue the tournament tomorrow night, okay?"

Deena gazed at Linc with the adoration of a fourteen-year-old with a brand-new crush. "I saw that car you rented. It's cool."

"Maybe tomorrow I can take some of you for a ride," Linc said.

"We *all* want to go, but we won't all fit! That's why we have a van," Linda announced.

"We could take turns," Marcie said. "Right, Linc?"

"Right." He glanced at Trudy. "Ready?"

"I'll get our coats." She was definitely ready. She had

some things to discuss with the man who was supposed to be her big-city sex object. This home-and-hearth routine of his was making her think of things she didn't want to think about. Not for years.

It wasn't fair that he should be so comfortable with her family and look as if he belonged there. Even Prince liked him. Watching him interact so enthusiastically with everyone made her get all soft and sentimental. He needed to cut that out.

They had a hard time getting out the door, with each of the kids wanting to ask one last thing, but finally they made it down the walk and out to the sleek black Lexus. Once they were in the car with the heater blasting, she directed him to the main road.

Then she turned to him. "Anybody would think you grew up right down the road from me! Where *is* all this homespun behavior coming from?"

He grinned. "Am I pulling it off?"

"Apparently so! My parents are snowed and the kids think you hung the moon. Me, I'm trying to figure who you are and what you've done with Lincoln Carlyle Faulkner, the Fourth."

He laughed. "It's all very easy to explain. When I was a kid with no real family life of my own, I watched TV to get what I was missing. I was a family-sitcom junkie." He glanced at her. "I know all the moves by heart, Trudy."

She fought to keep from melting at the lost little boy look in his eyes. "Is that why you wanted to come here, to get into the family thing?"

His gaze flickered and he returned his attention to the snow-packed road. "Could be. I've been asking myself why, and that could be a big reason. But I'm sure that's not all of it."

She had a feeling that she didn't want to hear his other reasons. "So how did you learn to do dishes?" she asked quickly.

"I don't know how to do dishes. The kids told me what to do, and I asked if I could be the washer as a special favor because I'd never done it before."

"No wonder they adore you. First you dazzle them with tales of the big city and then you let them teach you things they know that you don't." She sighed and leaned her head back against the headrest. "I thought you'd be appalled by this place."

"Then I guess you don't know me very well, yet."

She turned her head to look at him. "I guess not." And he was really beginning to worry her. Maybe the sight of downtown Virtue would take the shine off his romantic picture of life in the country. "Turn right at the next street, and we'll go through the main part of town."

"Okay."

"It's very dull."

"If you say so." He turned and gave her a wink before he made the turn.

"Totally dull," she said, knowing she sounded cranky. She wished he wouldn't be so damned charming all the time, which made her want to kiss him and stuff. Lots of stuff. Right now wasn't a good time to do that, when her emotions were a mess and she was thinking that Linc would make someone a terrific husband.

That was the problem in a nutshell. He was looking very matrimonial at the moment, and she didn't need that, thank you very much. For another thing, he shouldn't look so good driving this car. Coming out here from the airport and going into town tonight had been her only experiences of being a passenger in the car Linc drove. She'd discovered that watching him handle the car turned her on.

This trip might well be the biggest mistake of her life.

"Are you going to point out the sights?" Linc asked in the deep baritone that made her think of sex.

"Sure. There's the tiny little bank, and there's the tiny little department store, and there's the great big feed store, and there's the run-down gas station, and over there's the one-screen movie theater, and next door is the totally closed soda fountain and drugstore. You notice there are no people. We are the only car going down this street.'' She glared at him. ''Any questions?''

''Yeah,'' he said with a chuckle. ''Where's the nearest lonely farm road?''

18

LINC WASN'T USED to spending so much time with Trudy and not getting skin to skin with her. Tom had advised him that they'd have one option, and one option only, which was why Linc had rented a luxury sedan instead of a sports car. But he wasn't sure he could talk Trudy into it. After all, she had vowed never to have back-seat sex again.

Trudy looked over at him. "I can't believe you really want to go parking."

"Humor me. I've never done this before."

"That does put a novel twist on it. But you'd have to keep the motor running so we could leave the heat on. How's the gas situation?" She glanced at the gauge.

"We're fine. That's why I filled up at that station between here and the airport."

"You were *planning* this? I wondered why you topped off the tank like that. I thought maybe you were nervous about getting stranded in the middle of nowhere."

"Nope. I was hoping to get laid in the middle of nowhere."

That got to her, apparently, because she began to laugh. "Well, if I'm going to break my promise to myself, I suppose I could do worse than the back seat of a car like this. And just your luck, the roads have been recently plowed so you won't get us stuck. Plus the cops won't be out looking for lovers tonight, with the temperature below zero."

"See, we're fated to have car sex."

She grinned at him. "Okay, turn right at your next opportunity."

"You'll do it?" He started getting hard immediately.

"I will, but you might decide washing dishes is more fun."

"I sincerely doubt that." He turned on the road she'd pointed out and drove along next to a barbed-wire fence that seemed to stretch forever into the darkness. He glanced at her. "How far do we go?"

She gave him the kind of smile that made him want to rip her clothes off. "All the way, dude. All the way. Until you're dripping with sweat and hollering for mercy."

"No fair saying things like that. I have to keep my hands on the wheel."

"But I don't." She rustled around in her seat.

"What—what are you doing?"

"Taking off my jacket and my boots." She tossed them on the floor. Then she squirmed around some more. "And my slacks and panties."

He looked, trying to see what was going on over there.

"Eyes on the road, hotshot. Use your imagination. Mmm. Leather seats are *very* nice. I've never felt leather against my bare tush before."

He groaned and gripped the wheel harder. He should have realized that a world-class tease like Trudy would take this chance to make him crazy.

Turning in her seat, she reached over and slid her hand along his thigh under his coat. "I'll bet you've never been felt up while you were behind the wheel, have you?"

"No." With a sharp intake of breath, he took his foot off the gas. "Trudy…don't make me wreck."

"A real man can keep driving while he's being fondled," she murmured. "But if you're worried, go slow." She opened his fly.

He trembled with anticipation. "Then we'll never get there."

"We're almost there, and I want you to have the full sex-in-the-car treatment. Back-seat sex begins in the front seat." She worked his briefs down over his erection. "My, you are ready, aren't you?"

"You could say that." Having a woman stroke his penis while he was driving was wonderful and terrifying at the same time. He had trouble breathing, let alone steering. "People do this?"

"Sure."

He gulped. "On the highway?"

"Well, I wouldn't. Back country roads are the only place I'd advise it, and you have to be careful. But nobody's out here. And you're going—" she craned her neck to look at the speedometer "—three miles an hour."

"The rest of me's going a hundred and twenty. Stop a minute." He gripped the wheel tighter. "Take your hand away." He sighed as he got control of himself. "Are we there yet?"

She laughed again. "Almost. See that little path to the right?"

"Yes." He felt totally disoriented, driving along fully exposed and hard as a gearshift.

"That's where we turn, as long as it's been plowed." She cupped her hands around her face and peered out the side window. "Looks good."

He guided the car a short distance down the little lane. "Here?"

"Here."

He put the car in Park and switched off the lights. God, it was black out there. The glow from the dash was the only thing between them and total darkness. Even the stars were covered with a layer of clouds. They were truly alone, co-cooned in the night. His heart raced with excitement. "Now what?"

She unhooked her seat belt. "Well, I'm small enough to crawl between the seats, but I'm afraid you'll have to get out and get in through the passenger door. And watch your step. It's probably icy footing.''

"Right." He was shaking so much that he had trouble unlatching his seat belt. By the time he got it undone, he turned to see how she was doing and discovered the most delicious prospect—Trudy's bare bottom right next to his cheek as she squirmed into the back seat. "Hold it right there." He wrapped a hand around her warm thigh.

"Hold it? But I'm—"

"In a perfect position...stay like that. Please stay exactly like that." She was entirely too much in control of this encounter, but he knew a way to make her quiver as desperately as he was doing. He needed to try the unexpected. She was a sucker for that.

"For back-seat sex, you have to be in the back," she said.

"I want something else first." His coat was in the way and it was very close quarters, but if he could maneuver onto the console, get between her legs and scoot down...

"This isn't...how you do car sex." From the ragged way she was breathing, she'd obviously figured out his intent.

Cupping her bottom, he tilted his head back and made one long swipe with his tongue, right where it would have the most effect.

She gasped. "But I like it."

He made sure she really liked it. He buried his face in her heat, sucking and licking until she filled the car with her cries. While he drove her wild, the taste and scent of her did the same to him. The air from the car's heater teased his penis like a lover's breath. He made her come once, then again, wanting this to be the best she'd ever had in a car.

But at last he let her go. She was so dazed and limp that he had to help her into the back.

She tumbled onto the seat like a rag doll. "Oh, Linc, no one's ever...never done anything...like—"

"Good." He shook with reaction, but he managed to lean

forward and snap open the glove compartment. Grabbing the condom he'd stashed there several hours ago, he tore open the package and put it on with trembling fingers.

Then he closed his coat and lurched out into the stinging cold. He slipped once on the ice and clutched the door handle to keep from falling down. He didn't care about any of that. All he could think of was plunging into her. After wrenching open the passenger door, he climbed in, but there was almost no room for him with her stretched on the seat.

She was still struggling for breath. "Take...take off your coat."

He did, and threw it in the front seat.

"And your pants."

That took more effort because he had to ditch his shoes, as well. Objects went flying into the front seat and coins spilled out of his pocket to land God knows where. By the time he'd accomplished that and turned back to her, he discovered she was sitting up and had moved to the very edge of the seat.

"Lie down and bend your knees," she murmured. "Let me be on top."

He wasn't about to argue at this stage.

Once he was in position, she climbed astride and eased down onto his shaft. Ah. Heaven. As always, he wanted it to last forever. As always, he was ready to come immediately.

Her voice was husky as she anchored herself more firmly, her bottom brushing his raised thighs. Then she began unbuttoning his shirt. "Do you want it slow or fast?"

"I get to choose?" In the dim glow from the front seat he could just barely see her face.

Her smile was lazy and satisfied as she spread his shirt open and played with his nipples. "Any man who did what you just did gets whatever he wants."

Her touch galvanized him, but her words were even more potent. No woman had ever paid him such a compliment, but then no woman had ever inspired him to try the sorts of things he attempted with Trudy. "You liked that?"

"Oh, yeah. I'll never think of the space between the two front seats the same way again. So what would you like?"

You. Forever. The words seared themselves into his brain, like an unexpected bolt of lightning. He had sense enough not to say them out loud, and he also understood he was in a heap of trouble. Because he'd come to a realization. He'd fallen in love with her. God, how had he managed to do such a stupid thing? But there it was, plain as could be. He wanted her in his life, for the rest of his life. He'd never expected to feel that way, but he'd never expected to meet a woman like Trudy, either. And he couldn't let her know how he felt or she'd run.

He swallowed. "Take it slow," he said. "After all, this is my first time."

She began an easy rhythm. "And don't try to tell me it's better than being on a bed, because you know it isn't."

It *was* better. His legs were cramped and he had a crick in his neck, but none of that mattered, because he was making love for the first time in his life. "Take off your sweater," he murmured.

She paused and pulled it over her head.

"And your bra."

Arching her back, she reached around and unhooked it. Then that, too, was gone.

He stroked her breasts, gliding both hands down to her waist. She was so perfect, and at this moment, in the middle of a wintry Kansas night, she was his.

"I can't believe I'm getting aroused again," she murmured. "I thought you'd drained my batteries."

"I guess you're hooked up to the energy source."

"I guess." She flattened her palms against his chest and shifted her angle slightly. "Is that good?"

"Oh, that's more than good."

"Faster?"

He couldn't hold back much longer, anyway. "Yeah." He spanned her hips with both hands and looked into her eyes. "Go for it."

She picked up speed, and her lips parted as she neared her climax.

Damn, how he loved her. He watched her eyes, felt her tighten around him. When the first moan slipped from her lips, he let himself go. As he tumbled with her over the brink, he felt his heart go into free fall, too. And he knew it was too late to save it.

TRUDY DIDN'T HAVE another chance to go parking with Linc that weekend. They spent most of the day playing in the snow with the kids, and Saturday night her folks threw a party that ran late, which was fine with Trudy. She didn't dare go out on a lonely road with that man again. The game had changed.

Sometime during the party Saturday night she realized that he was a threat to her entire plan. Here she'd thought she'd have an affair with a sophisticated city guy. In the beginning she'd been in control and they'd had a fantasy relationship—great sex and no bonding. Whenever things had become a little too intense, she'd ducked behind her folding screen and put some distance between them.

But then he'd asked her to have dinner with his parents, and she hadn't ducked behind her folding screen since. Worse yet, she'd taken him to meet *her* parents, as if they were going through all the traditional steps that would end with a trip to the altar. Ack!

But all those events might not have worried her so much if she hadn't seen the look on his face recently. She recognized that look, because it reflected the way she was beginning to feel about him. Like it or not, they were falling in love, and that was the exact opposite of what she wanted.

She'd worked for so many years to get to this point—her own apartment in New York and the freedom to date a city full of gorgeous men. She could *not* fall in love with the first man she ran into, no matter how wonderful, handsome, talented, and good in bed he happened to be.

So what if her parents adored him? So what if her brothers and sisters thought he was the coolest dude they'd ever seen? So what if her heart ached every time she thought about what she had to do? She'd made a plan, and she'd sacrificed enormously for the plan. He was a danger to the plan.

She had to break off the relationship.

But she couldn't do it until they'd left Kansas. He looked too happy, and so did her family. She couldn't bear to burst everyone's bubble in one fell swoop, so she settled for bursting his later on.

Yet on the way back to New York he spent the plane ride talking about what a great time he'd had, so she kept putting off the moment. But when they arrived at JFK and walked out to the taxi stand, she knew she'd run out of room. She'd have to give him the bad news on the way into the city.

Of course, maybe he wasn't falling in love with her the way she was with him. Maybe this wouldn't hit him like a ton of bricks. She hoped not, because she didn't want to cause him pain. She just couldn't take a chance on having him around anymore.

Linc settled into the cab with a contented sigh. "I say let's grab something from a deli for dinner."

Oh, God. He'd assumed they'd have dinner together. Somewhere along the line they'd become a couple in his mind. This could be bad—really bad. Her throat hurt. She could just have dinner with him, maybe.

No. Because after dinner would come their favorite activity. She couldn't go to bed with him again. He made her feel too good, too happy, too ready to blurt out something damaging. Like *I love you.* Once she said that, she'd never be able to take it back. She couldn't say that and continue toward her goal of swinging singlehood.

She closed her eyes. Damn. Damn it to hell. Meg was to blame for this, and Meg was going to hear about it. She was going to hear plenty. Trudy sighed. No, she couldn't take her anger out on Meg. She was mad at herself. She could have stuck with her program and kept her hands off Linc, but no, she'd had to put her hands all over him. The memories made her ache with longing.

"Trudy, is something wrong?"

She opened her eyes and looked into his. Her heart twisted. Unless she knew nothing about men, he was in the same fix as she. This was going to be very, very difficult. But it had to be done.

"I've...I've decided we shouldn't see each other anymore."

He looked as if she'd slapped him hard across the face.

"I'm sorry," she said softly. "I didn't mean for us to get so involved. I know you didn't, either, but it's happening."

He said nothing, just stared at her with that dumbstruck expression.

Her own pain didn't matter, but she wasn't sure she could survive knowing that she was hurting him. "When we started out, we both said we didn't want anything serious, but I'm afraid that—"

His glance hardened. "What makes you think I want something serious?"

The blow took her breath away. She'd been so sure that he was falling for her, but maybe she'd been mistaken. Maybe she'd projected her own feelings onto him.

"You've been a lot of fun, Trudy." His voice was as icy as the streets they traveled. "I'm glad I had a chance to travel into the hinterlands, too. That was very educational."

Educational? She would have sworn he'd been completely charmed by small-town life. In fact, through his eyes she'd been able to see those charming aspects, herself. She'd never want to live in Virtue again, but now she could admit that she loved the place, warts and all.

"I…guess I misread your feelings," she said.

"I told you I wasn't interested in getting serious, and that's the way it is. If you want to stop seeing me, that's fine. But I think it's a shame to throw away the kind of good sex we've had. We both know how the other feels, so I don't see why we can't still enjoy each other." His eyes were unreadable. "Unless you can't handle it."

Her brain whirled. He was suggesting that they keep on having sex—uncommitted, lusty, fantasy-laden sex, the kind they'd had before. That was what she'd come to town looking for, wasn't it? So why did the whole idea sound like torture to her now?

She tried to imagine going back to having fantasy sex with Linc and then disappearing so that he could go home. No cuddling, no conversation. No love.

It wouldn't work. That kind of relationship was impossible now that she'd met his parents, now that she'd taken him to Virtue, now that she'd seen him standing in front of a sink full of suds while her brothers and sisters helped him with the dishes.

She gazed at him and fought tears. "I'm sorry, Linc. I guess I can't handle it."

Something flashed in his eyes. It could have been anger or agony. She was too busy battling her emotions to be able to tell. Without a word he faced forward. He didn't speak again, not even when the cab stopped at her apartment building and she told him goodbye.

But when she tried to pay her part of the cab fare, he gripped her wrist hard enough to make her wince.

"No," he said.

She didn't have the energy to fight him on it. After getting out of the cab, she ran into her building.

GONE. As the cab moved through the streets toward his apartment, Linc leaned his head against the seat and tried to cope. He still couldn't believe that Trudy was really out of his life. Surely he'd wake up back in that cramped little bunk in Kansas and find he'd had a horrible nightmare. Throughout the weekend as he'd been falling deeper and deeper in love, he'd tried to be so careful not to do or say anything that would let her know.

She'd guessed anyway. And as he'd known she would, she'd run like hell the minute she realized that he cared about her. In his desperation to hang on to her he'd proposed returning to a sex-only relationship, but she'd been smart enough to see through that.

Oh, God, he didn't want to tie her down. Yes, he did, but he knew that wasn't what she wanted, so he would have bitten off his tongue before he'd ever have said what was in his heart. His parents had taught him to hide his feelings, so how the hell had all those years of training failed him?

But he knew how. He'd never had to hide a feeling this strong. Apparently he couldn't do it. And now she was gone.

DURING THE NEXT TWO WEEKS, Linc pumped more iron and played more racquetball than he had in the whole previous year. He played racquetball with Tom as long as Tom agreed not to mention Trudy, but Tom didn't have enough free time to satisfy Linc's need for physical exhaustion. Linc paged through the roster of players at the club and phoned guys shamelessly, looking for a workout.

He couldn't be beat. By the end of two weeks nobody wanted to play with him because they said he was no fun— a grim competitor who seemed to take pleasure in annihilating his opponent. Only Tom understood, and even Tom's patience was wearing thin. Considering how easygoing Tom was, that should have been a warning.

Still, he hadn't expected Meg to come sailing into his office in the middle of a Monday morning, a don't-mess-with-me expression on her face.

"I've had it!" She flipped his door closed and turned to him, hands on her hips. "You're going to kill my husband,

and maybe yourself, but it's Tom I'm concerned about. And you should be, too. He's your best friend.''

He stood. ''Nice to see you, too, Meg.''

She didn't smile. ''What's wrong with you? Do you think all this macho stuff on the racquetball court is going to get you anywhere?''

''I'm not trying to get anywhere,'' he said quietly. ''I'm just trying to get a little exercise.''

''The hell you are. I know what's wrong with you, but what I can't figure out is why you haven't tried to contact Trudy.''

He stared at her. ''Why should I contact Trudy? She doesn't want to see me. She was very clear about that!''

Meg blew out a breath. ''You *would* be the type to think she meant it. Can I sit down?''

''Of course she meant it!'' His head buzzed. ''She wants to be free!''

''I'm sitting down, now.'' Meg lowered herself into one of the chairs across from his desk. ''Feel free to do the same. We need to talk.''

19

POWER DATING SUCKED. After eight dates with eight different men, Trudy wondered what had happened to the supply of gorgeous guys in New York. On the surface they all seemed attractive enough, but after about an hour in their company, she knew they would never do.

Their eyes weren't as blue as Linc's or their shoulders weren't as broad. They had no sense of humor or they laughed at everything. They talked endlessly about themselves or they couldn't manage a conversation, period.

She hadn't worked up enough enthusiasm to try kissing even one of them, let alone inviting any of them up to her apartment. Her plan wasn't nearly the amount of fun that she'd imagined. Meg had tried to get her to call Linc and pick up where they'd left off with uncommitted sex, but pride was getting in her way.

Okay, more than pride. The problem was that sex alone just wouldn't cut it. But she didn't want to get married. She really, really didn't. But if she *were* to consider marriage, which of course was out of the question, Linc would be the guy. Not that she was thinking of it.

Well, maybe she'd had a few dreams lately that involved wedding dresses and diamond rings. They meant nothing. So what if she looked at Meg and Tom with envy these days? So what if her apartment seemed incredibly lonely without Linc in it?

Linc didn't want anything to do with marriage. He might

be perfect for her, husband-wise. Yet knowing he wouldn't ever trek down the aisle with her would be hard to take.

When the phone rang early Monday night, she hoped it wasn't one of the losers she'd dated recently, because she'd made it clear that she wasn't interested. Apparently only one man in New York was good enough for her, and he didn't want a permanent commitment. And...damn, damn, damn, she'd have to come out and admit the ugly truth. She was ready for one.

She answered the phone, and the particular man who figured into her matrimonial fantasies was on the other end of the line. Her heart started pounding. She tried to tell it to quiet down, but it kept pumping frantically, anyway. "Hello, Linc," she said.

In the brief silence she imagined a million reasons why he might be calling. If by any chance he was calling to invite her to resume their no-strings-attached sexual arrangement, she would agree. She was desperate to be with him, under any conditions. Without him she was a total wreck. She could barely sleep in her big bed, because it was filled with memories of Linc.

"I—" He cleared his throat. "I was wondering if you'd return my coat."

Disappointment sliced through her. He only wanted his coat. How shallow was that? Here she was considering happily-ever-afters, which was a huge step for her, a complete reversal of her cherished plans, a reversal that was totally his fault, by the way, and all he wanted was his coat.

She'd meant to return it before this, but she hadn't been able to bring herself to give it up. It wasn't the coat she'd grown to love so much as the association with Linc. "How about your card table and chairs?" she said, not able to keep the sarcasm out of her voice. "I suppose you want those back right away, too?"

"No, you can keep them. Forever, actually. I'll never have any use for them. But I do need the coat."

"Okay." She could work it out so she didn't have to see him. "I'll give the coat to Meg, and she can give it to Tom, and Tom can give it to—"

"I don't want to wait that long. I want you to bring it over tonight."

"Tonight?" Boy, he was getting demanding.

"Yes, tonight." His voice sharpened. "ASAP."

She frowned in irritation. What a dictator. Good thing she hadn't become more involved with him, after all, if he could be so bossy. Maybe he'd make a terrible husband, come to think of it.

This was going to cost her taxi fare, but he didn't seem to care. "All right. I'll bring it right over." She caught herself before she added *your majesty*. She wouldn't give him the satisfaction of knowing he'd gotten under her skin. "Goodbye."

After she hung up she stomped through the apartment, flung open her closet door and pulled out the trench coat. Then it hit her. He couldn't possibly be that desperate for the coat. He had others. Waiting for the coat to travel through channels wouldn't have been such a hardship.

Which left only one alternative. He wanted to see her. Well, that shouldn't come as such a surprise. He'd indicated on the ride in from the airport that he wouldn't mind continuing their sexual relationship. But considering the current wedding-bells direction of her thoughts these days, she really shouldn't think of having sex with him again. She could get burned.

Okay, she'd risk getting burned. Two weeks of being without him had weakened her. She shouldn't have gone cold turkey like that. Tapering off made more sense. She'd have sex with him tonight, then skip a couple of nights, then go to bed with him again, then skip three nights. Eventually she might be able to go a whole week and not ache for him. It could happen.

In the meantime, she would take his coat back and try

out that sleigh bed of his. She began to quiver with anticipation. Then she took a deep breath. She had to go in there
cool and collected. She might be hopelessly in love with
him and crazy about his body, but he didn't have to know
that.

Still, it took her an embarrassingly short time to put on
her parka, snatch up the trench coat and get into the creaky
elevator. Soon she was in a cab headed for Linc's apartment,
and she was quivering again. She took more deep breaths and
worked on a jaded, big-city chick attitude. Fake It Till
You Make It. This would be the ultimate test of her motto.

By the time she rang Linc's doorbell she'd done so much
deep breathing that she was sure her blood must be super-
oxygenated. It certainly was racing madly through her body
right now.

The door opened, but she saw no one, only flickering
shadows. "Linc?"

"Come in."

She still didn't see him, but that was definitely his voice,
so she stepped into the foyer. The flickering shadows were
created by small votive candles surrounding the statue she
liked so much. Set up this way, it looked like an altar to
sex. She shivered.

"Thank you for coming." He stepped away from the
shadows surrounding the door.

She gasped. He stood there in tight black leather pants
that laced up. Behind the laces an impressive bulge revealed
his growing arousal. He also wore a leather vest over his
bare torso, and...a black mask. A thrill of primitive passion
ran through her.

So she'd been right. He wanted to continue their sexual
fantasies. But she'd never in a million years imagined that
he would dream up the scenario himself.

He closed and locked the door.

Because he was so obviously in charge, she didn't know

her lines. Heart racing, she held out the coat. "I...I brought your coat."

"Good." Behind the mask, his eyes raked over her. "Now I want you to take off all your clothes and put the coat on." He gestured toward the living room. "I'll be in there, waiting for you."

She tried to maintain some control. "What if I don't want to do what you tell me?"

He pinned her with his gaze. "You want to. I know what sexual desire looks like on you, and you're very hot right now." Then he walked past her and into the darkened living room.

She was stunned by the way he'd taken over. Stunned and excited. All this time she'd thought any fantasies would have to be introduced by her, but there were depths to this man she'd never suspected. He would be a constant source of surprise, even after years of...no, she couldn't let herself think like that.

All she had was now. And a leather-clad man waiting for her. She took off her clothes as he'd directed and left them in a pile next to the table holding the statue. Then, already wet and excited, she slipped on his trench coat and belted it around her waist. The effect was so sensuous she wondered why she'd never thought of it before.

Glancing at the statue, she took courage from the marble woman's uninhibited stance. "Wish me luck," she whispered. Then she walked into the living room.

Candles were everywhere here, too, making the antique furniture look gothic and tantalizing instead of sedate and stuffy, as she'd categorized it on her first visit. Or maybe it was the tall man standing with his back to the window who made the room seem drenched in sex.

"Sit over there." He pointed to a Victorian sofa covered in burgundy velvet.

She did as she was told, her bare toes whispering across a soft Oriental carpet. As she sat on the sofa, she briefly wondered if he was concerned about the lining of his coat. She was becoming very, very wet.

"Now lie back and slowly open the coat. Only let me see a little at a time."

Pulse racing, she leaned back against a pillow tucked into the corner of the sofa. With her gaze fixed on that dark silhouette by the window, she gradually untied the belt on the coat. She couldn't see his eyes, but she could feel them, as if they were burning each inch of bare skin she uncovered. At last she lay with the lapels of the coat completely open.

His voice was thick and heavy with desire. "Now..." He paused and cleared his throat. "Bring yourself to orgasm."

Her heartbeat thundered in her ears. "And if I don't choose to?"

"Do it," he said. Then his voice softened. "Do it for me."

Closing her eyes, she slid her hand between her thighs and the leather sleeve of the coat caressed her belly. He was daring her to be wild, and she would show him how wild she could be. She cupped her breast with her other hand and squeezed her nipple. Then she began stroking that hot, wet cleft that demanded attention.

The sound of his harsh breathing carried across the room, reminding her that he was there. Knowing he was watching propelled her even closer to her climax. She began to pant and her fingers moved faster. Surrounded by the scent of his leather coat, she imagined that his hand instead of hers was coaxing her to a shattering orgasm.

She began to swell and tighten, and her thighs began to shake. At last, with a frenzied cry, she arched upward, coming in a rush of moist heat.

"Yes," he murmured, by her side now. "Yes, my love."

While she continued to quake, he moved onto the narrow sofa, unlacing his pants as he approached. He lifted her leg over his leather-clad shoulder and guided the other to the floor as he probed her quivering folds and pushed home.

"Look at me, my love," he demanded.

My love. The first time he'd said that, she'd wondered if she'd imagined it. She hadn't imagined it this time. She looked into those intense eyes, made even more dramatic by the dark mask.

"I know you want many men," he said. "So let me be all of them. I can be anyone you want. Tell me what your fantasy is and I'll be that fantasy. I love you, Trudy. I need you. Please give me a chance to prove that I can be enough for you."

She was speechless. He *loved* her?

"Maybe you don't love me yet, but we'll work on that. Meg says you do, but—"

"Meg said that?" She'd kill Meg. Or maybe not. No doubt Meg was responsible for this awesome leather outfit of his. "Meg has a big mouth."

"So she's wrong." The glow left his eyes.

Trudy cupped his face in both hands. Her heart swelled with love for this sweet, sexy man. "No," she murmured. "She's right."

"She's right?"

"Yes, but I would have liked to be able to tell you mys—"

"She's right?" His smile was so bright he wouldn't have needed a single candle to light the room. "About everything?"

"Uh, like what sort of everything?"

"Like you wanting to marry me."

"How could Meg know that? *I* didn't even know that until a couple of hours ago!"

"So you do want to."

"Yes." She abandoned herself to the inevitable. Meg would gloat, and she would let her. Nothing mattered but spending the rest of her life with this man. "Please love me, Linc."

"I can't help myself." He began a slow, steady rhythm within her. "I love you so much."

"I love you, too." She felt the sweet slide of leather along her thigh. "You still have on most of your pants."

"Uh-huh. When you unlace the front, the rest sort of…stays on. Do you like it?"

"I'm crazy about it."

"I mean it, Trudy." He increased the pace of his thrusts. "I can be anyone you want. Any fantasy."

She felt another climax hovering near. "I think…mostly…oh, that's good…I want you to be my fantasy…husband." Then she wrapped her arms around him and hung on tight.

OKAY, so all her cherished plans were in the dumper. Trudy grabbed a plastic glass of wedding champagne and gazed across the crowded dance floor to where her husband was dancing with her sister Deena. Never in a million years would she have imagined that within six months of moving to New York she'd be standing in the Grange Hall drinking pink champagne at her own wedding.

And she never could have imagined that she'd be this happy.

Incredibly, her aristocratic in-laws had agreed to attend this wedding. In fact, they'd loosened up quite a bit since the raucous rehearsal dinner the night before, where Linc had challenged his dad to a beer-drinking contest and Glenda had cheered her husband to victory. At the moment Glenda and L.C. were dancing with each other, and it wasn't even a scheduled parents-of-the-groom dance.

Meg nudged her. "Your in-laws are thawing."

"I know." Trudy took another sip of champagne and decided it didn't taste bad at all. "Isn't that wonderful?"

"It's because of you, toots. You may work a little miracle there."

"Linc tells me not to get my hopes up."

Meg put an arm around Trudy's waist and gave her a squeeze. "He's right, but you never know."

Trudy glanced at her matron of honor. "I should put you on the case. They'd be canoodling in no time."

Meg looked totally unrepentant. "Let's see. There's something I've been meaning to tell you. What was it? Oh, I know. *I told you so.*"

Trudy rolled her eyes. "For the five hundred and forty-second time."

"You were so asking for it, toots, after the way you hassled me about Tom. And speaking of my love slave, look at him dancing cheek-to-cheek with Meredith. He is nutso over that kid."

"Like you're not." Trudy's heart gave a funny little flutter whenever she looked at Meg's baby. Probably indigestion. "You won't even let Linc and me baby-sit."

Meg grinned. "Get a kid of your own."

"Hey, wait a minute. You just got us married off. Don't be trying to get us into the baby business already. I want to have some time to goof around first and play games."

"If you say so." Meg smiled her know-it-all smile.

Trudy gazed at her friend. Her prying, bossy, scheming friend. "Don't you dare try to talk Linc into having kids already."

"I don't have to say a word. Just see how he's looking at Meredith."

Trudy glanced at her tuxedo-clad husband and, sure enough, he was making cow eyes at Tom and Meg's little girl. Come to think of it, when they'd had back-seat sex a couple of nights ago for old time's sake, he'd mentioned that he was getting tired of using condoms.

"Relax," Meg said. "With a man like you have, the fun and games will go on forever."

"Especially if you keep giving him tips. I can't believe the two of you cooked up that whole masked-man thing."

"It worked, didn't it?"

"Yes, but I think that you—"

"Time to dance with me, bride." Linc appeared and swept her out on the floor.

She looked into his eyes, still not quite believing they were husband and wife. She loved the concept—she just couldn't completely accept that it had happened. "Do you feel like you're going to wake up and none of this will be true?" she asked as they swayed to the music.

"I sure hope not." His gaze was tender. "This is my fantasy."

"Mine, too." She linked her hands behind his neck. "Is Meg trying to convince you that we should have kids right away?"

He smiled. "Yeah. Turns out she used to watch *Family Ties* and *The Bill Cosby Show,* too."

Trudy had a feeling she was fighting a losing battle. "So *has* she convinced you?"

His smile broadened. "Yeah."

"*Linc.* You know I want to wait." But her body tightened with anticipation at the idea of making love to him and conceiving a child.

"I know," he murmured, gathering her close. "We'll still use birth control if you want."

"I do." At least, she sort of did. Maybe. Then again...

"Unless..." Linc nuzzled behind her ear.

"Unless what?"

"Unless sometime...like during our honeymoon...you feel like acting on impulse."

And she knew, as she snuggled in his arms, that was exactly what she wanted to do.

Who needs Cupid when you've got kids?

Sealed *with a* Kiss

A delightful collection from *New York Times* Bestselling Author

DEBBIE MACOMBER

JUDITH BOWEN

HELEN BROOKS

Romance and laughter abound as the matchmaking efforts of some *very* persistent children bring true love to their parents.

HARLEQUIN®
Makes any time special ®

Available in January 2002...just in time for Valentine's Day!

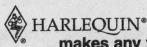

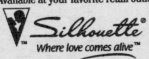